HOPE FOR NEWBORNS

Rodge Glass was born in 1978. He is originally from
Cheshire but has lived mostly in Glasgow since 1997.
Hope for Newborns is his second novel. His first, *No
Fireworks*, was published in 2005 and was nominated for
four awards. Since then he has written for a number of
newspapers and magazines, and has recently published a
biography of Alasdair Gray. He is currently completing a
PhD at Glasgow University.

also by Rodge Glass

NO FIREWORKS
ALASDAIR GRAY: A SECRETARY'S BIOGRAPHY

RODGE GLASS

Hope for Newborns

ff

faber and faber

First published in 2008
by Faber and Faber Limited
3 Queen Square London WC1N 3AU

Typeset by Faber and Faber Ltd
Printed in England by Mackays of Chatham, plc

© Rodge Glass, 2008

Hope for Newborns emblem artwork by Dave Turbitt

A CIP record for this book
is available from the British Library

ISBN 978-0-571-23821-7

2 4 6 8 10 9 7 5 3 1

For Amber

PART ONE

A Way of Life
2004

I

Aftermath of an Attack

Our place stood between a bar and a grocer's shop in the centre of the city. A sign above the door just said VICTORY; underneath, in the front window, black lettering on a Union Jack background read:

THE VICTORY BARBER SHOP, MANCHESTER

**PROUDLY SERVING GREAT BRITISH SCALPS
SINCE 1945**

*PROPRIETOR, C. J. PASSMAN. COME IN FOR A
SMILE AND A SERVICE, SEVEN DAYS A WEEK*

Two windows facing the street displayed framed popular images from the First and Second World Wars, each lovingly maintained by Morta, Dad's new Lithuanian assistant, who prided herself on her ability to spray, wipe and dust surfaces more efficiently than anyone born east of the old Berlin Wall. There were hundreds of photographs for her to look after. Processions of returning soldiers riding through the streets, waving. D-Day celebrations. Women working in the munitions factories. The Queen Mum in the East End. Nothing too bloody. Underneath the pictures was a carefully scattered selection of ration books, wartime adverts – 'Dig for Victory!' – and an impeccably presented display of Grandpa Harry's commemorative stamps. Winston Churchill himself looked down on customers from his place above the welcome sign, photographed in a jeep in Berlin in 1945, waving at a grateful crowd. It was never mentioned that, despite his many attributes, Churchill was in no need of a haircut. And neither were many of the shaven-headed members of the front line grinning out from the surrounding photographs and newspaper cuttings on our walls.

Winston and his men covered half the space; the rest was taken up with wartime maps of the changing shape of Europe, spattered with red and black arrows pointing in all directions, and some local newspaper cuttings from the time of the Blitz, Dunkirk, VE Day. Along the left wall was a bench for customers to wait on, Grandpa Harry's old wartime jukebox featuring hundreds of hits – 'We'll Meet Again', 'This Is the Army, Mr Jones', 'There'll Always Be an England' – and opposite were three barbers' chairs. The most important things lived above the till. The collection box for servicemen. The tips jar. The scissors. Water, gel, hair spray. Amongst these were a couple of official regiment photographs of Grandpa alongside colleagues and superiors, two of his three brothers and one of his cousins, all of whom died in service, apart from Great Uncle George, who became a general, so escaped direct bullets.

'We were a real army family,' Grandpa Harry used to say, snipping at some strange head, talking to me via the mirror. 'You know, Lewis . . . Britain accepted us at a time when most other places were either kicking out Jews or killing them. The least we could do was die for this country.'

Today, the modern Passman family would return to see almost the same shop front that had stood there since Grandpa first cut the ribbon on opening day in front of a crowd in 1945.

'Ladies and gentlemen – welcome to the Victory Barbers,' he said to thunderous applause. 'Now get inside and empty your pockets!'

Dad was still a boy then, standing by his father at the entrance as they cut the ribbon together.

'Dad?' he asked. 'One day, can I have the shop?'

Grandpa looked down at his only son and said, beaming, 'Clive, this is Great Britain. You can have whatever you like.'

I wish I had been alive then – you knew where you stood with things – or at least it seemed like it. Hitler had just been defeated. The National Health Service was up and running. A majority Labour government had been elected for the first time. We were on a roll, so we thought: an example to the rest of the world. The British were even arranging for a state to be set up, a place where Jews could feel safe, something which hadn't been achieved in thousands of years. Perhaps the Jews would have felt less heat if they'd accepted the centre of the earth as a homeland, but those who knew that at the time either didn't speak up or were ignored, so the arrangement went ahead in 1948. I was a teenager before I was told we British had been in charge of Israel until then, and that maybe its inhabitants were pleased to see us leave.

'Nothing is clean,' Grandpa Harry said whenever the subject of 'that place' came up. 'Sometimes you've just got to choose the least dirty option and be thankful you've got any options at all.'

These days, everything seemed dirty. Especially since my eldest brother Charles (or Chuck, as he now preferred to be called) followed in the family tradition and joined the army, in America, his new home. The brash shop front and 1940s-style interior he and his twin, Philip, left five years ago now seemed hopelessly out of date – a relic of something it was getting harder to believe really happened – a war everyone agreed had been a good idea. Modern ones were messy, gory affairs. It was difficult to know who to support. I preferred the old kind. Towards the end of his life Grandpa had been trying to persuade me that all our history was equally covered in muck and spit, but, like the rest of the family, I wasn't ready to believe it yet.

We were all nervous about today. Chuck, Daisy and Tampa Bay were due in at the airport mid-afternoon. Dad said he'd drive them the short journey back to the shop, which is also our family home, and I took the afternoon off work to prepare, going back to my flat to pick up a few things before heading round there. But straight away there was a setback. Just as I was unlocking the shop three kids on bikes raced past and threw a brick through the front window. So instead of putting out streamers and balloons I spent the time before they arrived carefully covering up the big hole in the window with several layers of masking tape, then going out to the pavement and sweeping up the last of the shattered glass with a dustpan and brush, still in my suit, scrambling around on my knees for overlooked shards. I was thinking about being somewhere more spectacular, but recently I always felt I was supposed to be somewhere else. Like it was some terrible mistake that I found myself wherever I was, doing whatever I was doing.

I was so exhausted from work most days that sensations of any kind seemed to pass through me with little effect. It was amazing I had the energy to talk at all, really, but occasionally I did. Usually to Anna, one of the company secretaries. Lunch hours, moments between meetings, a few minutes early morning before anyone else got in – especially over the last few months, while we'd been discussing a trip away together. Anna was part way through travelling Europe, she was impatient to move on to the next place, and couldn't understand why I was so reluctant to give up the job and go partying. We were a strange couple; hardly a couple at all. We didn't know the simplest things about each other. Sometimes I thought Anna was my girlfriend, but even that basic detail wasn't clear: sex usually came before relationships these days, and we'd not even been close to it. We'd only kissed a couple of times.

I didn't want to ruin things by asking for clarification. It was always easier to let things go on as usual than to put questions I might not like the answers to. I spent my professional life doing that anyway, so usually I didn't even notice myself doing it. Absorbing, controlling. Absorbing, controlling. Pleasing clients. My boss. My parents. The customers and hangers-on at the Victory. I did whatever was necessary to please those around me, keep things easy. Not take any risks. A month or two ago Anna decided to make me her new pet project, and she set about transforming a stiff, proud man who acted older than his years into a carefree young one ready for good times.

'If I can't wake you up,' she said, smiling confidently, 'then no one can.'

But I was harder to shift than expected. I talked about wanting to travel but really the thought of leaving my desk for more than a few days made me queasy. Eventually Anna got impatient, saying she was leaving for Europe without me. That was this afternoon.

'Where are you going, then?' I asked.

'Not telling you.'

'When do you leave?'

'Tomorrow.'

'Well – aren't you going to tell Marcus?'

'Rule number one,' she said, brightly. 'I owe no loyalty to bosses who only call me "sweetheart" because they can't remember my name.'

We worked on for another hour in virtual silence, punctuated only by the sound of tapping on keyboards and the occasional sigh. Then I left the office without a word, and walked to the shop, choosing to stay smart for the arrival of the folks. Every so often it was worth reminding them that some people took me seriously.

I noticed I'd missed a bit of glass on the pavement, so I retrieved the broom and swept it up, without anger. I never quite got used to it, but the initial shock of attack was long gone. Now I kept sweeping the road, though there was nothing left to sweep, as the teenagers in school uniform passed on their way to the bus stop. Sometimes I just wanted to draw all the kids to me. Break the bad news gently. The old folks too. They all looked sad, even when they were smiling. The poster Dad had insisted on keeping in the window – SUPPORT OUR TROOPS: BE PROUD! – had been taken clean out by the brick, and now lay on the inside of the shop, face up.

HOPE FOR NEWBORNS

BECAUSE THE LOST JUST WANT TO BE FOUND

To be found, go to www.hopefornewborns.com

and enter the password: RESET

CC 2004

HFN-I: #001

2

The Arrival

The family meal was our first together for five years. Chuck
had a short period of leave and was coming over from his
Texas base with wife and toddler for a long weekend in
Manchester, before going down to London to see the sights –
he knew they wouldn't be able to stomach us all for longer
than that. Later in the day Philip, younger by four minutes,
was due to arrive from Toronto, where he had left his partner
Stephen in their stylish modern city apartment watching the
kids and the cats. I didn't have to come far; most of my life
took place within a couple of miles of the shop, and I spent
much of my spare time there anyway. Especially since I'd started doing weekend shifts again. So in some ways it felt like a
normal day.

Each brother was returning to celebrate Mum's fiftieth
birthday – this, she showed us in her own way, was morally
wrong, as nobody knew exactly when her birthday was, and
apart from us there was no one to invite. All my attempts to
track down some blood family in time for the party, an elderly
cousin or distant great aunt whom we could wheel out from
behind a door and shout 'Surprise!' had failed.

On a recent home visit, her social worker had tried to
explain her reticence over the party idea. 'How can you get
going to where you're going to go,' she said, nodding sadly,
'and make merry where you are, if you haven't come to know
where you've come from?'

That sounded stupid enough to be true – but to Mum, it
wasn't the where that mattered. If she couldn't know for cer-

tain *when* her life started, and *who with*, she had no interest in
marking it. That seemed to pass everyone by. But we went
ahead anyway, on Chuck's insistence.

'Even foundlings have to have birthdays,' he bawled down
the phone, 'She'll have a good time whether she likes it or not!'

Mum just wanted to hide away, pretend she wasn't getting
older, pretend she didn't know who she was. But once Chuck
had booked tickets it was going ahead whatever anyone's
opinion was, so Philip offered to come home too, and I began
preparations for what was now a reunion as well as a birthday.
Just a few drinks at the house, then dinner close by; something
to show we cared. There were few opportunities left to do that.
Which was why Anna would be flying alone.

When the car pulled up on the main street I welcomed
Chuck, Daisy and Tampa Bay with hearty hugs and kisses,
insisting on carrying their bags and generally acting like there
was nowhere in the world I'd rather be. I always seemed to be
on the verge of tears for one reason or another, especially with
members of my family. More since the trouble. A few threatened to make themselves known as I held Daisy close, saying,
'Come in, come in. It's wonderful to finally meet you.'

The taped-up window might have unnerved her, or she
could have been anxious anyway. Daisy followed me through
to the back room.

'What the hell happened here?' asked Chuck, pointing at the
mess.

'Just kids,' I replied. 'Leave it.'

Chuck walked purposefully towards the phone, but I
blocked his path.

'No. Morta can get someone in to repair the window properly on Monday. Anyway, we're supposed to be celebrating!'

'Who's Morticia?' asked Chuck.

'She's from Eastern Europe, you know. And so are you, I
suppose, if you go back far enough. Come on in!'

My brother bounded through to the back room, took my
skull in his big hands and kissed me hard on the crown.

'Good to see you,' he said. 'Now wipe your eyes.'

'Get off. I'm fine.'

I laughed as he ran his fingers along the three lines that were scored deep across my forehead, each slightly wavy, like shapes drawn in the sand with a stick. I wasn't used to that kind of contact any more.

'Suffering for us all again, Lewis? Go on, tell us what you're worrying about.'

'Well . . . they do say confession is good for the soul,' I said, not able to stop another smile breaking out. 'But then, who's to say that's not just a rumour spread by priests to get us to reveal all our secrets?'

Following an hour of us men slapping each other's backs and saying loudly how great it was to be together again, we began to run out of ways of being cheerful and the energy to keep it up. By late afternoon a new depression was quietly taking hold of everyone apart from Chuck, who seemed determined to be happy, no matter what, at least for now. He and I joined the family's new arrivals in enduring Dad's obligatory, never-ending tour of the shop – he still took so much pride in his little empire, which he told Daisy was 'a collection of memories celebrating the best of British' – even more post-siege. Since Dad's poster of pride, a small gang had taken to writing slogans on the door and the sign above it. Yesterday he'd seen one of them running away, but didn't get a good look at who it was – though he said he had his suspicions. One hand on hip, the other clamped round a bottle of beer, like a cowboy dreaming of high noon, he said he was determined to get them next time. There was no mention of that today. They were beating him again.

While Dad explained the history of the Victory to Daisy, how long the shop had been in the family, what his grandfather did on first arriving in England during the Russian Revolution, we all pretended to forget the multicoloured damage painted outside:

NAZI'S
TROOPS HOME!
100,000 DEAD

He explained the history of each piece like it was a work of art, focusing in on a few favourites, particularly the photograph of Grandpa Harry's regiment circa 1943, taken in France. Since Grandpa opened up sixty years ago on returning injured from that war, the living museum we exposed to the public every day had become more like what most families use a dining room for – the place where everything important got done or said; the fulcrum of the home. So it wasn't unusual that we should be expected to stand on ceremony and watch while Dad presented a wartime postcard, pacing back and forth, hands clasped together behind his back, like an officer giving a speech to his troops. The postcard was from Grandpa, saying that he was down to his last roll-up, but he reckoned the Jerries were nearly done for and hoped to be home by Christmas to smoke until he was sick.

'So was he, then?' asked Daisy, trying to show an interest. 'When he got back from the war . . . did he get ill?'

'Oh no . . .' said Dad with great pride. 'Never sick a day in his life. Made of strong stuff, the Passmans. Apart from Lewis, of course. There's always one!'

He ruffled my hair like I was still a small boy and went through to the kitchen to get us each a bottle of beer. Daisy wasn't offered one, so went and got one herself from the fridge. Chuck visibly swelled with pride.

'Yup,' he said, rearranging his crotch in his trousers, 'that's my woman.'

'For now,' she replied.

Chuck's smile turned into a full-blown grin, and he began to laugh.

The tour continued with Dad proudly retelling the fable of his grandparents' romance on the boat to England from Lithuania back in 1917, and regaling Daisy with details of barbering trends of the twentieth century. (The seventies were quiet. Everyone grew their hair long.) Daisy did a good job of seeming fascinated through this ordeal, which, unfortunately, encouraged Dad to keep going. He drifted into a version of one of his favourite speeches, hands back on hips, legs apart as if straddling some great steed.

'In recession time, we didn't get hit like some of the other industries did. A good reputation always helps, of course – a loyal fan base, if you like – this place was bubbling, not that you'd know it now. But my father made the shop a real community centre. Sometimes, men saw the sign and just came in off the street asking if we knew so-and-so from such-and-such a regiment. Often, someone knew who they were. We were a centre for all the ex-army folk in the area. You don't get community like that any more.'

Once he was in the flow there was no stopping him, but Dad's talk was convenient anyway as we were trying to put off explaining about Mum to Daisy. (It would have been out of character for Chuck to reveal something so unpleasant without being forced.) So we just stood and listened. There was a long afternoon ahead of us.

'Fashions change, of course,' said Dad, beginning to pace back and forth, as if dictating a letter, 'but it was mainly the short-back-and-sides that kept the family solvent. If my father got into barbering for a little variation in his life, he must have been bored out of his mind! Which might have been why he opened up the second shop, I suppose.'

Dad stood thoughtfully and almost, but didn't, put a hand round his daughter-in-law's shoulder.

'Daisy, my father was not an entrepreneur. He was trying to do something more worthwhile than just make money, see? And the second place didn't have the right atmosphere. Wasn't the same. Seemed fake, you know. So he closed it down and swore there'd be no more expansion.'

'This is the only one?' asked Daisy.

But Dad didn't hear her. He was far away in his own thoughts.

'My father seemed to fall in love with this place all over again then,' he continued, 'as if he was saying sorry to it, even adding some special features, like a customer toilet in the style of a bunker. That enthusiasm lasted nearly a year, then exhausted itself . . . but let me show you our special water closet!'

We all trooped through to take a look.

Welcome . . .

. . . and thank you for answering the call. Starting tomorrow you will receive information about Hope for Newborns, an organisation designed to help you repair your own damaged life and the lives of others.

Send the word 'YES' in reply to this message and wait.

It's time for a new beginning.

CC 2004

Freedom through Kinship,
Wealth through Understanding,
Love through Sacrifice

HFN-I: #002

3

Sunshine and Candyfloss

While this great show was going on Mum sat in her room above the shop, feeding the many hamsters, rats and amphibians she looked after full time, and reading celebrity magazines – inspecting this week's blown-up snaps for evidence of stretch marks, running make-up and bumps where no bumps should be. That was my fault, like everything else: after all, who took her order and delivered it?

I went in to check on her every half-hour or so, inviting her to join us each time, but with no success. It had been a bad day: one of her goldfish had died this morning. Suicide, probably. Just jumped right out of the bowl onto the carpet first thing – took a great leap and wriggled itself into the next world while Mum stood above, silently horrified. Something had changed in her since then. She realised the animals could escape her not only through natural death, but voluntarily as well. Now a few hours had passed, and I tried every persuasion and bribe I could think of to get her downstairs, but no – she was in mourning. Since the American contingent arrived she had come out of her room just once, looked at everyone grimly, picked up a magazine and gone back inside again, hardly giving a glance to the decorations I had bought and carefully put up – LIFE BEGINS AT FIFTY, HAPPY BIRTHDAY SEXY – or to her new granddaughter, who was sitting on a lounge seat cheerfully rolling her neck around her shoulders, testing out its strength. Philip arrived then, pulling up in a taxi that rode up onto the pavement as it parked. My brother came through the front way and, ignoring the sign reading BLOOD

ON YOUR HANDS above the entrance, said, 'So! Good to be home!'

Nobody apart from him felt that it was, and soon neither did he. We opened the champagne anyway, but the party poppers stayed in the packet. Already I was grateful that it was only a couple of days we had to fill, not a week, or a fortnight.

After Mum's gentle rejection we tried to make Daisy feel welcome in other ways, desperately trying to drag afternoon into evening by asking her all the questions we could think of about her daughter. These were mostly answered with 'No's. No, she wasn't speaking yet, though there had been a few gurgles and once she could swear she was asking for a handbag. No, there were no signs of unusual intelligence. No, Tampa Bay wasn't a religious name – it was where she was *brought into the world* – they went on holiday there once.

Dad changed the subject, asking if they were being treated well at the base.

'Yes,' said Daisy, 'very much so – the nurses are used to new arrivals. Especially unexpected ones.'

'Unexpected?' said Dad.

'Oh yes, Clive – you don't think I'd give up my career on purpose, do you? I'm only twenty-five!'

Daisy sat perfectly upright at the kitchen table, green crinkle party hat dead straight, daring someone to reply. No one did.

'I love my baby,' she added.

Beneath her hat, Daisy was dressed conservatively in a flowery summer dress ill suited to the North of England in October, but spoke in a clear, unashamed, forthright voice that showed she thought what came out of her mouth was more important than what practical clothing decisions she made, taking hearty slugs of her beer as she talked. I could see why Chuck had gone for her. Some men need a doormat. Chuck needed a sparring partner.

'Time for dinner, then?' said Dad, standing.

It was still before seven, but we all said yes anyway.

Mum was not prepared to leave the house, so we all hovered

by the door to the shop, coats on, waiting. How a woman who hardly ever exits her room can be short of make-up time is a mystery to me, but she always seemed to manage lateness on the rare occasions she was forced out into the world. After a few minutes I was sent in find out what was going on – but, opening the door after the usual knock, I saw she was not even fully dressed.

'Five minutes, okay?' I said, eyes down. 'Hurry. I'll come up and get you.'

If Mum could do this, I'd never ask for anything again – come along, raise a glass, smile, go home. Prove everyone wrong. I explained to the others that we were going nowhere just yet.

'What's up?' asked Philip.

'You can't tell the birthday girl what to do, right?' I said, trying to joke. 'I'll call the restaurant and get them to hold the table.'

There was no need to do that, though. Everyone knew we weren't late. Without comment Dad, Chuck and Philip went through to the back room to watch TV – anything but anything to do with the war, though that was harder to avoid these days. Daisy followed, holding Tampa Bay. There was some noise, a few questions about the attack on the shop, but Dad didn't want to talk about it, so nobody did. Trying to think calm, pleasant thoughts that would take my mind away from the evening ahead, and Anna packing for the sun, and the day's messages from something calling itself Hope for Newborns. I stepped into the bunker-cum-toilet Grandpa had designed so fondly, and Dad had shown Daisy round earlier on, looked up at the painted-on, pretend trapdoor on the ceiling and wished I could escape up it and out of the city for ever. But if I went, where would I go?

The shop seemed less vibrant now. It was at its best in the early days when Grandpa Harry was still in charge and nobody doubted what we were. Some families revolve around the identity of a single person and fall in on themselves when that person dies. Ours was like that. He was the cheerful one who reminded us there was no need to be so grim all the time. Grandpa said he was happier than the rest of us because he'd seen so much sadness in his life that he didn't have the energy to get irritated any more by small, inconsequential details like profit margins, who said what about so-and-so and which idiot happened to be running the country this year.

'When you let go of that, my boy,' he said, 'all that's left is sunshine and candyfloss.'

I laughed at that, but these days my greatest thrill is skimming my two per cent from a deal nobody needs, and if he were alive Grandpa would be ashamed of how I make a living. Though of course he wouldn't say. That would be the Russian thing to do, and, as we were always repeating to ourselves, we were British as British could be, which meant we had to buy into all Britain's silly silences in places where a good shout, scream or cry would better serve.

To the sound of the TV buzzing, I leaned back on the barber's chair, stretched out my arms and closed my eyes, dreading dinner. I hadn't slept properly for days, and could hardly think about food. Too tired to do that. Too tired to do anything. Tired made me emotional, and emotional left me saying and doing things that, when stronger, I knew how to stop. 'Sometimes when you see an opportunity you've got to just grab it,' Grandpa used to say, before catching a nap between customers. We'd wake him up by poking him with his old backscratcher, saying, 'Hey! Dribbler! It's trim time! Get up!' And he'd bolt awake, stand, slap himself about the face with his hands, turn to the customer and say while making a mock-salute, 'The V-V-Victory Barber at your thervice, Thir!'

There's something about being in the shop alone that seems to bring back everything that ever happened or was talked about in there. Every family member, customer, visitor, seems to hover in the air. Mum pottered about above the bunker, stalling, and in the next room the family sat in front of the box, waiting on her.

It had been nearly twenty-four hours now since she came for me. Sent me that note from out of nowhere, saying almost nothing, asking me to join her. Of course I wanted to, but when I tried to reply my messages were just sent back. I had to wait for Christy. And it was her, I knew it. Who else could have made up Hope for Newborns? Who else could CC be? If those initials hadn't appeared at the bottom maybe I would have deleted it straight away. Put it in the virtual trashcan along with all the other promises to make me happier, thinner, bigger, stronger, sexier. But the initials were there. The name was there. And that was enough.

Just then my work mobile rang and I picked it up, snapping into my recruitment voice and attitude fast. If the others had heard me they'd probably have thought they were going mad. This wasn't the voice of the person they knew.

'Lewis Passman speaking – can I help? . . . Ah, Greg, I'm glad it's you – I was just about to call. I've spoken with them this afternoon and they're *very* interested in your CV . . . oh yes . . . well, early days, Greg, early days, but with a little push I think we could get you the figure you want . . . Ha, patience! . . . What's that? . . . Well, I'm at a conference all next week, but – yeah, nothing sexy, just a load of men in grey sitting around talking about *growth* – yeah, yeah, I know – but I'll be back in touch before the following Monday. Leave it to me. Anyway, how was your holiday? . . . Good . . . Did you try that restaurant I recommended by the sea? Yes, the food's excellent, isn't it? Nowhere quite like Greece this time of year . . . Right . . . oh . . . a call on the other line, Greg . . . must go . . . speak soon.'

Sometimes if you don't cut these guys off, they'll talk all day. Trying to get at facts they don't want to know.

As I pressed the 'Off' button on the phone, a loud noise brought me back to reality. Dad was shouting from the other room.

'Lewis! Go and check on your mother!'

'In a minute,' I moaned.

22

When I was small he'd pull up a spare chair and tell me all the reasons why he loved Mum, while he clipped steadily away at a regular. I listened in wonder then – but he couldn't even go and get her from her room any more. Eventually I got up off the chair and went upstairs to tell Mum she could hold off no longer. She came without a fight, standing sadly in her all-black outfit when I entered, insisting (by standing next to the bowl and gripping the side of the glass) on giving the remaining fish their tea before leaving. We fed them together, then I put Mum into her coat one arm at a time. I picked her handbag off the desk and said, gently enough, 'You know, you should be nice to Daisy and Tampa Bay. You can be like this with the rest of us, we're used to it, but you have a granddaughter now. Isn't that nice? You always wanted one of those.'

Mum picked up the packet again, emptied the rest of the food into the tank and her little treasures hovered round it in a way that showed they wanted dessert but weren't entirely sure it was the done thing to accept.

Dad drove Chuck, Daisy and Tampa Bay to the restaurant in the larger car my parents used to share; I took Mum and Philip in my battered newer one. This vehicle division suggested itself as naturally as anything did in our family, as Philip and Chuck only spoke to each other when necessary, which was not often, and when forced out of her room Mum always came with me, mainly through a slightly greater mistrust for everyone else. Whatever other crimes I was known for at home, dishonesty was not one of them.

As I drove, answering Philip's cheerful probes about my love life with monosyllabic 'Yes's and 'No's, I was relieved not to be in the other car, listening to Dad and Chuck act all rigid and distant and polite with each other. When we were children, dour, practical questions about how life moved from one day to the next were given much more attention than anyone's feelings – these were considered an extravagance indulged indecently by the kind of politically correct liberal sissies that were to blame for the decline of the Empire. Nothing much had changed as we grew older, though we no longer had to stand to attention and call our father 'Sir', so Dad's talk with Chuck would probably just be a safe, adult version of an old one they used to have before he left for the States. He would be far more comfortable asking him how that new additional room or redecorating job was going than entering the dangerous conversational arenas of politics, relationships, love.

I preferred to be with Philip, the most touchy-feely of all of us. Touchyness and feelyness was avoided by everyone else. Especially since Chuck got stationed close enough to the trouble for nobody to want to know exactly where he was. Just in case we saw it on the news, or heard a customer talking about it; all the things the papers said soldiers were doing; how we shouldn't be there in the first place. Now with every spoken word came the chance for someone to slip up and mention how they *felt* about Chuck doing what he was doing. There were no pictures up in the shop of that war. Too inflammatory. Especially now. One poster had been enough provocation. In the other car, Dad would be simply trying to think of a way to show his son he was pleased to see him alive and on leave without seeming to touch him on purpose. I was better far from that suffocating bloody manliness that ruined everything so effectively. Meanwhile, if Philip's questions got too uncomfortable I could always mention lightly in front of Mum that he was a . . . well, you know. One of *them*. Not that I'd ever do that. All the defences would come down then. We'd rip each other to pieces.

LP: You disappeared. I thought I'd never hear from you again.

CC: Well then, you must be luckier than you thought. How have you been?

LP: Fine.

CC: I have an idea, Lewis. Something I want you to help me with.

4

The Meal at Benny's

We parked outside Benny's.

'Right, Mum, shall we go?'

I helped her into a standing position.

'You know,' Philip said to me, taking Mum's other arm in his, 'If you keep proving you're prepared to do anything for her, she'll have no need to change.'

'Please, Phil. You're not here much. I know what I'm doing.'

'Is this going to go on for ever?'

'She's not well.'

'I'm just saying . . .'

'And I can hear you. But I'm not the only one.'

Maybe she was enjoying all this. Not in a cruel way, just in the way I'm told mothers enjoy having family around them on special occasions. The kinds of mothers who insist on doing washing for adult sons, always making sure they leave after a visit with a meal or two in plastic containers and tin foil; asking them if they need any money. Slipping some into a pocket anyway, even if they refuse. Our mum couldn't do any of that, but a small sign that she was pleased we were together round the same table, for her, would have been nice.

'Ready, Mum? Now. Let's have fun tonight, shall we? Would the birthday girl like a drink? Why not, eh?'

She looked up at me with the same blank, childish sadness as always.

'Okay then. Let's go.'

As we walked towards the front door my phone beeped and I checked the message. From Rakesh, of course. I don't have many friends: EAT WELL, LIVE LARGE, DON'T WORRY. R.

For a moment I wished Rakesh had come with us, but he'd probably sent that message from some party, already having more fun than we ever could. I flipped the phone closed, opened the door to the restaurant and ushered Mum through.

The others had already arrived and were sitting at the table, waiting. Daisy started clapping when she saw Mum shuffle through the old revolving door, and everyone else followed her example, cheering like she had done something amazing we could hardly believe. I found it difficult to raise my arms from my sides to join in, but made myself do it, feeling the muscles ache, wanting to resist. It was a miracle having us all together. I should have been happy. Enjoying myself. Relaxing. I looked at Mum's face to see if there were the beginnings of a smile anywhere. A standing ovation! Even Dad was clapping! Who wouldn't be pleased?

Benny's was a poky, dirty restaurant near the more fashionable part of town – Dad used to go to school with the owner so we always went there, no matter how bad the food or service was – that's what Dad calls loyalty. Mum never liked the place. It had been nearly thirty years since she'd knocked back Benny's advances in a Wythenshawe car park, but she doesn't forgive so already the atmosphere was tense, though we were only just in the door. I looked around at the other tables, mostly empty, surprised at how sad the decrepit look of the place and the few customers in it made me. The chairs were upholstered with a dusty dark-red velvet that might have seemed stylish in the sixties but now was just a sign the owner was out of touch or unable to afford a refit. Even the positioning on the street – between an underground jazz club and New York-style deli with seating out on the pavement, showed up how out of place Benny's was. It was bound to be swallowed up soon, become flats or an independent clothes shop, but for some reason, as I approached the table with Mum's arm through mine, that was depressing rather than exciting. These days I felt like a set of party balloons being pricked repeatedly, popping and

27

popping and popping. Anything set me off.

After seeing Mum to her seat, I took the place between my brothers. They argued too much for me to have the easy life I was after but there weren't any better options. Dad headed the table at one end, opposite Mum and between Chuck and Daisy; Tampa sat quietly on Daisy's knee. She was such a happy child. I wanted to cuddle her but didn't know much about children apart from that they break easily, and I didn't want to be responsible for anything as dramatic as a breakage before dinner. So I just smiled.

'Aren't you gorgeous?' I said to my new niece.

Having Phil around was already having an effect on me. I could feel myself going soft. We each took a menu and pretended to be engrossed by it.

Seeing us all together, I realised that most of my family didn't look like each other, apart from me, who was an obvious composite of the others. Mum and Dad had such a different build. Where Dad was small, skinny, wiry, Mum was a big woman – over the last few years she had become bigger through lack of exercise – with thick fingers, broad shoulders and round back, as if weighed down by a heavy head containing too much anger, sadness, unnecessary additional weight. Chuck, who was about twice the size of his wife, had inherited this trait the most, making him seem like a great grumpy mulleted rhinoceros, one fat single eyebrow furrowed as he tried to pick something to eat – but his physique was the only one in the group that was still mainly muscle. Philip was the inverse of Chuck – a thinner, more stylish model apart from the receding hairline he pretended didn't bother him. It was obvious he wasn't the army type. There used to be a mole above his lip, but that had been removed since we were last together. Looking at his new, moleless face, it seemed strange that he didn't look like anyone at all, least of all Chuck. I only know one other set of twins: Fiona and Catriona, two girls from the old Academy crowd, who are both nurses now. At school, those twins had similar names, same clothes, same faces, voices, hobbies, and mostly traded the same boyfriends since primary school. My twin brothers looked like they'd arrived from different worlds.

I was a stick-thin weed compared with Mum and Chuck, though Dad and Philip considered me fat. In other company I was that familiar kind of slightly overweight twenty-something whose expansion starts with a small bump of the stomach in the teens and increases by degrees over the decades until you're so big you can't be sure you still have toes. That's how it happened with Grandpa, who was, as he always told us, 'lean, mean and hungry' in his army days. (Hungry enough to eat solidly for twenty years once he came home, said Chuck.) Dad handed round a basket of half-stale bread. We all took a chunk and busied ourselves.

'You ready?' asked the waiter, a sullen teenager who looked like he had been put into his cheap bow tie and creased shirt by force.

'Oh yes!' we replied. 'Good timing!'

We were pleased to have the opportunity to talk to a stranger, and the others asked many questions before finally settling on a dish. 'What exactly is in a Car-bo-na-ra?' 'Is it possible to get half a pizza for half the price?' 'And how much is the cheapest wine?' 'Yes, we are celebrating, but we don't want to go crazy now, do we?' The waiter looked terrified. As always, I picked the first thing on the list from both the starters and mains menu, the melon and the pizza margarita, doing the same for Mum, who was looking at me with an expression of extreme panic. Once her meal had been written on the waiter's scrap of paper she relaxed a little. Margarita is often the opener on the menu in Italian restaurants. It's bland and usually done badly, but that's a small price to pay for peace of mind. With a clear system it's easy to make the kinds of decisions that used to send me into a state of panic, and sometimes still can – what to eat, what to drink, how much to spend, what out of the billions of things in the universe to do *next*. The first dish on the menu is never the most expensive and it's rarely got meat in it, so you're safe in so many ways: Mum doesn't eat

29

meat, and when I'm nervous the sight of anything that used to breathe makes me feel ill.

The food came. Mum seemed far away from us all, at one end of the table with the spare seat to her right, but that's where she had shown me she wanted to be – sitting next to one of us was effort enough. Occasionally she reached across Philip's plate for the salt or pepper (she added too much to all the meals I prepared as if to remind me that she, not I, was in control of her diet – and she retained the habit now we were out), but otherwise continued like none of us were there and she was having her normal nightly meal alone with the animals. She missed out on conversations about Philip's fast-developing popcorn business in Toronto ('It's the most profitable thing on the planet! Do you know what the mark-up is on a regular cinema tub? You'll die when I tell you!'), Chuck's plans for once he left the army and, mostly, the situation with United in the light of last week's disappointing draw. It was only October and Chelsea were already running away with the league.

'They might as well just print the balance sheets instead of the league tables,' said Dad. 'It's not a proper game any more.'

I tried to include Daisy in this last conversation, explaining, in the best way I knew, how a game with no goals in it could be described as a good result for the away team, wondering aloud why we all spent so much time talking about a sport we would never dream of actually playing, and that it was possible to watch for nearly two hours without having anything to cheer.

'Men have got to talk about something, I suppose,' said Daisy, with a gentle smile in Mum's direction. 'Can't sit in silence all the time.'

And then she realised what she'd said.

Daisy explained how she came from a big ice-hockey-mad family, and how there were usually lots of goals in hockey games; but the season had been cancelled over a wages dispute so her brothers were getting interested in football. That excited everybody. Dad had an excuse to be friendly without seeming inappropriate and Philip could quiz her about her Canadian heritage. Chuck had kept that detail about his wife quiet when they got married at the base back in 2002, surrounded by flags, in full uniform, to the sound of Jimi Hendrix playing the 'Star-Spangled Banner'.

'You lose the accent after a while,' said Daisy sadly. 'You lose who you used to be.'

'True enough, love,' said Dad, so loudly that Mum looked up from her dinner. 'That – is – true – enough!'

After a bit more sports talk we ran dry again, with Mum breathing deeply, eyes half-closed, clinging to her part of the table so tight that her knuckles were white. Every time she looked up Dad was there, grinning falsely, continuing as if everything was as it should be in a close and loving family that was welcoming in the new generation for the first time. That grin was Dad's only remaining weapon in the ongoing silent war between him and his wife. Mum concentrated on her margarita, reaching for her wine glass without even looking up to see where it was, so as not to get an accidental glance at her husband. That was why she spilled her drink twice. The first time, nobody said anything and the waiter saw to the mess, apologising repeatedly as if it was his fault. The second time, Dad got up.

'For Chrissakes, Marion . . . for *Chrissakes* . . .'

Dad went round to the other side of the table, picked up the glass and dabbed at the red mess with his serviette. Everyone else stayed still. Mum didn't look up.

'So nothing's changed, then?' said Chuck, half-laughing. 'We all still see to Her Ladyship?' He raised his voice. 'It's pathetic. There's a world out there. Some of us are fighting to keep it!'

'Don't talk about Mum as if she's not here,' I said sharply. 'Have some respect.'

But Chuck had been hoping for that. He threw his knife and fork down and spoke boldly.

'If she has something to say, let her say it. God knows we've come far enough. She could at least say hello to her grand-daughter.'

He pointed at a smiling Tampa Bay, who was sticking her tongue out, seeing how far it would go. She was waving a spoon and had food in her hair. She was the kind of child that made you want to go out and get one of your own.

'Her granddaughter! . . . You think it's cheap to come over here? Do you know how much this cost me?'

'Eat your food, Charles,' said Dad calmly, brushing a little sauce from Mum's chin before returning to his place. 'God knows what Benny will think of us if he hears this racket.'

'Aren't we *paying* to make a racket?' said Chuck, raising his voice further. 'Actually, aren't *I* paying to make a racket? God, this family hasn't changed one bit!'

Dad looked down, talking steadily, without animation. 'You could try harder to understand us, you know.'

But Chuck felt he was trying hard enough already, and had shown it by paying for three return tickets, Dallas, Texas to Manchester, England in cold, hard dollars he'd earned on the battlefield. What more evidence could there be?

'Daisy,' Chuck snapped. 'Every bit of that gunk you give the baby dribbles back out or ends up on her clothes. Isn't there something you can do?'

Daisy cleaned her daughter, put her carefully in the pram, then winked at me.

Sometimes I misunderstand things, but at that moment I was sure she meant: *You and I both know that man is a brute. One day we will be rid of him.* Or maybe she just loved Chuck and could see that I didn't; not all that much, anyway. A love main-tained through obligation can be a weak one, and mine for my brother was sometimes hardly worth the word. It was more like a fragile agreement to tolerate. He set about the rest of his steak with enthusiasm, leaving the vegetables to one side, as always, and I began to feel sick. I didn't see him look up at his wife the whole time he ate – if I had one like that I wouldn't risk looking away, just in case she escaped while my guard was down – but Chuck acted like he didn't need anyone or anything. Being in the army seemed to do that to most members of my family, and I was glad I had not emulated them, though it had been a close thing. I got as far as the medical, then ran – and I've been running from it ever since. I tune out when they're talking about it. I don't even know what rank my brother is. Why would I want to?

'Everything okay over here?' said the waiter nervously.

'Oh yes,' we all said, nodding, 'Lovely. Just fine. Good. Great.'

'Tell Benny,' said Dad, beaming proudly. 'The food is the same as always.'

At the mention of that name, Mum snapped her gaze upwards, eyes bulging as if about to pop from their sockets. She still noticed things when she wanted to. And there was no need for her to speak, really. Everyone enjoyed complaining about her silence but she expressed herself in other ways. As well as her appointed birthday (Philip suggested the same one as Julie Andrews some time in the eighties – he says lots of foundlings choose a birthday in that way), it was also another anniversary – eight years since she had spoken to anyone except her pets and the occasional word, I suspected, to her social worker. She'd go on in silence as long as the family insisted on not seeing why she was doing it.

'Would you like dessert, Mum?' I asked. 'How about some cake? It is your birthday, after all . . .'

She tapped the table once with the base of her fork, which I took to be a 'Yes', and when the waiter came I ordered cake all round. Twenty minutes later most of the dry, flavourless desserts lay partly uneaten apart from Mum's, whose plate was spotlessly clean, making me feel like at least one good decision had been made.

LP: Why all the mysterious messages?

CC: All new members get that. Don't be put off, it's just for security. You're different – I trust you already.

LP: Are you going to tell me what all this is about?

CC: Soon. How's your mum these days?

LP: The older she gets, the worse she is – I don't think anyone can help her now. You're the only person I know who understands that.

CC: Yes. But what if I were to tell you that you could help foundlings like her, and like me, and rescue yourself at the same time – all without having to leave the computer?

LP: How did you know I needed helping?

CC: We all do. Why would you be any different?

5

The Party Goes on Too Long / An Unwanted Memory

Philip had been waiting for a moment to make his speech and give out his gifts, but all that presented itself was quietness. Mum wasn't entering into the intended spirit: it was like having a sullen child at the end of the table, unconcerned about spoiling the atmosphere for everyone else. It was stupid to try to have a good time if she wasn't going to, but what did we expect? Faced with her stillness, even us brothers struggled for anything to say to each other:

'So, how's the army treating you then, Chuck?' Philip asked.

'Good.'

'Good.'

'Yes. You should have stuck the army out, Phil. It would have made a man of you.'

'I'm very happy how I am, thanks.'

'Like I said. The army would have made a man of you.'

'What does that mean? I mean, have you killed anyone?'

'I love my job. At least mine is necessary. Who needs popcorn? . . . There's no movie theatres in the Afghan mountains, you know.'

Dad cut in. 'Charles, why do you talk like you've swallowed a copy of the American Constitution? *Movie theatres*. What the hell's a *movie theatre*? I'd love to know!'

'Pop, that's how we speak.'

'*Pop?* What am I now – a bottle of Coca-Cola? That's not how I brought you up!'

'America is my home now. It's assimilate or die where we live.'

Dad looked desperately to Daisy for confirmation. 'Are the Texas suburbs at war with each other now?'

'Everywhere is,' said Chuck, interrupting his wife before she could answer. 'Whether they know it or not. Everybody knows that.'

'Enough!' Dad smashed his knife and fork down into the abandoned cake. 'You're on the Queen's property now – *I will have RESPECT!*'

And this was supposed to be us making a big effort. We were all too selfish to do it properly, I suppose. For Mum, anyway. Mostly, we didn't feel she deserved it. Dad neatened his cutlery.

'Why do my boys talk like Yankees?'

'Canadians aren't Yankees, Dad,' said Philip.

'Damn it, why are my children not at *home* any more?'

'I am, Dad.'

'Yes but *apart* from you, Lewis. Of course *you're* here. But what about these two? Is the country of Churchill and Dickens and Bevan and Shakespeare and Bobby Charlton and Fleming and James Watt and bloody God knows who else not good enough for anybody any more?'

Philip interrupted. 'Actually, Fleming was a Scot, Dad. So was James Watt. That's exactly the kind of confusion that happens between America and Canada all the time. The achievements of the poorer country always get absorbed by the rich neighbour, while . . .'

Dad listened to this speech sitting down, then stood, redfaced as Philip's sentence stumbled to a halt. He said, with frightening steady clarity. 'I am going to the lavatory. When I return we will all be nice to each other. Is that clear?'

The box had peeped open, then been firmly shut again.

At first I had absorbed these awkwardnesses more easily than others, sometimes barely even registering the painful, gaping absences between each forced comment, the horrified look on Daisy's face as she slowly realised how the family she had joined communicated; I dealt with these things every day, without agitation. I tuned out, mainly. Operated unaffected.

37

But now even I was finding it difficult. And Philip was, too. He had fidgeted, sighed and tutted his way through the meal so far, unable even to manage an hour in Mum's quiet, steady, determined presence, where I had to look after her for days without a break. Take her tea. Talk. Make sure she had supplies. Philip seemed to have forgotten how controlled she could be in company and looked on in amazement at her lack of movement, expecting her to react in some way, to something, being continually shocked when it didn't happen. At last he decided the time had come – if only to avoid more emptiness – to give out his presents. Like Dad, like me, he just wanted everyone to *get on*, regardless of what they were thinking or feeling. We were continually smoothing over the little frictions that threatened to turn into big ones and end us. The speech Philip had planned in Mum's honour was sensibly abandoned, but the presents couldn't be. Or else he'd have to carry them back to the car.

Philip reached under the table and brought out a big bag of goodies, handing out each one with an explanation, just as he always did on his annual returns home, only this time with the addition of Daisy and Tampa Bay: 'I thought you could use this in the garden,' 'I know how much you like that colour,' 'A voucher for the Aquarium, Mum! Just let me know if you want me to change it . . .' (twice the usual amount because it was a special, round-number birthday). Philip couldn't just be generous; everything had to be a performance. But he was making the effort, and was the only one among us not too ashamed to show a little emotion.

'This is for the little one,' he said, passing a crumpled old Polka-dot blanket over the empty wine bottles to Daisy. 'I thought it would be nice to pass on.'

The rest of us just kept eating – so much Philip did was taken as embarrassing and obvious evidence of his sexuality to those of us who knew about it, and unexplainable weirdness by those who didn't – but Daisy liked the unusual gift.

'If it's important, surely you'll want to keep it?'

Daisy looked at Mum for some indication of approval, but she was busy negotiating her wine glass, twirling it round at the base with one finger from each hand.

'You're family now,' said Phil. 'Take it. She's so beautiful. I'm a little old for it these days!'

The blanket went straight in the buggy and Tampa Bay seemed to reach out, snuggling back into position with her little arms wrapped around her present.

'Aah,' said Philip. 'What a sweetie. Why don't you introduce her properly? She's doing no harm.'

He peered over.

'Come and say hello to your uncle Phil, darling!'

Delighted at the opportunity, Daisy took her out of the buggy and passed her over, while I wished I had done the same earlier, and Chuck fumed. He knew how to deal with big nasty animals but not gentle effeminate ones. Philip, I thought, as he bobbed the little girl on his knee, would have made an excellent drill sergeant. He got things done. The Maple Leaf Popcorn Co. would do just fine.

Even in this period of great attention for the baby, Mum hardly looked at Tampa Bay, who was continuing with life wonderfully unaware, trying to clap her hands but missing one palm with the other each time, enjoying movement, just beginning to learn how to use her arms and hands. I hoped she would do something impossible to ignore. Tie a knot in a handkerchief. Breathe fire. Write the winner of next year's Grand National on the table in crayon. A new addition to the family might have forced Mum out of herself a little – I imagined her seeing the little girl arrive at the house, running to meet her, embracing Daisy and child and crying out, 'Welcome to England!' – but I was beginning to realise that she wasn't going to break, or even crack. I looked at Mum and tried to give a smile of approval.

'You know what? I think Tampa Bay has your eyes.'

But she knows my methods and doesn't succumb. Mum grinned as if to say she knew what I was up to and it was a nice try, but one that would, like all others, fail. She returned to her glass twirling while I felt the beginnings of tears forming. The words *Because the lost just want to be found* seemed to flash before me as I tried to blink them away. Dad came back from the toilet and sat down with an exaggerated, satisfied sigh that meant his bowels had moved in a way that had made him, at least, feel infinitely better.

'Right then. Everything okay? Good. Everything's oookay.'

He filled his glass to the brim from a newly arrived bottle of wine, and soon it was empty again.

It seemed like Philip had been giving the presents out for ever. The last one was for me – a traveller's pack including a miniature map of the world, a globe key ring, copies of *The Beach* and *Teach Yourself Spanish in an Hour and a Half* and a large string of multicoloured comedy condoms which Philip slipped under the table. My brother put his hand on my shoulder and whispered, 'For if you ever get round to going on that trip. Hope it comes in handy, buddy. Make sure you get plenty while you're away!' He lowered his voice even further. 'But if you want to be a *proper* traveller, avoid the English. And the Australians. They infiltrate, everywhere. Poison everything. Charge in and get drunk for a year, pull a moonie and head back to Oz . . .'

Now he pulled away and continued talking, but much louder, so Chuck could hear, 'And *God*, the *Americans*. Ugh!'

Philip turned to Daisy and Tampa Bay and said charmingly, 'Present company excepted, of course.'

Daisy nodded, amused. Tampa Bay clapped. Chuck could take no more of being ignored and retaliated sarcastically, 'Oh – *your lot* are okay, apparently, but then you would say that.'

He faced Daisy. 'Phil loves Canadians. Even the murderers.'

It was a long-standing joke between the three of us that we only saw the good things in our countries of choice and were unable to accept that, say, people in Toronto (in Philip's case) were not the best golfers, or physicists, or window cleaners on the planet. This extended as far as crime, considered as much a skill as anything else in our game: before anyone left home Chuck used to wind up Philip by saying there was nothing Phil liked more than an efficient, organised Canadian murderer, whenever something gruesome came on the news. 'Even if one broke into our home and murdered us all in our sleep,' he said, 'Phil would stand at the gates of hell blaming America.' Chuck was more serious these days, but he was as dumb when it came to sensible analysis of Texas life – 'The best, kindest, most honourable people in the world and no mistake!' he'd say, pounding the table with his fist. 'Show you sorry bunch up as like the miserable stick-in-the-muds you are.'

He never missed an opportunity to make us look ridiculous.

I hadn't noticed myself drifting out of the conversation and into my own thoughts, only beginning to notice people were talking again just as they were getting annoyed with me.

'Aren't you going to thank me?' said Philip, turning. 'Are you too well paid to lower yourself to our level now, or have you just given up on travelling?'

'Thanks,' I said, trying to catch up. 'I'll find my own way.'

I was confused. Phil seemed to sneer, 'Sure you will.'

I wasn't sure the edge to his voice was imagined, but I couldn't be polite to anyone any more. 'You probably had a bad time,' I said, getting my thoughts together, 'because you walked through the world with your eyes patched over with maple leaves. My experience will be different. Thanks for your gifts.'

But as soon as I'd said that, I wished I could take it back. I was ashamed, and didn't want to spoil the meal any more than it already had been.

'I'm sorry, Phil. I don't know what's wrong with me . . .'

My brother laughed loud and hard, hand firmly back on my shoulder. 'Stop it, will you? It's tiring. You're allowed to be annoyed for longer than that, you know. Dear *God*, somebody sling another big fat slice of *repression* on the barbie, eh?'

He burped.

'Do you think I could get another drink?'

41

I didn't know what to say, apart from, 'Yes, yes. I'll see what I can do about that.'

The fury sizzled and bubbled inside me. Another bottle of wine was ordered.

I never even realised I was angry until I was shouting – and then the rage was gone, so quickly. That's what my temper has always been like. Long periods of quiet, then a brief explosion, then back to silence. From the very first morning at the Academy I sat obediently next to Christy in every class, keenly raising my hand to try and answer questions the teacher asked, trying to prove I deserved to be there, amongst all the other clever children who had been plucked from ordinary schools and brought to this special one. I usually behaved. Nearly always. But one Monday morning, after being marked out to solve a simple maths puzzle, I gave an answer so wrong that everyone started laughing; even the teacher let out a smile. I stood up and screamed, then sat back down again: that's what I felt like doing now. God knows what happened inside me to trigger the overflow back then – the break-up, probably – it's sad, but everything, if you look back far enough, is because of your parents, I reckon. Talk politics all you like, but if the Russian president's mother doesn't return his call, he gets upset and presses the nuclear button, we're all done for, bunker or no bunker. These days it's safer for me to stay quiet – because even now, once I open my mouth, I never really know what's going to come out. Except in the office. That's different. That's another world.

Now it was Dad's turn to get annoyed again. 'What's this about a holiday? If you're going away I shall need some notice so I can get cover for you at the shop. Will it be longer than a week? Because if it's a week then maybe we can get by, but any longer and you're really costing us. Things are tight enough already without you swanning off somewhere to get a suntan.'

For a table where so little had been said, there seemed to be a lot of people keen to chip in with an answer.

'Has he not told you, Dad?' said Chuck, first in the queue.

'Lewis has been planning a trip to *find himself* or something. He was supposed to be going three years ago. Then two years ago. Then last year. Now he wants to go off with some girl to *feel* things, or feel *her* things at the very least. The last I heard it was postponed till January. Really, you don't know about this? He'll be gone much longer than a week if he ever has the guts to go.'

He gulped at his wine gleefully, then turned to me. Chuck was drunk.

'You'll never go though, will you? You're afraid. Of course you are. Too afraid to join the army, too afraid to stay in school, and now too afraid to go and be a hippy somewhere in the fucking mountains, smoking pot and talking about truth and justice like they're brand-new words no one's heard before.'

Dad pushed his drink away.

'Is this true, Lewis? When were you going to break the news? Does nobody tell me anything? *Well?*'

I was proud of what I did next. I got up from the table, raised my glass, said 'To Mum!' – drained it, took my jacket off the back of the chair and put it on with calm assurance, kneeling down by my mother and saying, 'Happy birthday. Your other children will have to take you home tonight. I'll pick up the car in the morning, then bring you breakfast a little earlier than usual, okay? And don't worry. I'll remember the fish food.'

She extended her cheek to be kissed and raised an eyebrow as if to ask why her routine would be disturbed.

'I'm going for a swim in the morning, there'll be no time later. I have to work on my presentation. It's due on Monday morning. Remember me telling you?'

She smiled slightly, I think. Sometimes you have to look close for how people feel in our family. I peeked back at Chuck for a moment, seemingly enjoying the breakdown of this most simple of moments, and then at his wife, who wasn't enjoying it at all.

'I'll be in O'Toole's,' I said to Philip. 'Someone from the office is having a leaving party. Come if you like, but don't bring a crowd, okay?'

Whatever you do is selfish though. There's always someone screaming at you from the direction you didn't choose, reminding you what you've done to them. That's what Mum said when I chose to live with Dad after the split. Look what you've done to *me*. She said it in a low, barely controlled voice with clenched fists, like mine tonight, stiff by her sides.

'No more, Lewis. I don't have to take any more. Nobody should have to put up with what I have. You'll never know what it's like to be a mother but I'll explain it to you in the best way I can. It's like being punched in the stomach and face and back and legs until you feel nothing of yourself is left. You give and give and get nothing back. I can't do it any more.'

Dad appeared and led her into the bedroom.

'Ignore her. She's ill.'

'When will she be better?' I asked.

'Not all diseases can be fixed. Some are in a place no scalpel can get to.'

There were screams, then a silence, then more screams. She didn't have to listen to him any more, she said. He didn't want her. Nobody did. So why couldn't we leave her be? She burst out of the bedroom they had shared all my life, clutching clothes to her chest, and dropped them in the spare room. I stood, unmoving, while she went back and forth with her things, emptying out whole drawers onto a pile on the floor, until everything she called her own was in a heap in the spare room. Skirts, eye shadow, a few magazines and catalogues. She looked at me coldly, then closed the door. Her new home just yards from the old one. Then she stopped talking to us.

I've had a long time since then to reflect on how Mum might see things, giving up her own ambitions to raise the family she needed, becoming trapped in a nightmare she volunteered for. She even pretended to be interested in converting to Judaism for a while after she and Dad got married, even promising a second wedding ceremony and everything after she'd been let in the club – but then Grandpa Harry died and nobody cared enough for it to matter any more. We were busy assimilating as quickly as we could, scrubbing ourselves clean of anything that wasn't Britishness. Anyway, it was another sacrifice, or would have been, if things had turned out different. I always felt she would have been happier if we all believed in something else apart from the army, the Union Jack, all that. She never really bought into it the way the rest of us did. She just wanted to have something to share.

There's no point trying to explain to someone with no family tree that they don't need one – you've got to let them be, no matter how crazy it makes them. When Mum decided the unit she'd carefully put together with years of hard work had turned on her, she caved. You think something will fill a hole. It just turns into a bigger one. You fill it with sand and it still grows. What do you do? I often thought of shutting myself off – the break-up and all that came after it was a good excuse for her to do it. I quite respected her eight-year sulk, controlling her environment, surrounding herself in that one room with living beings that could not (until now) abandon her, say nasty things, sleep with customers' wives and old family friends. I even admired the way she refused to leave the house, challenging Dad by her stubborn silence behind that door to pick her up and throw her into the street, which he didn't have the courage to do. She had won, we all knew it, and she was at a kind of certainty none of us could reach. But that final look said something more, that now I think might have meant this: a speech I have practised in my head, altered, refined, until it is as right as I can imagine. It's not how she would have said it, after the break-up. It's what I imagine she would have said if she'd opened her mouth and spoken the way she used to before she returned to being ashamed of herself – using fewer words, saying less:

45

Giving birth unleashes a new wave of unpredictable sad-
nesses upon yourself and new, imagined people who cannot
be expected to love you the way you need. It is a selfish, cow-
ardly distraction. There are enough unwanted children
already in the world without bringing fresh ones in. How
can anyone do it? I don't know, but I did it myself, bearing
three I do not recognise any more. They are nothing like the
babies I cradled in my arms, put to sleep at night, told my
secrets to in the dark. They want things I can't comprehend.
I should have searched out three foundlings, raised them and
then set them free. I understand why my own mother left me
now. You disgust me. I disgust me. Enough.

I was still standing in the doorway of the restaurant, hovering.
What to do? I could have let my plans pour out, but how could
I be sure to get the words right? Anyway, I might change my
mind again – as Chuck had reminded everyone so smugly, my
first wasted plane ticket was bought a long time ago. There
had been several since then. I was supposed to just empty the
savings account and go. Get on a plane to Paris and take it
from there – off to all the more beautiful, more glamorous,
more satisfying, more interesting places on earth than the
Victory Barber, England. But I was required. I still am. The
business depends on my support; not everyone can run away.
And my parents need me, though neither of them will say it.
That's how people like things sometimes. Unspoken. I understand that because I too have a long list of things I mean to say
that can't ever seem to find a way out. I didn't tell Dad about
my plan to leave with Anna this week because he would have
complained, then complained some more, then insisted I go,
then never forgiven me for it. He'd just said the opposite, but
that was different. That was in public. That was when it was
just an idea, not a reality.

I left without another word to the family, quietly paying
Benny at the door so Chuck couldn't have the pleasure of
insisting on it in front of everyone once I'd gone. Benny asked

if we'd had a good time. I looked him in the eye and said Mum hadn't been so happy in years. A voice at the table, Dad's, said, 'How selfish. And on tonight of all nights.'

Philip now: 'Do you think he's okay?'

Chuck: 'As okay as anyone else, right? If he wants to go, let him. He wants to spoil the evening – he doesn't care what he does to us. We've come all the way from Dallas to be walked out on.'

I left the restaurant and walked down the road, crossing at the lights and stepping up onto the wet pavement, the puddles splashing water onto the bottom of my suit trousers, making them damp. I thought about whether there was anywhere else I could go but the place I had already told Phil I would be. I wasn't sure whether I wanted to see everyone from work.

CC: You feel trapped – but that's normal. I did too. I felt the world was too big and rotten and doomed, and I was too small to change it. We're made to believe that by rulers and advertisers, but it's not true.

LP: So what can I do?

CC: Forget previous immoral living – guilt does no good. Great visionaries don't sit around feeling bad. They battle the future. They don't avoid problems. They don't run away. What you need to do is: learn to see the scales. When I open my eyes – *really* open them – all I see are scales that need to be reset. Little ones. Big ones. Ones so faint you can hardly be sure they're there. But believe me, Lewis, they are. The world is full of injustices waiting to be righted.

LP: Maybe, but you can't solve everything everywhere. Isn't it better to concentrate on one thing and do it properly?

CC: Yes! Yes! And that's what Hope for Newborns is all about.

HFN-I: #013

6

O'Toole's

When Anna asked me where they should hold Belinda's leaving party – somewhere the decor would explain, without anyone actually having to say it, that we were all pleased to be rid of her – I thought of O'Toole's straight away. But I didn't think I would be joining the party. For once I thought I had somewhere to be. When that wasn't the case any more, I was drawn back to O'Toole's; choosing the familiar stops panic. It's almost like not choosing at all. Anyway, I was trying to save money, I heard Marcus had put a tab behind the bar and I wouldn't know if I really wanted to see Anna until she was close by. She says there's an Irish place like O'Toole's in every big city these days. In the one near her old flat, the James Joyce, nobody knew what Ireland was, never mind who Joyce was. Like that one, O'Toole's is a large high-ceilinged place that used to be something else, maybe a bank, and had recently been taken over by a chain that heavily advertised Irish-sounding drinks, Irish-sounding theme nights, and played modern, corporate-endorsed versions of Irish bands on a loop until 1 a.m. every morning. During term time it was full of students. On football nights it was full of the football crowd. Late on a Friday and Saturday a DJ took over from the jukebox for a few hours, then packed up and moved on to the next job. The rest of the time it was dead.

Belinda, a tall, awkward-looking woman in her thirties, had a surprisingly high turnout and was having a good time. The DJ knew he was in for one of his better nights and encouraged people to dance between records – 'Grab that special lady and get on down!' – but only a few were drunk enough to think it was a good idea. Still a little early for that. I watched Danny from Accounts as he danced girlishly in circles and played air guitar to *I just want your . . . kiss*, sliding along the dance floor on his knees like a child, while others cradled drinks, standing at the side, laughing. I just watch, think, try not to feel a lot. There's a lot I don't want to see or hear. In work today, Anna slammed the phone down on a client and shouted across the floor, 'I think I've travelled too much . . . I hate everyone now.' I didn't know what they were like in the places she'd been, but it was hard to imagine the idiots of Asia or Australasia or South America were any more easily suffered than Danny from Accounts, who was now pressing himself drunkenly onto a woman I didn't recognise, saying, 'Come on, baby . . . everyone wants a piece of the Danster pie . . .'

I don't know many people from the office any more; they come and go quickly and I don't socialise much, so I managed to get to the bar without anyone noticing me. Most of these people didn't know I was the one earning the money that helped pay their wages, which paid for their drinks and their ugly pin-stripe suits and power boots. I looked too young for that. Too nervous. Not a flash spender. Not a serial fucker of underlings. Nothing like the go-get-'em, wham-bam shark they think you have to be in our business. But my strength is that they don't suspect me. No one does. Niall the barman thought I was in for my regular quiet hour or two and greeted me as usual – I wondered if he knew I had a job at all. The thought that Niall, the only real Irish thing in the pub, might think me a harmless waster, not a hotshot city recruitment consultant, left me with a tingling, satisfied sensation. I was one of them but walked quietly among the human race, unsuspected. It was one of my few remaining pleasures.

'How you doing?' I asked.

'Looking for another job.'

'Oh yeah?'

'Have you seen our life-size blow-up Leprechaun? The

brewery sent it – for a promotion . . . If my parents knew I was working here they'd roll over and die.'

I looked round for hidden sprites in the crowd.

'Can't see it,' I said, laughing. 'Must have gone to the Gents.'

I sat for a while in the quietest corner with my lemonade. Others around me knocked back shots, sipped cheap cocktails, flirted. I can't remember at what point in my life I changed from enjoying anonymous company to needing it, but these days I could only think when surrounded by people. I always read my travel books in public, sometimes even sat in O'Toole's to make business calls, pay bills, chat by text to friends I'd met on personal sites on the internet and probably wouldn't want to meet in real life. Sometimes you've just got to get out, and, even if you don't drink, where is there to go at night but pubs and clubs? Most days there was a reason to reward myself with a soft drink and an hour watching the crowds. I wanted to go further than this place – see the Eiffel Tower, the Taj Mahal, Grand Canyon, Ayers Rock, the Pyramids, the nightclubs of New York, the Japanese underground, the Great Wall of China, the North Pole. Why not? After years of having to bail out the Victory Barbers every time a few pounds had been saved, I finally had some money to do it. But then, after the last couple of days, what was the point in doing anything like that? If I couldn't get on with family at home, what hope was there of making friends in some unknown place? Might as well go nowhere, think nothing, do nothing. I sipped my lemonade and made the same contented noise after swallowing it that Dad had done after his visit to the restaurant toilet, though I didn't feel satisfied at all.

A young woman stood above me. She was wearing an all-in-one black glittery dress that almost came down to her knees and seemed to shine under the cheap lighting, making her glow. She was light-skinned and had freckles on her face, arms and neck. As she came closer I saw it was Anna, smiling, holding a hand out looking for a dance partner.

'Bet you didn't recognise me, dressed up like this?'

'You know I don't dance. You do look good though.'

Anna sat down in the seat opposite and made herself comfortable, smiling defiantly. I didn't know to do. When we saw each other out or at office parties, Anna always acted just the same as she did at work only in different clothes. Everybody likes her for that but it can be hard to tell how she's really feeling. I'm bored of having to guess.

'I *really* love parties,' she said, talking loud to be heard over the music. 'I thought you were with your family tonight.'

I was nervous, but didn't want to let on there was something wrong. Anna is always bright and treats problems like they're no problem at all – which can be frustrating, but keeps bosses calm. No matter how intelligent secretaries are, they threaten no one, so it's easy to be nice. It doesn't occur to most of the guys on top that if the secretaries didn't turn up for a single morning there would be anarchy. And if they took the afternoon off as well, there would be no company left to come back to.

'I should go,' I said. 'I hate Belinda.'

'Don't worry, me too! Well, maybe you'll get things done around the place now she's gone, eh? Look . . . don't leave. The only reason most of us are here to celebrate is because we're so happy she's finally off. Funny to think, this is my leaving party as well, but nobody knows it!'

I only know how to be confident at work, protected by a phone and my rank, behind a door with my name on it. I backed away slightly, bringing my drink with me.

'Go back to the others.'

'What's wrong, Lewis? Didn't you come here to see me?'

'Yes. No. I don't know. I'm going, I'm going . . .'

'Wait,' she said, blocking my way. 'Don't take things so badly. I haven't gone just yet. Maybe we can spend some time together?'

'It's not that . . . it's just been . . . a bad night, that's all.'

The song began to skip, but the DJ was busy chatting someone up at the bar between songs. *Love me like you used to doooo* played repeatedly in the background until he ran through the cheering crowd of Belinda's leaving party, who were starting to have a good time. I thought of whether everyone was still at Benny's. What they were discussing. Whether I even made it into conversation in between all the army talk. I put my hand on top of Anna's, which was cradling her drink.

I said, 'I'm so sad.'

She pulled her hand away, but with no great aggression. 'Stop it.'

'Everything is my fault.'

'That's stupid,' she said. 'Watch . . . I'm going to go over to Belinda and give her a big hug and say I'm sorry she's leaving, that I'll miss her, and I'll insist we have a bit of a dance – that'll be *a big fat lie* and there's *no way* that can be your fault.'

'It doesn't work like that . . .'

But she was already gone, running off to the dance floor, throwing her arms around Belinda and dancing to the new song that had replaced the *Love me like you used to doooo* one. I got up and went to the bar, ordering another lemonade for me and a drink for Anna too. When she was gone I felt empty. When she was around I felt more capable, humming and buzzing with juice, even when I was acting miserable.

The dance floor emptied. The song was changing to something more uplifting: the words *Jesus walks with me* blasted out of the speakers – a rapper backed by a gospel choir: *Lord, the devil's trying to break me down.* I only listen to hip-hop these days – say what you like, but at least it's music made by people who aren't ashamed of themselves. That's the difference between black and white music. Pride. When Anna arrived back she came in beside me and slipped her hand through mine.

'I hate that song. So miserable!'

The DJ, in a fit of panic at losing dancers, cut the song short and replaced it with more of the usual: *If you wanna taste my kisses in the morning . . . Jump!* Anna looked down at the stirrer and wedge of lime and made a face.

'Thanks, but I don't drink girly drinks. The patriarchy starts with diet tonic and ends with rape and bulimia. Don't you agree?'

'What? I can't handle alcohol.'

'Well if I were you I'd consider giving it another try. It might help you forget yourself a little . . . Listen, don't you feel better now you've seen something you can't be blamed for?'

Was this flirting? On my first clumsy night with Anna, I don't remember any of that. She just grabbed me, pushed me up against a wall, kissed me and demanded to know what I had in my fridge. It was wonderful. For a few minutes, anyway, until she changed her mind and ran home, bottle of wine in one hand, high heels in the other. Anna took a sip of her girly drink then spat it out again, right back into the glass.

'Ugh! Do us all a favour and get me a pint, will you? Be nice to someone . . . that's what I always do when I feel guilty. It always makes me happier, even if they don't like it.'

'I used to be nice to people. I made friends.'

'Then what happened?' she asked.

'Everyone moves on after a while – they've always got to rush off to Macedonia or Cambodia or to do a course somewhere, and you've got to start all over again . . . Do you know how many people have worked at the desk opposite me in the last year? It makes me not want to even bother saying "Good morning".'

She'd been in the company four months. It was amazing I'd never said this to her before. But there's not much time for real talk between meetings – I tend to talk about work with work people – and I don't see Anna much out of work hours.

'You talked to *me* on my first day . . .'

'Yes. Well . . . can you believe Malcolm left as well? Said he wanted to spend a year on a Greek island to "get his soul back". This is before your time, but he was in the job before Mark, who was before Stephen, who was before Simon. I liked them all. We'd go out sometimes. Mark and I did the '03 to '04 business plan together. I don't keep in touch with any of them, though; they leave the desk and they leave your life for ever.'

'I know what you mean,' said Anna, talking even quicker than before. 'I used to worry about that too.'

'How long were you travelling before you got to England?'

'A few months. I did most of Europe then got offered the job here – it's been, like, *for ever*. Can you believe it?'

'That's nothing. I've been at the company nearly seven years – too long. I'm only twenty-two . . . I feel so *old*. I've never done any travelling, but it seems like everyone I meet has. I want to do the same. It's so dull here.'

'You're only saying that because you live here and never leave. This is one of the best cities in the world! This city is beautiful! Did you go to university? That's movement, at least.'

'I left school at sixteen. Now I look after Mum at home. Can't leave.'

'See? I said you were nice and you didn't believe me. What's wrong with you? Want to know what I do when I get depressed and dull?'

Anna came closer, cupping her hand around her mouth, planting it on my ear as if imparting a very important secret. Her breath was hot and she smelled of the same perfume she wore every day in the office and wore the night we first kissed – I'd recognise it anywhere, even mixed in with all the smoke. There was something beautifully honest about wearing the same scent both day and night. You got the same girl, no matter the setting.

'I just pretend the new people I meet are versions of my favourite old ones,' she whispered. 'That way I can be friendly straight away. I don't bother being weird with people.'

She backed off, smiled proudly, as if she'd just said something astonishing. She spoke up. 'You know, mix people around. For a while, you were a combination of three: one guy called Sam I met on Kos in the summer, one called Gareth I spent a few days with in France – *very* romantic, with these great big blue eyes, like yours – and someone I met on the train when I first came here. He didn't tell me his name but we had a good chat about where to get the best value fake stuff. You know, handbags, watches, trainers. He got off at the stop before me.'

'I don't want to be anyone but me.'

She pulled further away.

'Why not? Those guys were all lovely. And so are you, when you want to be. Look, I'm leaving tomorrow. What are you doing later?'

'Nothing. When are you coming back?'

'I'm not sure if I'll come back at all – I've been thinking about it. I'll go back to Sydney . . . eventually. Probably via Thailand. Maybe take in Vietnam on the way – is that on the way? Maybe stop somewhere and do something *worthy*. Anyway . . . I don't want to – I mean you could – what I'm trying to say is, Lewis, don't be sad about all this. We were never really together. And, I think, we should be *free* in this life, don't you?'

I clasped my hands tightly together and lowered them between my knees.

'Have you *ever* had a proper girlfriend, Lewis? And I don't mean one you met on the computer . . .'

I didn't answer.

'Well you bloody well should have,' said Anna, dropping her handbag on the table and folding her arms crossly. 'I'm setting you free for Chrissakes – I thought men wanted to be set free!'

I started picking at the candle in front of me with my penknife, sulking.

'Stop it!' I said. 'Stop it! Stop it!'

'Are you finished now?'

'I told you not to come over.'

'Yes,' said Anna, cheering. 'You did. But all those other people are even worse conversation than you are. I have to talk to somebody, right? And how are you going to get over me if I don't help you?'

'How am I going to get over you if you don't leave me alone?'

She kissed me on the cheek, chuckled, patted me on the back and made to leave.

'Hold on,' I said, getting up. 'Don't *you* have to say something now?'

'Okay. Do you want to dance?'

'You know I don't do that.'

She laughed as if this was the most obvious thing I could have said.

'Fine. Goodbye then, Lewis. Have a nice time – perhaps I'll come and see you later on? By the way, you never asked how *I* was tonight, did you?'

LP: I'm afraid.

CC: I know – you've become used to ordinary living. But any-one can be shaken out of that. We're going to do great things.

LP: You want me to give up my job, don't you?

CC: Yes.

LP: But I like it. I'm good at it.

CC: Leaving is just the first step. Think of it this way: every second you spend in that office is one extra second that someone like your mum, someone like me, but someone young enough to be saved, has to wait for help.

LP: Okay, okay. But not yet.

7

The Pure-Hearted Patriot, Son and Grandsons

Anna disappeared into the middle of the dance floor, where the other secretaries met her. I felt scooped out to empty and part of me wished she'd not come over at all, though a tiny freedom seemed to be breaking out somewhere. Energised and annoyed, I imagined going over and kissing her right there during 'My Way', but huddled deeper into the chair instead, hoping no one from the office would see me and want to talk. I might have been in love with Anna – and she'd given me plenty of chance to have her – though maybe if Belinda came over I'd find a way to love her too. I looked up to see Philip and Chuck coming towards my booth.

They pounded over purposefully as if expecting to rescue me from a gutter, find me limply holding a near-empty bottle and swearing at strangers, or fighting at the bar – but not everybody deals with problems noisily. As in the restaurant, my brothers placed themselves next to and opposite me and were instantly more relaxed once separated, Chuck lighting up a fat cigar with a naughty grin, seemingly not annoyed at me any more. They sat down without speaking. The space around us was empty. Everyone was on the dance floor – the party was really getting going.

'Why do you still come here?' said Chuck eventually.

'Is there anywhere else to go?' I said, turning away from Chuck towards Phil. 'I told you not to bring him, didn't I?'

But Chuck was first to answer, not the slightest bit offended.

'There must be a million places better than this, even in Manchester . . . Cigar?'

'No thanks.'

Philip took the one offered to me, and they sat there puffing steadily, like gangsters who'd just got away with a big bank job, not two grown men running away from Mum and Dad.

'So what did I miss?'

Chuck tapped a little ash onto the floor and let out yet another one of his cheeky smiles.

'Nothing you couldn't imagine yourself . . . Dad danced on the table . . . Mum announced she was pregnant . . . Want a drink?'

'There's only so much lemonade a man can consume.'

'Good,' said Philip, 'Because we're here to take you home. Father's orders. He thinks there's a problem. Even talked about giving you next weekend off.'

'A problem with me? *I'm the sanest of the lot of you!*'

You can get away with a lot if you say things in the right way. Philip replied, soft and kind, with his hand back on my shoulder.

'Now, now, Lewis . . . it's saying things like that that's getting everyone worried. So come on home – we'll have a nightcap with Dad, nice and quiet, no big deal, and then you can get back to your hovel.'

But I wasn't ready for giving up quite yet.

'You should come and see my place. I've really done it up. I have a plant now. And a carpet. No need to watch out for the nails any more . . .'

'Sounds like a palace,' said Philip. 'Far too good for the likes of me.'

One thing I'll say for my brothers is they don't hold grudges for long. Though Chuck had huffed and puffed, it didn't occur to either that me leaving the restaurant would be anything to do with them – and even if it was, they didn't care enough to let it spoil rare moments together once some time had passed. Every time, we just started again, maybe Phil a bit more readily than Chuck – but both of them always came round. It was less effort than being angry. Though I wasn't having one and I hated smoking, somehow the cigars helped; with each puff the tension seemed to dissipate further, and something so smelly and big as a cigar says clearly, to everyone around, *I do not care what you think*. Which is a sentiment that even I enjoy from time to time.

'Where are Daisy and Tampa Bay?' I asked. 'You didn't leave them alone with Mum and Dad, did you?'

'I put them all in a taxi. Said we'd get the bus home. Everyone's had a drink, you know?'

'But . . . were they *talking to each other*? Poor Daisy!'

Chuck snorted. 'Poor Daisy nothing. That woman's like a demolition truck. Squishes up trouble wherever she goes, one way or another. Don't pity her. She'll have 'em both on leashes by now, smackin' 'em with a stick if they don't behave.'

I finished my drink, knocking it back like it was Scotch, and we got up to leave.

'Does she want a job?' I asked. 'We could do with someone like that in my office.'

'Listen to him,' laughed Chuck, getting up. '*My* office. Ha!'

And he got up to leave.

Anna had been dancing with a few others; everyone looked like they'd had a few drinks now. On the way out she waved from the dance floor, mouthing something that could have been 'Have a good time!' Or maybe she was just singing along to the music. I waved back and felt warmer inside. I didn't bother saying goodbye to Belinda; soon she'd forget us all. I just kept my head down as we moved towards the door.

'Who was that waving at you?' asked Chuck.

'Colleague.'

'Bullshit.'

'Watch your language,' said Phil.

'Shut up,' said Chuck. 'Pair of faggots, you two. Come on, let's go.'

'You sound like Grandpa . . .'

'That was tasty,' said Chuck, ignoring that, getting up and stubbing out his cigar in an ashtray by the door of O'Toole's.

'Tasty like a thick stick of shite.'

Philip smiled and put out his own.

'That's not quite how Grandpa would have put it,' he said.

We all stepped out into the night.

Grandpa Harry lived to be eighty-seven – towards the end he told me, sitting among all the show of the shop, that he wished he could rip the whole thing down – if he'd known about some of the things we did in the name of king and country, in order to win that war he and his brothers had been so proud of, and many others, he would have lain down to die on the battlefield in shame. 'There had to be other ways to defend freedom apart from attacking it,' he said, spitting his words. Dad never knew he felt that way, and, no matter what the conflict, had always thrown his weight behind the services as if his entire soul depended on it. No matter the scandal, we were always reminded, 'The British Armed Forces are the best in the world, boys – and don't you ever forget it!' It was Dad who taught us we were living in the greatest country on the planet. That we could do whatever we wanted and be proud – I believed that the most, because for a few years he thought I was the cleverest and told me more often than my brothers that the world was mine to drink, if I wanted it. That's why they sent me to Kindler's Academy. Why they made me apply in the first place. So I could fulfil my potential.

'Only in Great Britain,' said my father, opening my acceptance letter, stifling a laugh. 'Only in Great Britain.'

Grandpa tried his best to shatter the childhood illusions he had helped form in me: the British could have blocked the lines to Auschwitz and chose not to, he explained; Churchill carved up Europe with Stalin on a piece of paper; the British army massacred hundreds at Amritsar, India; Suez was a lie. The BBC pretended we weren't bombing there for forty-eight whole hours! *No news today! No news today!* Shortly before they took him away to hospital for the last time the old man spat on the ground and said he wanted nothing more to do with our shop, but by then everyone thought he was crazy. Anna would have liked him, I think, in those last days. She's part German and is always going on about Dresden, saying we like licking our lips and telling foreigners off but don't know how to look at ourselves and see how ugly we really are. Anyway, as I grew up Grandpa's memory was kept alive as the pure-hearted patriot who fought for our freedom. He even got a photo up by Winston. During the Falklands, watching developments on TV, Dad was convinced those boys over there were like Grandpa. In 1990, he told us the boys in the Gulf were like Grandpa – doing good work. In the mid-nineties, he said the same of those serving in Bosnia. Come the next major war, his eldest was involved.

LP: How do you know this is right?

CC: Because when I close my eyes, I see thousands of sets of scales. Which is why we're going to build a great network, worldwide. Set up HFN branches wherever they're needed. You, more than anyone, should understand that.

LP: I think I do.

CC: Foundlings are the most forgotten of people; in every country. Every time we help one, we're putting a small part of the world back to its original state. Of course you understand.

HFN-I: #024

8

The Night Bus

O'Toole's was close to Benny's but too far away from home to walk it, especially in the rain. So we left the club and stood under a bus shelter, hoping a bus would come by and take us out of the cold. We would have got a taxi but I was short of money, Philip didn't want to spend any more and Chuck had made it clear that he'd spent quite enough getting over the Atlantic. After a while the night bus appeared and we stepped on; Philip paid for himself, I paid for Chuck – as he kept saying, he'd not come thousands of miles to pay his own bus fare. The air was thick with the stench of alcohol breath – like everyone was on their way to, or on their way back from, a night out on the lash. We took seats near the middle of upstairs, with Chuck on a seat in front and Philip next to me, closest to the aisle. The time, their drunkenness and the fierce jolting back and forth made it difficult to concentrate on anything but keeping the night's dinner in my belly, so I was quiet, which made it more difficult to speak up when I had a reason to. Several stops after ours a man of about thirty got on who made Philip and Chuck seem sober. Taking a seat just behind us, he burped, zipped up his jacket and pulled out a pair of thick sunglasses with the words COOL DUDE running along the stems. It was almost dark outside. The man was carrying something that looked like a phone but was blaring out music like a mini ghetto blaster; the song was some old house-music tune; I tightened my grip on the bar of the seat in front. My brothers might have forgotten what it was like here so late on a weekend, but I had not. You learn to smell danger, smell the crazy harmless from the crazy dangerous. Chuck's bulky presence made me feel a little less nervous, and that was a strange feeling – to be pleased he was there – but it didn't last long.

'Hey, you!' said the voice.

None of us turned round. The guy was talking to someone sitting on the front seat.

'Hey you! You! Hey you! Hey you!'

I tensed up further, and the young man at the front he was now talking to, who seemed more like a boy, did the same. He was wearing what looked like a school uniform. It was hard to tell from where we were sitting. Surely it was too late at night for that? I didn't know what Chuck and Philip were doing at this point because I fixed my eyes on something going on out of the window, a couple having an argument in the street. I tried not to see the man and hoped my brothers were doing the same. No eye contact. No facial expressions. Don't give them anything to notice you for.

'Can you hear me, you fucker? Hey! I've seen your picture in the paper. You're that, fuckin' . . . don't think I don't know who you are!'

Still no response, from anyone. I watched his reflection in the window. He waved his music player.

'Do you like my new toy? It was free! A feller gave it me!'

The man got up off his seat and went forward, almost toppling over as the bus jerked, forward then back, then side to side, like a juddering train swaying on old tracks. He leaned into an old man who had just got on. I tried to get Chuck's attention, but he was sitting forward, still, looking down, with one hand clapped to his waist as if looking for his army gun but finding no holster. The man in the sunglasses was right up close to the boy now, spitting while talking, saliva dribbling down his chin as he pointed, pointed, pointed, with his singing phone puncturing his insults with the thumping sound of crackling dance music, the beats blistered by the high volume and tinny sound. The other seats had filled up now, each stop bringing a new wave of witnesses. Old passengers sat with steely expressions facing forward, new ones stood as far out of the way as they could. All other conversations had been abandoned. An old woman held her shopping bag tight; two teenage boys wearing a similar kind of tracksuit to our man made themselves look as small as possible, hoping he wouldn't switch his attentions.

'Hey! Hey, you deaf?'

The boy at the front of the bus just continued looking forward, not acknowledging, not even wiping his face clear of spit. Like a professional who'd done this many times. I thought about getting up but decided it was probably better to stick to the code.

'Don't ignore me,' said the man. 'I don't like being ignored. I hate being ignored, you hear me?'

The boy attempted to stand, but the man pushed, sending him crashing into the side of the bus. The boy rebounded back off the side window and collapsed back into his seat, curling up into a ball to protect himself.

'You killed my dad!' shouted the drunkard. 'You killed my fucking dad! You think I'm gonna let you off killing my dad? I'm gonna kick you to death, you little Paki fuck!'

Finally, somebody unfroze. Philip stood up, and said calmly, as if saying hello to a friend on the street, low and cool, friendly, 'Hey . . .' and at that the man forgot the boy and came towards the three of us. It doesn't take much.

'What's that?'

'You must have had a tough night,' said Philip. 'Everything's all right here. Nobody killed anybody.'

Philip's manner was steady, calm, unflinching, even when the man feigned a punch, but I could feel Chuck shaking through the seat in front. I wanted to kill Chuck almost as much as the stranger.

'Hey, relax, man,' said Philip, palms open and outward to calm the man. 'Okay? He's just a boy. This is crazy.'

'Relax? *Relax?*'

Still Philip didn't back away, but the colouring of his face

68

did become paler as the man turned off his phone, put it into a back pocket and pulled out a thin, rectangular object he hid underneath his coat, pointing it right at us and screaming, 'You think I wouldn't? Hey? Hey?'

'No,' said Philip, 'I'm sure you would. But I'm asking you not to.'

It didn't look like anyone else on the bus would have cared or even noticed if any of us was murdered. Nobody else, including me, was prepared to do anything to stop all this, not even Chuck. Without a weapon he was impotent and seemed pathetic, sitting there, face forward, like the old women and children surrounding us. What was the point in all that training if he couldn't stop a drunken idiot waving a knife? The man was dancing around now, the point poking outwards from under his coat.

'Come on then,' he whispered. 'Come on, come on and hit me . . .'

I could smell his stinking breath, feel it mixing up in the air with mine, with my brothers'.

Philip put his arms above his head and said, 'Okay, you win.'

'Damn right. And don't you forget it, homo.'

He spat in Philip's face, then saw where the bus was and ran down the stairs to get off – even violent maniacs don't like missing their stop. If complete strangers could tell Philip was gay, I thought, watching him sprint from us, then how come our parents couldn't? The man turned and threw something up at the bus window to get our attention.

'Hey, cocksucker!' he shouted.

The man took the point out from under his coat, waved his little phone at Philip, who was peering downwards with a look of rage and fear on his face, and grinned.

'Got yer!'

Then he was gone. Philip opened the small window as far as it would go and was going to speak – he even opened his mouth – but changed his mind and closed it again without making a noise. Only then, sitting back down, did he begin to shake like the rest of us.

After the bus had moved on the other passengers around continued stony-faced, as if nothing had happened, and the kid up the front didn't move either except to clean his face, which my brother did as well. After a minute or so, Philip had to do something to get the tension out. I get that too, so I understand what he did next. He got up and went to sit down next to the kid, moved his face close and whispered sharply, 'Well? *Well?*'

But the kid just looked back, petrified. I wondered if he could even see Philip at all.

'Whoa! Calm down,' shouted Chuck from his seat, on the way back to his old self. 'Take it easy. What did *he* do? It's not his fault.'

Philip didn't reply to that. He just shot Chuck a look, and tried to get his breath back, gasping. Sometimes you can lose your breath without even moving much. From something almost happening.

'Let's go,' I said, and we all got off three stops early, walking the rest of the way to the shop.

It was dark and cold and none of us spoke for a few minutes, just pressing onward, hands deep in our pockets, collars up to protect ourselves from the rain, wanting the day to be over.

'I hate it here,' said Philip. 'You wouldn't get that in Toronto.'

'No, not in Texas either,' said Chuck. 'This country's a fuckin' mess.'

They picked up the pace and I followed. It was the first time they had agreed on anything all night.

LP: Where are you?

CC: In Latvia, at an orphanage, negotiating. But don't be in such a hurry to join me. Get yourself right first.

LP: It's all right for you, you're seeing the world.

CC: Lewis, Hope for Newborns is a company like any other. Everybody has different jobs. We need you to do yours.

9

Home Again

We were walking up the street to the shop, about a hundred yards away, still not talking, when we saw three small figures in the dark – two going at one side of the shop with hammers (puncturing my patch-up job from this afternoon), the other one spraying what was left of the door of Victory Barbers with graffiti. Half the shop front was clean, half was in pieces. Then they went for the other side. The scene reminded me of what happened when newspapers printed details of rapists and paedophiles then left them to the mercy of vigilantes, finding out later that their name was spelt differently, they were innocent, they were someone completely different.

Chuck broke into a run, shouting, 'Let me deal with this one, boys.'

These were young teenagers, so Chuck was braver. Maybe that's unfair, but I'd witnessed enough I didn't like recently to believe anything Chuck did was just more evidence of what I wanted to see. He caught the kid with the graffiti can from behind with a crack to his skull from his right fist, then when he dropped to the ground began kicking him in the head and chest, threatening to do things I hardly understood but was sure I didn't want to watch. I imagined him in his uniform; thought of those news reports that make soldiers look like animals and terrorists like frightened rabbits.

Dad appeared out of the darkness of the staircase, standing in his dressing gown, mouth open, horrified. The other two boys were too scared to make a move in case Chuck turned on them, much like the people on the bus had been. Chuck stopped for breath and surveyed the wreckage. I found myself pointing down at the kid, whose mouth and nose were bleeding. His two friends ran away.

'What are you doing here?' I asked the kid below.

I felt strangely calm, but Chuck's foot was on the boy's chest and his friends had gone so I was in no danger. He tried to get up but Chuck moved his foot to the boy's neck and he collapsed back down.

'No,' I said. 'Stay down there and listen. Leave us alone, we're peaceful people.'

'Yeah, right,' said a small, weeping voice.

'You did this!' I replied. 'You attacked us! You're damaging our property!'

'This isn't a conversation,' said Chuck, taking his foot off the boy's windpipe.

Before anyone could react, the boy was up and running after the friends who had abandoned him.

'That's right, fuck off,' Chuck shouted at his back. 'And don't come back.'

We stood on the street, watching him run.

'Stop the war!' he shouted as he disappeared into the night. 'Not in my name!'

I called after him, letting out a mighty roar.

'I agree! I agree!'

Above us, a light came on and Mum could be seen peering down from her room with a hand over her mouth. When she caught us looking she disappeared again. I wondered if she would come down the stairs when she was sure it was safe, maybe see if we were all okay. Someone did appear, but it was Daisy, holding a crying Tampa Bay. Chuck sent them back to bed with a gentle kiss for each.

'It's okay, baby. Daddy's here. Go to bed now. Bed.'

I had only known Daisy for a few hours, but I already felt it was unlike her to take that comment without question. Maybe she could see it was not the time for argument. Maybe she just wanted to get away. Maybe Chuck was her protector, and she liked it that way. She climbed the stairs and was gone.

Dad, Chuck, Philip and I sat on the barber chairs, just like we used to years ago. When we were children, before Mum's breakdown, Dad used to sit us down where the customers usually were, flip the chairs round, pour out glasses of fruit juice for us to cradle while he told old war stories in the near-darkness and we listened, proud, amazed at what our father knew about the world. We never finished our drinks: they were just for effect – like the lamplight he shone on the ceiling – we pretended we were drinking whisky, like Dad. Now it was no secret we were there, and there was no storytelling. We just sat, in shock, glass everywhere.

'I've already cleaned that up once today,' I said to nobody.

Outside, the city went on as normal. People walked past on their way to weekend pubs and clubs, glancing through the smashed window on one side at the mess on the floor of the shop, and the four of us just sitting there, looking at it. One man stopped to ask if we were all right. Nobody answered him. Then the neighbours turned up. The duty manager from the bar next door, Tsunami, came to make sure we were okay, then returned to his shift once he saw no one was dead. Rakesh came running from the other side with his parents, Aarav and Mira, and stopped in for a few minutes – Dad sent me to pull up some chairs for them and put the kettle on. They didn't say much. Didn't need to. It was just good to have them there, knowing they cared, even if no one was dead. It was like a death house anyway.

'No respect,' said Aarav, shaking his head, inspecting the damage, picking up a few things and putting them back in their rightful place. 'No respect at all. They got my windows last week. Little bastards.'

'Why did they get you?'

'They don't need a reason.'

'Do you think it was the same kids?'

Rakesh spoke for the first time. 'Same ones . . . different ones . . . what difference does it make?'

He and I were the same age, but he was more mature. When Rakesh said things like that, I wanted to be like him. He knew more about the world.

'Thanks for coming,' I told him. I wanted to say something more but worried that if I moved I would burst into tears, so instead I just gave a tight little smile, which was enough for him to understand perfectly and return a tight smile back.

After a while Rak and his family had to get back to their own business. Dad understood. Peak hours and all that, Friday night. Drunken idiot time. They had recently applied for, and got, an alcohol licence, and were beginning to regret applying for it at all. Dad hugged Aarav before he left, while Chuck and Philip looked on, amazed to see him touch someone they hardly knew, the two of them clasping each other tightly as if they'd done it a hundred times before. Somebody must have called the police when the noise started up, because some time after everything had died down two uniformed men appeared to find out what had happened, swaggering into the shop through the debris as if in full control. The police are never there when you actually need them – only to document crimes that can't be undone.

While Dad sat in his chair by the till looking defeated, head down between his knees in silence, Chuck became the measure of calm, superior authority. There was little opportunity for the policemen to ask any questions. Chuck did all the talking, his voice slipping back into the kind of stiff, almost comical officer-class speech he used to use at home, a voice similar to the two men now standing in what remained of our doorway.

'Good evening. My name is Charles Passman. On behalf of my family I'd like to report a crime. My father's premises have recently been assaulted on a regular basis by a small group of hooligans – they are probably all on your records – they looked like regular troublemakers to me. My father is greatly distressed at the moment so perhaps he can talk to you later? But my brother and I will be happy to give you detailed descriptions of our attackers. I have been a serving officer in Her

Majesty's Army, and am currently on leave from service. I am now an American citizen. My youngest brother', he pointed to me, 'is a leading member of the local business community and also a partner in this, the family commercial concern. Unlike our attackers, nobody in this family has ever been in trouble with the law. We are upstanding citizens. Search the place if you like.'

As Chuck continued talking to the officers and Philip chipped in with the occasional remark about tiny minorities spoiling things for a perfectly respectable movement, and it probably having nothing to do with the shop, and he was sure it wouldn't happen again, I went over to Dad who was sitting on his barber's chair, head clasped in hands, both between his knees. It had been a long time since I'd had occasion to touch him, but I did it now without thought, maybe because Aarav had been there first. Dad's body was shaking.

I knelt down by his side and whispered, 'It's okay, we'll get this cleared up.'

'No.'

'I'll make it look like new. And we'll get them, Chuck will see to it. If nothing else, he's good with the law, eh?'

'I understand.'

'How can you? It's disgusting.'

His voice stayed quiet, but became more insistent.

'I understand why they did it. I know those boys.'

'Let's talk about this in the morning. The morning, okay?'

It was getting late, and a cold wind was blowing in through the hole in the shop front. The officer spoke up, addressing everyone, just as Mum reappeared.

'Right, we'll be off then. We'll come back tomorrow.'

Afterwards, Chuck explained it was usual for police officers to take statements, but that he had reached an understanding that meant we didn't all have to go through that nastiness. Not just yet, anyway. Maybe tomorrow.

After the police left, things happened fast. One minute we were all standing amongst the debris, looking at each other, wondering what to say; the next Philip and I were dragging Dad to his bed in the same way we used to drag Mum after her episodes started. Restraining someone we wouldn't normally handle at all didn't feel right, but if you open a door like that, it's hard to see how it will ever close. Once the police were gone, Dad began to smash anything in the shop he could get to – before we could stop him he shattered one of the main mirrors, swept all his instruments off the table and put the till through what was left of the outside window. The Churchill photo wouldn't give way, though. He threw that on the floor but the frame didn't break.

'Typical!' he screamed. 'Stubborn git.'

Philip and I managed to get an arm each while Chuck took Mum, bottom lip quivering, back to her room, meeting Daisy and Tampa Bay at the top of the stairs. Each parent fell asleep quickly, like a couple of kids, exhausted after staying up too late and getting all excitable after a party. Everyone gathered in the lounge for a post mortem, but I was not in the mood for one. Without even wishing my brothers goodnight I picked up my coat from the barber's chair, stepped through the gaping hole in the window and left – back to my flat, wandering side to side on the pavement, singing softly to myself. Though that made me feel no better, I had to do something, make some noise. To convince myself I was really there.

CC: I wish I could make you feel better.

LP: You do. But I think you should tell me the rest now.

CC: The rest of what?

10

The Truth About the Truth

Some things you don't forget. Some dates don't slip your mind. Some memories linger in the mind, eating you up cell by cell.

On the night he found out about Mum's affair, Dad began to feel less guilty about his own. He set things in motion without permission, sitting each of his three sons down on the barber's chairs that very night and explaining the situation as he saw it. Mum gambled on him not having the courage to kick her out, saying she'd given up her life for him; she could have done great things; most women these days do. Did he really appreciate her so little that he'd end their marriage because she had spent a few afternoons in the arms of a kinder man? Well, yes. Though our house was too small to have missed any of their arguments, he argued his case to us as if we knew nothing; like we should have been covering our ears for the last six months out of respect. It was the week after I had returned from Kindler's Academy for good – it wouldn't open again, not as a school anyway. Soon I would go back to the place I'd left a few months earlier, but I knew well what was going on at home.

After a brief explanation of the situation as he saw it and a businesslike summary of the reasons he would not have his family's finances ravaged by lawyers who wanted to turn us against each other, Dad said, 'Now, gentlemen! There is a choice before you, and you must understand that choices are very important things. Make them with certainty, or else risk falling into the murky ravine of Chamberlain-like appeasement. Understand?'

Not understanding at all, we nodded. Chuck and Philip

were nearly fourteen and I was twelve, but at that moment each of us felt much younger and very afraid of our father. He was a lot stronger then, and that threatening bite in his tone turned us into obedient little boys, no longer savvy teenagers with an answer for everything.

'Good,' he boomed. 'So look inside yourselves, boys, be brave, and speak your minds . . . Your mother and I are going to be living separately from now on, because she is a whore without respect for this family. She will tell you different – she will accuse me of awful things, she'll be clever with words – but don't listen to her.'

He sighed, pacing the shop floor.

'Still, worse things happen. There's no great drama in the business. We must be able to adapt to changing circumstances. You must each elect who you wish to reside with during the week from now on. You will see the other parent twice a month on the weekend. This probably won't go on too long . . . you'll be grown up soon. And we should not presume to live long either. That is unwise. Now, Charles?'

He turned to my eldest brother, who jumped out of his seat and made the military salute. When Chuck moved I noticed I was frozen still, and could not understand why the prospect of moving seemed like the most frightening thing imaginable. It was all I could think of.

'What's your choice, boy?' said Dad.

Charles, almost in tears as he spoke, said, 'If it pleases you, Sir, I'll live with Mum. I think she needs me more.'

Dad flinched.

'Philip?' he said.

Philip got up and stood beside his twin.

'The same.'

Dad breathed in, long and slow, through his nose, then let the air out, even slower, through his mouth.

'Good boys,' he said. 'You have proved yourselves to be men. I'm proud of you. And you, Lewis? What do you have to say to your father?'

I thought of Dad working alone in the shop and how empty it would be without anyone to work with – brush up the hair off the floor, take the money, remove customers' hats and coats then give them back. I stared up into his stern face, challenging me to make the same decision as my brothers – asking without asking whether I was made of the same stuff. I was overtaken with fury at being the youngest; boyish tears filled my insides but, thank God, none could get out. Better to keep them down. Tears were cowardly. Un-British. I tried to think as clearly as Dad needed me to; look into myself and see what was there. Some small voice told me it was unfair to leave him. Though he was the sturdier of the two, no person should have all three of his children side with their mother in this situation. Should they? I reached down into myself to feel something for him, though it didn't seem like he was able to feel anything for me. He drew closer. Shaking, shivering, breathing in short, sharp stabs, I could no longer see the whites of my father's eyes – only their brown centres, staring me down. There was no deviousness there. No trickery. It just hadn't occurred to him that there was any hurt but his own – everything in his world. Sadly, I stood up as straight as I could and spoke in the most confident voice I could summon.

'Dad – I want to stay here with you.'

As if instructed to do so, my twin brothers bolted upright and stood beside me, saluting. Occasionally they showed evidence of being born together. I wanted to thank them both. Instead, I fainted and hit my head on the sideboard, my last thought before passing out being that maybe if I hit myself hard enough I would get a couple of days in bed. A while off school. A little attention.

I had misjudged both my parents. After I came round, Dad treated me no differently from the two sons who had defied him. I had hoped for some kind of favour, but he remained as equal as ever, though in the following years I stayed at home, worked with him, listened to him talk – enjoyed his company, even – while they ran as far and as fast as they could. When I left school and began at People4Jobs, a recruitment firm on the other side of the city, I still worked in the shop. He did not seem proud.

Meanwhile, Mum had taken my choice as the final rejection. 'I can't even rely on the loyalty of my sons!' she cried on that horrible night, hearing the news from her husband. He delivered the information coolly, like he was passing on a message about what he had decided we were going to eat for dinner that night. '*What did I do wrong?*' said Mum, sobbing. '*What did I do?*'

It was as if her other two children had done the same – it was no comfort to her that Chuck and Philip had taken her side. If she didn't have the full set, she'd failed as a mother, or had been failed by us. One and the same thing. And though she would never admit it, I was the favourite – for being the most dedicated out of the macho bunch she had spawned. For being the smartest, who had been sent out to the special school in the country where I had learned how to be a gentleman, and returned, so quickly, not good enough. My failure, and rejection, broke her. It was my fault. Nobody doubted it.

In the following days, weeks, months, nobody budged. Nobody moved out. We existed in numb limbo. Were they splitting up or just playing chicken? The house began to smell because Mum was not cleaning it any more and none of the rest of us had cleaned anywhere apart from the shop before. We ate takeaway most nights, and separately. Nobody checked our homework. Mum retreated into her new room, becoming quieter and quieter and finally, totally, silent. I took over most of the chores but only because I had to – there was a big hole where life used to be, everyone else was too afraid to fill it and I wanted to put something into the space where the Academy and my family had been, so I began to take Mum meals, look after her, make sure she was comfortable. Dad kept running the shop. Chuck and Philip looked after themselves, avoiding Mum like she was an embarrassing disease that might be contagious. Even now, years later, I still went round to see Mum at least twice a day. Tried to persuade her to change, be more positive, meet new people, go out – *talk*. I was still doing it. It was no use, but I couldn't have left her. I don't understand these children who think the world owes them a good time. Everything else has to be sacrificed to save them from not being able to go out every weekend. If we were still religious, they wouldn't have been allowed to do that anyway – but by then religion had become a faraway place we could no longer be bothered to travel to. If we decided to make the trip, no one would even be able to remember the way there. We still had Jewish customers, but increasingly the community was moving out of the city centre, into bigger homes in the suburbs where other shops would absorb their trade – and even the few who stayed in town never talked about God. There was a strange absence of God. Even the religious seemed embarrassed to mention Him. That word – religion – was an indicator of chaos. Of idiocy that made people do crazy things – invade, bomb, retaliate, attack.

All the details of that night of the beginning of the change circulated in my mind as I walked back to my flat. After climbing the three flights to my room and fumbling the key into the lock, I inspected my door, which still had a large crack up the side, almost splitting it in two. The landlord had been promising to do something about it since the week I moved in but it looked too expensive to be urgent, so I had dealt with it myself. I painted around the problem using the crack as the stalk of a flower, under which I had written LOVE. (The landlord had said nothing. Neither had my neighbours. I called that a victory.) After a night out, I always feel weak. After a bad one, pretty much anything makes me go to pieces. The door fell closed behind me and I collapsed on the bed, tugging at my hair so hard that I could feel the roots straining.

But nothing lasts for long. After my moment of self-pity I got up, took my clothes off and ordered them neatly in a pile on a chair already heaped with folded shirts, trousers and underwear from the previous three days – it was annoying that I had no wardrobe and no wash basket, but it was still possible to keep things something approaching tidy if I tried. I took some clean clothes off another pile and got dressed, leaving my feet bare, enjoying my own stink. This was the single guilty freedom I had from living alone. Then the light bulb went out above me. I didn't want to be alone any more. Better to have some life to share in, someone to share it with – someone that might change things unpredictably – than to sit in the dark sniffing yourself.

LP: This philosophy of yours – it's braver than I am. Sometimes I look at these walls and I'm sure that life is closing its hands around my throat.

CC: Forget those feelings. What have you done for us recently?

LP: Today I broke into my first account. A savings account in Hungary. It hasn't been touched in three years.

CC: You didn't take too much, did you?

LP: No. Like you said – just a sliver. And then I set it up, the same amount, on the first of every month from now on.

CC: See? Life is not closing its hands around your throat at all. You are closing your hands around life. How did you feel?

LP: For a second – just for a second – I felt a hundred feet tall.

HFN-I: #050

An Attractive Studio Apartment in a Sought-after Locale

It was Anna who first suggested I leave the Victory. I had always kept a firm line on why I didn't move out: my parents needed me and, more importantly, I was able to save while I was there. Unlike work colleagues of similar age, I had no debts. No student loans. No overdraft. No rent to pay. 'Come and stay with my family for a few days, then you'll appreciate what you've got,' said Marcus whenever I complained about life at home. 'You live in bloody paradise.'

But in paradise you don't need to keep bailing out your folks. I remember Grandpa Harry saying when I was very little, 'You owe your parents nothing, Lewis. They owe you. They brought you into the world – nobody made them do it – you remember that. Now grab all the biscuits you can and run!'

But there wasn't much time for escaping responsibility – I had to grow up quicker than most. The business needed constant investment to keep it going – the idea it paid for itself was now a dream no one pretended to believe in any more – so there was never quite enough saved for me to go far. How long can you live on a couple of thousand these days anyway? Instead of a rent payer, I became an investor, a shareholder, in Victory Inc. Not through invitation, but grudgingly, because my dirty recruitment money was needed to keep the shop in business. It was easy to hand over the occasional bonus as I didn't have many outgoings and sometimes I made the equivalent of a month's money just by cutting a couple of extra deals. The company gets ten per cent of the client's wages for the first year. I get ten per cent of that. They're usually highly paid jobs. It's easy money. As Marcus always said, 'Scratch that itch all you can, Lewis, because some day people are going to work out what we actually do – and before you know it we'll all be on the dole. Well, *you* might be. I'll be in the Bahamas!'

So I worked hard and occasionally put some of the profit into the family. It made me feel good. And meanwhile, I turned twenty, twenty-one, then twenty-two in the same old bedroom. Dreamt. Surfed the internet too much. Walked to the office on weekdays, worked in the shop on weekends, looked after Mum in between. In lunch hours I bought books on travelling; started courses in Spanish, French and German in my spare time (and gave them all up soon after); at nights I planned the route I would take round the world. But all from the safety of the shop.

'For God's sake,' said Anna. 'It's indecent, a strong young thing like you, wasting away in Mummy's house. There's something creepy about people who live with their parents too long.'

'But I want to save money, not spend it!'

'Then rent a rabbit hutch. Dig a hole in the ground and climb into it at night. Just get out of that place . . . you're beginning to smell funny. Like, of old people or something.'

That day I went looking for a place of my own, and soon learned that the adverts in the newsagent's shop window bore little resemblance to what they advertised.

At the beginning of the summer I moved into a place on the second floor of a large old building that used to belong to one rich person but now housed nine poorer ones. Every room was occupied by a single tenant, who for one reason or another had lost track of the rest of society. Even the landlord, a sad-looking thing in his mid-forties who insisted on doing the odd jobs himself, was a man alone. He liked to knock on the door in the evenings, pretending to check we were all okay, but really just wanting someone to remind him he still mattered. He was always talking about his ex: how he only saw his kids for a couple of hours on a Saturday and thought about them for the rest of the week, how he was missing them growing up, how there's nothing as bad as missing your kids. He was the kind of person I couldn't be around for too long without getting depressed, and though it makes me ashamed to admit it, sometimes I held my breath and pretended not to be in when he came by for a coffee and a chat. What do you pay your rent for if not to be left in peace?

Most of the tenants were quiet men who mostly kept themselves to themselves. The one directly above me told me once that his wife died years ago and he didn't want to live without her. The one across the hall used to have a wife but she left him. The one next door to him used to be married as well, twice maybe – the others weren't interested in having a wife or couldn't get one. I must have been one of those. On each level three men shared a bathroom that contained bath, sink, wooden floor covered in part by an old stretch of carpet and one small cupboard to keep toiletries in, which most were too clever to put anything inside. My room was next to the bathroom, prime spot – so any time someone washed or went to the toilet, I was the first to know about it. As I noticed when I pulled a sickie once and stayed in bed as an experiment, only a couple of the guys went out to jobs during the day. Some didn't get up till the afternoon. Some didn't get up at all.

There was an unspoken agreement between the men in the building not to bother each other or joke in the way people usually do about what was going on in our lives – we each suspected everyone else's was as miserable as our own and we probably didn't need reminding of it. Day to day there was little interaction between us. We said hello, politely, made sure there was no one in the bathroom before using it and tried to keep the TV down after ten o'clock, but that was it. No prospect of friendship between these similar men of different ages and backgrounds, no interference, for fear that any one or all would break down at the first sign of it. Just like home. All surface. This arrangement was strong and even lasted when, on rare occasion, the man in Ground Left brought a guy back for an hour or two. The walls were so thin we could all hear what was going on – even that sounded sad somehow – but I suspect we felt it was a good thing that one of us was getting a break, and it would be bad form to mention it. Also, he might not have been getting what he was getting for free – so why say something and risk embarrassment?

My room looked like a teenager's, not that of a fully grown man with a job, responsibilities, a bank account in the black. The stained old wallpaper, peeling at each corner, was covered by pictures of places I wanted to go to, like a photo album of memories not yet had, printed fresh from my favourite travel websites. Though I scrubbed the place regularly, I always felt that dust covered every surface and polluted the air in my flat. The wood around my window was rotting, though that was partly covered by piles of books recently transferred from home and awaiting a shelf to perch on, which would probably never be built. It was enough to get through each day and into the next. Pay bills. Meet targets. Iron shirts for the week. Who the hell had time to put shelves up? Anyway, the whole place was dark, dingy, too small to be worth cultivating. I had no space to keep my belongings and there was no radio except the one available through the computer I used for working out of hours: sometimes I lay in the dirt and worried that Dad would just turn up one day, unannounced, and the state of things would cause a fight. Not because it was ugly – he would prob- ably be expecting ugliness – but because I knew showing it to him would make me gloomy. He had little patience for that emotion, and I was unable to hide it whenever it took me over.

I got up, stood at the window looking across at the brewery near by and told myself I was staying here for a reason. The dirty cheapness of my little space reminded me that my money was going to something more worthy than carpets, curtains and matching three-piece suites. The strange baked-potato smell the brewery brought through the windows at night had the same effect. In the meantime there was something satisfying about knowing I was scraping by on so little, letting my wages sit there, waiting to be squandered in more exciting places. In the last few months I had thought of seeing those places with Anna. Now she was going, I was staying, and I was alone again. A wave of regret passed through me and I wanted to be back in my old spot at home. Every so often I rebel against the wandering feeling that takes up so much of my energy. Why was everyone always trying to escape? Who was to say the world outside my flat, the Victory, Manchester, was any more exciting than what I had always known? At Kindler's Academy a philosophy master taught that happiness was in the mind, not on a map – that sank deep into me and made sense because I still believed I could achieve everything I always wanted from home. I loved everything about the Academy. The morning routine, the stiff traditional ways which magically never seemed to get in the way of all that free-spiritedness. Everything was possible. To think I had once answered the careers adviser's question 'What do you want to be when you grow up?' with the line 'Prime Minister of Great Britain!' The careers adviser was an Irishman who reminded me that not every one of my future electors felt proud to be part of the Union, and suggested I might take a few hours to read up on how one great British prime minister, David Lloyd George, tore Ireland apart, and how still nobody knew how to put it back together. I looked the Irishman in the eye and said, 'Perhaps I will find a way to do that.'

I went through to the kitchen, looking at the pile of dishes in it and the empty meal-for-one packets in the bin. My dinners were made in the only machine fit to make them – a brown microwave from the eighties that was almost the size of the fridge – a small oven was crammed in the corner of the room, unused. It had been broken since I moved in. Once, my flat had been bigger but the landlord divided it in two before me in the hope of doubling the rent money. Which he did. So where there had been a bedroom, small kitchen and living room there was now just a bedroom and half a kitchen, dividing my place from the other where a fat man in his forties who never introduced himself watched television all day and night. My sink was actually half a one – when dividing my room from the new one, the landlord had not thought about plumbing. That meant I had to put up with a flimsy plasterboard division, made damp by splashes from the tap. Because the pipes were on the other side, I had nothing on mine but a hole where a plug should have been. A bucket below caught dirty water that I emptied out in the bathroom toilet. What was I doing wandering from room to room? Sometimes I did this for a long time, too tired to do anything else.

Smelling something foul, I checked below the sink to find the bucket was nearly full with brown gloop and reached in to remove it. I went through to the empty bathroom next door, poured the liquid into the sink, ran the water to wash it down, then collapsed to my knees, bucket in hand, panic rising from my insides. Finding no exit, it sank back down again. Sometimes there's no need for movement. No need yet, anyway. Christy said she wouldn't send the next message until the morning. I muttered under my breath, 'Freedom through kinship, wealth through understanding, love through sacrifice.' There was not much kinship anywhere any more. Most people thought it silly to believe in anything. Better to laugh at the world than risk taking it seriously. But Rakesh had a friend who wanted to die in a religious crush on the other side of the world, praying to God; did that make him brave or stupid? I could have stayed on my knees, thinking all night, drifting in and out of consciousness, hoping someone was coming for me. But then the guy from First Floor Right knocked on the door and said, 'Anyone in there? You all right?'

I dragged myself upright and opened the door. At first I didn't recognise him, though I'd seen his face plenty of times before. It was just a forgettable face. I walked past him and went back to my room without a word or even a polite nod, then lay back on the bed and closed my eyes, feet throbbing, head pounding, the events of the day slipping away into nothing.

LP: It's not just outside that frightens me, it's everything inside too. I hate what my body does, what it wants.

CC: That's just being a man, Lewis. It can't be helped.

LP: But I get these horrible desires . . .

CC: Do you want to be violent?

LP: I want to be in control.

CC: Yes, men are taught they deserve that. It's not an instinct. You can be rid of it.

LP: But it makes me afraid . . . of being close to anyone.

CC: In time, all of that will die. Just concentrate on our work.

12

I Can See All the Way to Freedom!

I woke up with a dry, sour feeling in my mouth, hearing a banging noise from outside the room.

'Hey! Let me in!'

'Anna?'

'Who else?'

The other guys would hear this. I was contributing to the life of the block. I quickly put on a pair of jeans and a T-shirt and said, 'How did you know where I lived?'

'Easy.' Anna raised her voice further and hit the door again. 'I control all your files,' she shouted. 'You think I don't have your address?'

'Why won't you leave me alone?'

'Because I'm just too goddamn *good*. Now let me in!'

I reached over to the bedside table for a glass of water and gulped it down quickly, then got up and let her in.

'Hey, Lewis . . . it's party time!'

Anna flung her arms around me and kissed my neck, almost pushing me onto the floor in one move – not out of desire, just drunkenness. She bumped into the desk, then bashed the closing door, then the desk. Everything was close together.

'Whoa!' she said. 'No room!'

Anna's make-up was running; it looked like she had been rubbing her eyes, crying perhaps, but there was pure pleasure in her face as she edged past me to check out the view of the street from the kitchen window, a tight little ball of energy with nowhere to bounce.

'Well then!' she said brightly, peering down at the street.

'What have you got to entertain me in your hot new pad, Lewis?'

I thought of the mini-fridge propping up the microwave, and was angry my home was so shabby.

'Not much.'

'Have you got anything to drink?'

She brushed a finger across a dusty windowsill, inspected the brown residue, flicked it away, then went over to the fridge door and opened it, pulling a disgusted face.

'I'm just *dying* for a beer. The bar closed ages ago. Hey, you should have stayed at the party. Belinda found her boyfriend shagging in the toilet and battered him with a high heel in front of everybody. We all cheered her on – it was like a bullfight or something. He had *no chance*.'

I crossed my arms, sulking.

'Oh come on, Lewis, loosen up . . . I could snap you!'

I was tired of being told how tense I was when everyone else could only operate with the help of drugs. Everyone's so ready to give orders.

Anna looked around my place. 'Well, Lewis, it's not quite what I'm used to, but . . .' and here she employed her poshest voice, 'a girl can slum it from time to time – as long as she knows she can return to her palace when she gets bored . . .'

She staggered, though there was little space to do it in, then danced back into the bedroom, jumping onto the bed and sitting on it, cross-legged, waiting for me to do the same. I did. We faced each other. There was a brief moment of seriousness before Anna flopped backwards, arms behind her head, and lay over the side of the mattress. Facing upside down, body stretched out so her belly edged into view between a shirt and skirt she had not been wearing earlier.

She sighed and said, 'Oh, Lewis! I'm here for my one last night of passion. Are you going to give it to me?'

'But you're leaving.'

'Exactly.'

'So you want to *use* me?'

She sat up. 'You talk like we're strangers, Lewis. You sound horrified. But you've been chasing me for months!'

She raised her voice even more, though it often seemed she could get no louder. I just wanted her to quieten down.

'I have been a paragon of virtue!' she cried out.

Anna's legs now lolled to one side and came to rest on mine.

'Is there something wrong, Lewis? Do you think I'm a slut? How dare you call me a slut!'

There was nowhere else to look, so I concentrated on the mattress. She asked, 'Don't you like sex?'

'You have to do something to find out whether you like it, I suppose . . .'

She laughed at that, took my head aggressively in her hands and kissed it, moving her hands down to my buttocks, which she clenched tightly through my jeans, kneading her fingers about the flesh as if testing a peach for ripeness. I put my arms unsurely around her waist.

'I want to be held by a man, not a wimp!' she ordered, grabbing my arms.

'But I *am* a man!'

'Then hold me like one!'

I kissed her back, hard, my teeth banging against hers, making a sound like two swords clashing.

'Yes, that's it! Pretend you want me . . .'

'But I do! I love you! I've loved you ever since—'

Anna let go of me and put her hands down by her sides.

'Oh for God's sake, Lewis. You don't have to say that kind of thing these days – sex doesn't depend on it. And anyway, you only think that because I am the only woman in the office who isn't married, or old, or ugly, and you sit facing me all day. Now get me out of these stinky clothes and give me something merry to think about while I'm off saving the poor Vietnamese babies!'

I held her firmly by the shoulders, ripped her shirt off, sending a button flying, and dragged her skirt down, bringing a pair of tights with it.

She called out, 'All right – *now* we're getting somewhere!'

The men in the block might have been enjoying themselves, and it was thrilling, I suppose, in an unclean way, but I was mainly angry, not excited. I felt battered into submission, not gently persuaded into bed as I wanted to be. Anna was like an excitable doll, too cheerful to be anything like the passionate romantic I always hoped she would be. Congratulations after every garment removal didn't help things either.

'Well done! That's it – now the knickers! Keep going!'

And, 'Lewis, you animal – *liberate me of my socks!*'

It was all concentration, all effort, all ridiculous. I had expected to be taken on a secure, agreeable ride where I would not have to *work* at getting to the glorious end. But everything about it was so much effort. So much exertion. So uncivilised. So much . . . *nothing*. After several frantic attempts at trying to copy the kind of thing I have seen on television, with her up on all fours and me behind her trying to find a way in, Anna finally calmed and took action. She jumped up, turned round and said, in that comforting, stern secretarial tone I have come to adore, 'Never mind, Lewis. Let's try something else, shall we?'

But her new idea was less enjoyable than the last, and though a more orthodox initiative took us closer to the usual end there was little joy in it. All that senseless gurning and jolting and bumping and thrusting – I wanted to be held gently, whispered romantically to, taken to Paris and kissed at the top of the Eiffel Tower. Here I had a specific job: to move back and forth, swiftly and efficiently, without enjoying myself enough for the process to come naturally to an end as my body wanted it to. Her job was to cling on in the meantime and cry out wildly as if the end of the world was coming and she couldn't wait for it to arrive. It was horrible – there's nothing more foul than being aroused – but it wasn't just that. The closer I got to the end, the more emotional I became. Visions of Dad crying in the shop, Philip shouting at the boy on the bus, Aarav and Mira and Rakesh surveying the wreckage in the shop, the graffiti, the look on Mum's face as she arrived at Benny's – all these things cluttered the space where desire should have been as I pumped frigidly and repeatedly into the person I had romanticised about for months: Anna's contorting features, sweet-smelling perfume, the same both day and night, her skin, insistence on 'More!' were no match for the nightmares. My first experience of 'finishing' was ill-timed, and felt more like cold, painful, blameworthy release than ecstatic abandon. After Christy and I had our little fumble in the school library ten years ago, I had taken a safety pin from her sewing kit and secretly punctured my skin with it rather than go back to my room and do what most boys would naturally consider their right. I had done that thing a few times since, to release tension, lower body temperature, purely for biological reasons, but it was always followed by such guilt and self-disgust that I came to believe it was not natural at all. Anna got up and asked where the bathroom was, wrapped a towel round her and braved the corridor. I had an urge to search the flat for a safety pin.

Never one to make a fuss out of a bother, Anna didn't act upset by my failure to provide her night of passion. When she returned from the bathroom she suggested a cup of tea and 'a bit of a tidy up'. I agreed this was an excellent idea. I offered her my old blue dressing gown, popped the kettle on, put the day's clothes back on again and took a bin bag out of a near-by drawer. She tied the gown around her and said, 'Okay – washing or drying?'

I noticed the small pile of pots, plates and cutlery, and tried not to think about whether Anna might be disappointed in me – I thought I'd cleaned up from the other night – but I had been forgetting a lot recently.

'Drying,' I said, reaching for a tea towel.

Already Anna seemed lovelier since we had stopped what we were doing a few minutes ago. The dressing gown suited her, and the flushed red of her cheeks made her vulnerable in a way I had not seen before.

'So,' I said, taking a dish. 'Are you excited about your trip?'

'Oh yes – I can't wait to go,' she replied, very definitely. 'Actually, I was thinking I might go for longer . . . I read this thing in the paper this morning about a route down by the Mahaweli river in Sri Lanka, and I thought, why not? I'm sure there are poor people there too. Everyone needs help, right?'

'What about the Vietnamese babies?'

She shrugged her shoulders, and without the slightest hint of regret said, 'I'll get to them in the end.'

At seven o'clock I woke up, aware of a presence to my left where space usually was. Sitting naked and upright in my bed, unashamed, shimmering, Anna seemed quite perfect. Her hair was gathered messily on the top of her head, held together by a clip, and she wore black-rimmed glasses half way down her nose to focus on an article in an old newspaper I had left lying on my desk. The underside of her breasts peeped out from under the duvet as if to say – 'See? Here I am!' I noticed she had left a T-shirt over the bed with writing on the front: I CAN SEE ALL THE WAY TO FREEDOM! There was a small bag I didn't recognise next to her as well. I didn't notice her bringing overnight gear when she arrived. Why did I miss so much? Why was I walking through the world with my eyes closed?

Anna finished off the rest of her coffee, folded up last week's newspaper and said, in a friendly way, 'Right then, you. I'd better be off.'

'It's still early. I thought . . . maybe . . .'

Anna laughed warmly and cupped my face in her hands.

'Oh no, it's too late for all that now, lover man. I have to go and make breakfast for my other boyfriend . . . I wouldn't usually, but it's the least I can do. Listen, would you mind giving me a lift?'

I was furious.

'How come you never mentioned him before? What's his name? I mean . . . is *he* going away with you now? Am I that easy to trade?'

'Oh don't be silly – he's going nowhere. Now get yourself together and help me out, will you? If I'm late he could be awake by the time I get back, and will want to know where I've been. You wouldn't want him to suspect, would you? He's really quite the jealous sort.'

So I got up, dressed and prepared to go, but I'd forgotten the car was still at Benny's and didn't realise till we got down to the street. Anna seemed annoyed at this and I didn't want to part on bad terms, so I hailed a taxi and offered to pay for it in advance – an offer she did not decline.

'I'll miss you,' I said as she kissed me goodbye.

'Oh, Lewis . . . you'll replace me soon enough. Just put yourself where you think the lightning's going to strike – life's more fun that way.'

'What shall I tell them at work?'

'Nothing. They'll work it out soon enough.'

'Will you write?'

'Probably not. But don't be sad about it.'

Back at the flat I went straight to the computer, firing it up in last night's clothes, thinking about Anna, her other boyfriend, and how on earth we were going to fill the rest of the weekend before Chuck, Daisy and Tampa Bay left. There would be a police statement to give as well. I logged into my account, fully intending to delete the messages from CC and block all future ones: I didn't need anyone. I didn't need saving, and I certainly didn't care about anyone else. I just needed to be left alone. But I never got to do that – there was another short email waiting for me – two passwords – and instantly I forgot to say No. As I saw those initials a sharp pain hit the pit of my stomach as if I had been injected with a needle there, and at the same time I began to feel hot – then the pain faded, the heat rose, a headache more like a migraine began to pulse at the front of my skull and for a few seconds I went totally numb. Like I had no body. No past or future. A note under the title confirmed my suspicions as to who my prophet was.

CC: Below - proposed introduction for new members. What do you think?

Dear Newborn –

Ever since a very male God made Adam out of 'the dust of the ground' and then chose to graft Eve from one of Adam's spare parts instead of the same dirt he made Man with, the world He Created has been on Tilt. The story of Adam and Eve is the story of the first imbalance, and the story of humankind is just more of the same. Here at Hope for Newborns we believe we must reset the scales, one by one, until all foundling Eves, everywhere, are returned to Grace.

Send the word 'YES' and wait.
You will not know where I am.
You will not be able to get to me.
Not yet.
I am always on the move, trying to make things better.
With help, I will.

Forever yours, whoever you are –
CC 2004

Freedom through Kinship,
Wealth through Understanding,
Love through Sacrifice

LP: Very powerful. But it sounds like you're setting up a feminist religion, not a charity.

CC: Yes. Clever, isn't it? I'll put it on the site tonight.

HFN-I: #o66

13

Day and Night

I sat still for a while, imagining Christy sitting at her computer, waiting for the 'Yes' from me to appear. Her face brightening when it did.

It was hard to picture her exactly – it had been so long since I'd seen her – mostly the vision I conjured up of the mature, womanly version of the girl I knew at Kindler's Academy was so exciting I could hardly concentrate on it. But for a few seconds my vision of her was clear – I remembered her as she was on the first day we met, on the school playing fields. How would she be now? I imagined she had kept her short school hairstyle; she had smooth skin made shiny by hot sun and taut by years of daily runs down the Champs-Elysées (I already had her living in a stylish studio flat in the centre of Paris). What else? Clear, big, brown eyes. A smile to bring you to tears of grateful happiness.

In my mind the off-hand, laid-back childhood intelligence she used to have at school had developed into a self-assured confidence. Her kindness had become forthrightness and determination to do the right thing, no matter what. The legs Christy had revealed to me just once, pulling down her tights in the library and putting my hand on where they led to, had become long, slender things of beauty that she crossed in a sophisticated way as she sat at her desk awaiting my call – and that desk could be anywhere in the world. Anna already seemed like a cowardly compromise. She was half-forgotten, and fading. Here was a *real* revolutionary! Christy was travelling the world, saving newborns, raising funds, seeing scales and resetting them. I promised myself I'd keep a record of her route on my map of the world, on my wall, above my bed.

I could feel her with me so strongly it was almost like being together. I'd tell her that. I sent the word:

YES YES YES YES YES YES YES YES YES YES YES
YES YES YES YES YES YES YES YES YES YES YES
YES YES YES YES YES YES YES YES YES YES YES
YES YES YES YES YES YES YES YES YES YES YES
YES YES YES YES YES YES YES YES YES YES YES
YES YES YES YES YES YES YES YES YES YES YES
YES YES YES YES YES YES YES YES YES YES YES
YES YES YES YES YES YES YES YES YES YES YES
YES YES YES YES YES YES YES YES YES YES YES
YES YES YES YES YES YES YES YES YES YES YES
YES YES YES YES YES YES YES YES YES YES YES
YES YES YES YES YES YES YES YES YES YES YES
YES YES YES YES YES YES YES YES YES YES YES
YES YES YES YES YES YES YES YES YES YES YES
YES YES YES YES YES YES YES YES YES YES YES
YES YES YES YES YES YES YES YES YES YES YES
YES YES YES YES YES YES YES YES YES YES YES
YES YES YES YES YES YES YES YES YES YES YES
YES YES YES YES YES YES YES YES YES YES YES
YES YES YES YES YES YES YES YES YES YES YES
YES YES YES YES YES YES YES YES YES YES YES
YES YES YES YES YES YES YES YES YES YES YES
YES YES YES YES YES YES YES YES YES YES YES
YES YES YES YES YES YES YES YES YES YES YES
YES YES YES YES YES YES YES YES YES YES YES
YES YES YES YES YES YES YES YES YES YES YES
YES YES YES YES YES YES YES YES YES YES YES
YES YES YES YES YES YES YES YES YES YES YES
YES YES YES YES YES YES YES YES YES YES YES
YES YES YES YES YES YES YES YES YES YES YES

It felt good to send that, but after the message had gone, speeding its way to her, I felt that there needed to be more words, more energy got out out out. I opened up another computer window and wrote the first thing that came into my head, as if I was writing to someone:

I don't think about it every day. Sometimes I can go for weeks without thinking about it. But I know it's always coming back. And I have to tell you – because how else will I know you mean it when you say that nothing could change your mind about me?

I used to drink like anyone else. Not often – I never much liked the taste – but when we were teenagers I still thought I would get used to it. Even Rakesh drank sometimes, and he came from a family that hardly touched alcohol at all. Some nights we'd go out, just the two of us, after work. The nightlife was so close to our shops, it felt like we were at the centre of the world. Some of the places in town had bands on most nights of the week. They were usually bad but the music protected us from our conversations being overheard. There was usually a DJ on afterwards as well, and if we were in the door early enough, we wouldn't have to pay. We'd take stools by the bar when the place was empty and stay till it was full, maybe only having a few drinks, maybe just one – it didn't matter. We never had too much. It wasn't about getting drunk. Not like some of these guys you see throwing it down their necks as if all they have to look forward to is puking up in the gutter at the end of the night. We just clutched our pints and talked about all the things we couldn't while surrounded by brothers, sisters, parents who had already decided what they thought of the world and weren't much interested in being told they might be wrong.

Rakesh was always more relaxed when we were out than with family; he always looked at me directly, spoke in a low voice and said I could tell him anything I wanted, as if he knew there was something I wanted to confess, but that I'd never tell if no one ever asked. Once, he shocked me by telling me he had lost his virginity to someone he didn't like, just to get it out of the way – *but he did it more like an exercise in conversation – like he was showing me it was okay to talk.* With all that noise, the chaos of a weekend, the bellowing punters, sneering bar staff, sweaty teenagers drinking and dancing around us, I could say whatever I wanted. If I wanted.

What I respected about Rakesh was how he would act if we met anyone while we were out. One minute we could be in deep conversation about something private, as if there was nothing else going on in the world of any importance – then the next minute we could be talking to someone he suspected was out on their own, or looked lost, or was just standing near by. He included strangers as if it was totally normal, and never struggled for something to say. He had this attitude with folks he met: always shook their hand, always touched their forearm, always asked their name. Once he had that name, he'd repeat it a couple of times, digesting it, testing how it sounded in his mouth – as if preparing himself for something – then he'd wait for a second, and smile widely. Then he'd act like he'd known that person all his life. His kindness was never-ending. He had no prejudices. He trusted everyone perfectly, until he had a reason not to. And despite that perfect politeness, friendliness, openness with others, he never made me feel like an outsider. He introduced me to new people as my oldest and greatest friend Lewis, put an arm round me, showed me off, as if I was a great source of pride. With that initial introduction taken care of, I was let loose, confident, into the night. Without it, I was lost.

We had some really good evenings, which always ended the same way. Near closing time, Rak would cover his glass with his hand and say, I'm too pretty to die young. Even that made me feel warm, and it made me stop drinking too. Occasionally we'd go on somewhere else with the people *we'd met, maybe to a club, but that wasn't really our thing. Too difficult to talk when the music's that loud. Too many druggies. So we'd say goodbye to new friends and go home. Sometimes, once we were alone again, Rak would say underneath his breath,* Thank fuck for that – I can't stand those guys. *Then he'd burst out laughing, and it was as if it had been just the two of us the whole time. Afterwards, I'd wonder whether he meant that, or whether he was just saying it to remind me that no matter how many people he brought close, no one could come closer than me.*

Then, I might not see him for a couple of weeks. Then he'd call on me, and we'd go out again.

We arranged to meet in a place called Day and Night after I'd fed Mum. She'd been having a bad week, sulking more than usual, refusing to let me in her room when I tried to take in her dinner – so that night I just knocked on the door, left the food tray on the floor in the hallway and crossed the road early. Thought that maybe I'd have a couple of drinks before Rak arrived. It was payday, and back then I was still new enough to the job to find it thrilling to have money in my pocket, waiting to be spent. I'd seen plenty of men in suits sit at bars, moodily drinking themselves stupid, emptying their pockets steadily of their earnings. It seemed adult. And maybe I could make some friends, all on my own – when Rakesh arrived, he would see. Well, *he'd say.* Someone's growing up, aren't they? *So I didn't bother getting changed out of my work clothes. I just went straight in. When I walked in the door the place was nearly empty, but it still took me several minutes to get served by the sullen barmaid, who looked at me with pity.*

'Bad day?' *she said, more in accusation than sympathy.*

'No,' *I said, trying to pretend I wasn't offended, slapping a note down on the bar.* 'Good, actually. What would you like? I'll have the same as you . . .'

But that didn't work. She sighed heavily and said, 'The usual way is for the customer to say what they want.'

For the first hour or two, I really thought Rak was coming. I bought a couple of drinks, picked up a paper off the bar, read it right through from front to back. (It was the week they weren't sure if Arafat was dead or not – someone somewhere was checking on it; some papers couldn't decide whether they thought he was a freedom fighter or a terrorist.) I checked my phone a couple of times, tried Rak's phone a couple of times, got nothing. It just rang out. I began to worry, but didn't leave my seat. Maybe because I'd already said I was meeting a friend. Maybe because I thought something terrible had happened, and because, as long as I stayed at my stool, I couldn't find out about it. What a coward. Anyway, this time Rak wasn't there to cover his glass and stop us going too far, so I drank too much. And as I soon found out, time seems to move faster after you've had a couple.

I was there all night. At seven, the bands started filing in, at eight the sound check started and at nine the first went on stage. By then the place was beginning to fill up a bit, with the usual hangers-on, girlfriends of band members and the odd supporter competing for the attention of the barmaid, who had been joined by three others just starting their shifts. When the music started I hardly bothered to twist my head to the side to take in the stage. I had no interest in it at all. By eleven the bands had finished, the lights changed, and there was hardly any room to move. Which was why she bumped into me, knocking my drink over.

'Sorry,' she shouted. 'Sorry, it's . . . there's no room . . .'

'It's okay,' I told her. 'What's your name?'

She didn't hear.

'Should I get you another one?' she asked.

'No, don't worry,' I shouted back. 'What's your name?'

A second time, no answer to that.

'Well, all right,' she said. 'I'm sorry. Have a good time tonight, okay?'

She breathed on me. She smiled. Then she was gone.

I watched her for a while after that. She returned to a group of friends. She went to the bar again. She danced a little. I finally left my seat and leaned up against the arcade machines by the fire exit, watching her jump and jerk to the music – trying to work out how old she was – about my age, I thought – trying to work out if she was there with someone or looking for someone – trying to think what I would say if I went over. Then she stopped dancing again and returned to the group of three or four girls. A couple of times I thought she looked across and smiled. The floor seemed to shift and soften beneath my feet; I could hardly stand. I lost my drink and didn't want to leave my spot to get another. I couldn't get to the bar anyway. I didn't need more. I felt sick, but excited too. The DJ played a local favourite, an old classic, the whole place seemed to lift and I was lifted with it. So much so that when she looked over a third time, differently from before, I was confident enough to go pressing through the mass of bodies towards her, hand out, so she could take it and we could leave together. It would be smooth, swift, delicious. Now I know that look was suspicion, not lust.

When she saw me coming, realised, pulled her hand away from mine, ran to the toilets, I didn't know what to do – I hadn't thought about being rejected. So I left and went outside, where something that had previously lain untouched somewhere at the bottom of me, waiting to come to the surface, began to make itself known. I felt angry. Furious. I hated her. I thought everyone in the place had been watching, laughing at me. I could feel myself going redder, redder, not sure whether to throw myself in front of a passing car or break down and cry or run home. Every emotion began to bleed into the next.

I didn't move for a long, long time.

At the end of the night the club emptied out and she came tumbling out, at least as drunk as me. I saw her, reached out and said, 'Don't think . . . please . . .'

But the words ended there. And she was already running

away, laughing, holding hands with friends, swearing at me as she went. Others might have chased her, shouted at her, attacked her, apologised – but I'm not that kind of man. I staggered down the main street, away from home, not yet ready to return, until I saw a side street with a few kids hanging round at the corner and slowed down.

'What you after?' said one of the kids.

He couldn't have been more than fourteen, fifteen at the most.

'What have you got?' I asked.

'Whatever you like.'

It was two, maybe three in the morning. He opened his jacket, unclasped his palm and showed me a small pile of pills that could have been anything.

'That's no good to me,' I said. 'Have you got a strong drink in there somewhere? Something that's going to kill me? Quickly?'

'No problem, mate,' he said. 'No problem. Whatever does it for you.'

I had already forgotten the girl; a bigger fear was gripping me.

When I woke up I was lost. I walked around the city for what felt like hours, getting more and more panicky as the sun started to creep up over the horizon and I felt like I was in another place that looked strangely similar to my home-town, but wasn't. The spinning, swaying sickness that came along with all those drinks made me see everything differently, and more than once I fell to my knees in the street, bottle in hand, begging the sky to fall in on me take me back take me back take me back home or somewhere like it. Did I end up at a tram stop? A bus stop? A train station? I don't know.

Eventually I recognised a street and began to run – but home was not the first place I went. Dirty white shirt half-open, tie undone, mud on my trousers and shoes, the last dregs of a bottle dangling from my right hand, I stood below Rakesh's window, threw stones up at it and shouted how much I hated him and how much I hated me until Mira came out into the garden, quietened me, hugged me tight and said her boy had spent the night in hospital with concussion after having a minor crash in his car, but that he'd be all right and I could see him soon.

I hid for days. I took time off work. I neglected Mum. But eventually I had to surface. So I did, but made sure I stopped drinking. And stopped looking for sex. Just the thought of feeling that hand pull away from me in the club and what I did to myself afterwards made me so ashamed of who I really was, and sent me into panic, just imagining what that person living quietly underneath the usual one was capable of.

For a while I thought about it every day. Now I don't think about it every day. Sometimes I can go for weeks without thinking about it. But I know it's always coming back.

It makes me want to change me.

I looked at the screen for a few moments, amazed at how much I had written. I wondered why I had written it at all, and thought about whether I should keep it. I almost did. But some things are better put out, then buried. I deleted the whole thing and went to bed.

14

Correspondence, in the Following Months

Before Christy I spent most evenings at my computer looking for companionship, but it was difficult to get close to it. Yes, I could join a site, talk to whoever was online, click on and become someone's friend, for a while anyway, but I couldn't really know them. Everyone's photo on their personal pages showed them as they'd like to be. Everyone's profile made them look popular, stylish, intelligent, funny, sexy – like they wanted to get close to someone, anyone, without having to show their real selves. It was a big twenty-four-hour virtual party where you collected unreal pals in the hope of having more than the next person on the next page; a big, ugly pretend pot for empty people to put their lives in. A place full of beautiful, invented people, vanity and loneliness. Or it used to be. Now, it was a way to save me: Christy and I began a furious exchange of messages that began with a few polite enquiries but soon became an avalanche of emotion. She didn't even send a picture. It wasn't about that. It reminded me how different she was from all those others. Mainly our correspondence was punctuated by my questions, which were usually returned with considered, calm answers that didn't always say what I wanted to hear but always, always made me feel better.

She told me most of what I needed to know. Yes, she had thought of me sometimes. No, I couldn't know where she was. Yes, she was sorry we had lost contact after the Academy closed down, but we were young then, and lost time was not lost now we'd found each other again. I promised to help in any way I could; she said Hope for Newborns needed me but I had to save myself first. Christy made Anna look like a part-timer – someone more interested in having fun and getting drunk than really making things happen – and at first I was angry at her for that. In those first few weeks it felt like something I'd forgotten existed was being reborn inside me, fizzing and crackling and making me buzz with excitement. Christy was always teaching me something. I learned that my life – especially the parts I wasn't thinking about – was nothing but a big advert for destruction. The shoes I wore were made by slave children. The food I ate was made by crooks. Everything I invested in was built on lies. Even my bankers were murderers. But most importantly, I learned I was not alone. She had been there all along. And I could correct the bad I'd been doing by joining up.

It was a confusing time. When Christy wrote to me I believed her, when I read her words on the computer they were the truth: our truth. When she described them I could see little scales everywhere, waiting to be made even. But I reverted back to the old me once she was gone. I looked over the precipice when I was with her, and backed away from it when she was gone. Back into my usual existence. I didn't mention the Victory to Christy out of fear she would abandon me – it was clear from the beginning, what she thought of our sort – the Empire we celebrated was not famous for its charity. Also, like my recruitment job, I suspected she would encourage me to cut all ties. Even try and persuade the family to close it down. But there was no chance of that any more. Dad may have wavered for a while after the attacks on the shop started, but there was no way I could address the issue now. And I didn't want to mention my brother, or his war. Christy called that the Great Distraction. The small news that covered the big news elsewhere: the bigger war that got no coverage – the war on abandoned foundlings. She made me feel like an idiot, but one who wanted to make it right. When I told her that, she wrote, 'And you will make it right. I know.' At work I was always flipping away from my recruitment screen to check my account, see if there was any more juice in the Inbox, or to see if she was online. At home, I rarely left my desk. Everything was serious with Christy, everything was urgent. I learned to be alert.

Then she started putting up short political essays of barely controlled rage on the Newborns website, for seemingly no reason. The first of these was typical of the messages that came after. It was called 'Understand Your Nation and Reject It', and was the reason for our first argument. I said this had nothing to do with Hope for Newborns. She said everything was connected. To which I said she was going crazy, and asked why – if that was the case – we weren't starting an international revolution.

She reminded me that we were, then didn't speak to me for three days.

Understand Your Nation and Reject It

The British project – if ever begun – is now over. Its prophets were false prophets. Its leaders were liars. Its language, its literature, its Empire, mean nothing. Its glorious past is myth, and its present is built on fiction. We have neither the right to speak freely nor the right to remain silent when charged with a crime here: if we want bail before trial we must pay, our land belongs to the Queen, and we need to dig into our pockets if we want to be educated, cared for in old age or granted a prescription from the doctor. Our women are paid less for work, non-whites and non-Christians are discriminated against as a matter of course, as are the Scots, Welsh and Irish, though they have fought the Empire's filthy wars for centuries, and new immigrants are treated like filth, though all of us are immigrants of one kind or another, if you go back far enough.

We own nothing here. The fields, the gold, the splendid artworks and the scrap heaps of Great Britain belong in the hands of the few who look and sound the same, and condemn any principle that limits their profits as unrealistic, old-fashioned, obsolete. Meanwhile, the world runs out of its key resource, the leading plunderer makes record profits and the share price goes down because bosses were expecting more.

Our governments cry freedom and squander money like drunken idiots with no plan but ruination. Newborns could be forgiven for despairing. Where do our taxes go? Not on feeding the foundlings, protecting the weak or upholding human rights, but on arming our enemies, raping the defenceless, excusing the inexcusable in the name of the same old cause.

CC 2004

Making up was a huge relief. It felt like we had passed through a key stage all romances must, and had come out the other side unscarred, closer, more determined to succeed. This, after three months of back and forth, was the first time Christy told me she loved me. And she didn't have to wait long for my reply.

PART TWO

A Family Pulls Together
2005

15

Bravely on the Field of Battle

If it was a thunderbolt, it was one that hit slowly.

Hearing myself saying this makes me doubt it can be true, but life seemed to get something like back to normal for a while after the initial shock of Chuck's death – he had not lived with us for years, so his absence was as ordinary as getting up in the morning, flipping the welcome sign, talking about the weather to customers who preferred not to discuss anything else. Upstairs, we detected virtually no change in Mum. For the first time in years, I left her for more than a couple of days – only Dad and I went to America for Chuck's cremation service, so it was easier for the rest of the family to pretend nothing had happened.

'What kind of idiot travels thousands of miles to watch his son burn to the sound of the Star-Spangled bastard Banner?' Dad said, visibly shaking. 'Not my kind! And anyway, who would look after the shop? You want us to mourn *and* starve?'

But he went. None of us could even be sure if Mum understood what had happened, and we weren't brave or stupid enough to spell it out – so Dad left the shop, and his wife, to Morta. On his return, he hardly mentioned it. What was there to say? When people made the mistake of asking how his eldest was, Dad just pointed up to the wall where his son's photo now sat between Winston and Grandpa, then tapped his heart solemnly with the round end of his scissors. But after a few months resentment began to bubble to the surface.

We had been given little explanation of what happened – the phone call just said Chuck 'died bravely on the field of battle', and the written version used the same description, word for word: Dad began to suspect there was more to know. He made several polite enquiries to Chuck's superior officers, without answer, before suggesting something might have been missed. But in time respectful mutterings turned to muted hostility, which in turn became outright conspiracy theories, usually offered up mid-haircut to whoever happened to be in the chair – Morta said this made slow trade slower, but these days Dad thought about more than profit. The only official information we'd been able to extract from the authorities was that Chuck had last been seen giving orders to a junior officer at a check-point not far from Kabul. No witnesses, apparently. No infor-mation. 'No bloody interest in having any,' Dad said.

He began to regret the interview he had given to the BBC the day after we got the news. Offered the chance to question the army's version of events by an interviewer, Dad had simply said this: 'England has lost one of her best. But my son died for freedom. I am very proud.' Another in the procession of par-ents who, even in grief, knew which side they were on. When he changed his mind, Dad found it harder to get on television. There was no opportunity for him to change his story.

'So many parents,' said the researcher, calmly. 'So many dead children. I'm sorry.' Dad shouted down the phone about how he paid his licence fee and what did he get for that any-way. But it was no good. Three days later Daisy arrived at Manchester airport, ashen white, with Tampa Bay in her arms, and Dad ran right through a security checkpoint to get to them and hold them tight and tell them they must never, never leave us again.

The British embassy wanted little to do with the business because Charles had become Chuck and turned into an American citizen. They were polite but said they could do nothing. When I took over negotiations, made a fuss, demand-ed to speak to someone high up enough to make a difference and asked what could be done, it had no effect.

'Charles is no longer our problem, Mr Passman,' said the

embassy representative. His voice was gentle, but his words were not. I had taken twenty minutes to provoke him into this kind of comment.

'When you switch your passport, you give up your right to waste my time. Dial America if you like, but they're a little bored of families creating a fuss when things go wrong. If you sign up, you accept you may be sent to war, and in accepting that, you also accept you may die in pieces somewhere in the Middle East. What else do people expect?'

The man was so civil in tone and had the kind of voice I had been taught was the perfect example of good old-fashioned British decency. So it seemed wrong to complain further – and that was the end of that. After several months of going from department to department, opening up the shop as normal, Dad finally broke and I had to take over; People4Jobs granted me leave shortly before I was due to go for that promotion again and suddenly I was a full-time barber.

At first we thought it wouldn't last long. Morta went full time too but only booked a child-minder for a week at a time, expecting Dad to storm back into the shop front at any moment and tell us to bugger off back to our usual places. We underestimated him. He spent weeks stomping about, looking for Chuck's picture in the press, wailing about injustice and competing for attention with customers like a spoilt child. He couldn't believe the death of a British soldier was worth so little attention, and veered between anger and desperation, complaining about the unfairness of it all to anyone who would listen, and some who would rather not. It might have been easier if Chuck had died in glamorous circumstances – saving a child, foiling a bomber – but he was not that lucky. Just a photograph, a caption giving age, wife and child's name, and a note that circumstances of death were unknown – the following day fifty people died in Iraq and the news skipped grimly on to the next tragedy. 'My son is gone!' said Dad, spitting at a close-up picture of someone else's disaster on the front page of his daily paper. 'My son! My son! He's gone!'

With Mum, it was harder to tell the difference between old behaviour and new. In an early phone call about it, Philip said it was obvious – she didn't care about her children any more; then he changed his assessment, saying she had probably just shut down the part of her brain that grieved. As Christy says, if you stop hoping, you stop living; but then, if Christy knew I had a brother, if she knew he was dead, if she knew why, she'd say we had bought into a lie and been punished for it. There were times when I was close to confessing, but Chuck's death seemed like small news next to plans for the first ever HFN home in Romania, so instead we focused on her plans and my part in them. It was easier. Instead of explaining about Chuck to Christy, I promised myself to do five good things. That was something else that came from Christy. She had challenged me to reset five sets of scales a day. These were the first things I decided to do:

1 – Give Morta a rise in wages while I was in charge of the accounts. It would be hard for Dad to retract once he noticed it.
2 – Start shopping at the more expensive supermarket in town, so Mum could enjoy a better class of vegetable in her meals.
3 – Offer to baby-sit Tampa Bay once a week so Daisy could enjoy some time to herself.
4 – Make more of an effort with Philip's partner, Stephen. Send his kids birthday presents – they were family now too.
5 – Write a letter to the Foreign Secretary to appeal for an investigation into Chuck's death.

I'm not sure these were exactly the kinds of things Christy had in mind, but scales were scales, people were people, and I was sure she'd understand.

The Foreign Secretary did not reply, Mum showed no signs of pleasure at my upwardly mobile supermarket tastes and Stephen's children didn't mention the presents. When Philip tried to force them onto the phone to thank me they screamed, ran away and shouted, 'You're not my daddy!' as Philip talked over the noise, saying sorry repeatedly. I pretended not to hear, and told him I didn't know what he was apologising for, but not to worry about it. The only person I helped was Daisy, and even there I got the impression that I was getting more pleasure out of looking after my niece than her mother was getting out of a few hours off. Since Chuck's death, Daisy clung to her daughter more desperately, as if she thought a gentler cuddle would leave her open to kidnap.

After a couple of months of stagnation, Dad returned from lunch one Friday afternoon and announced, in that old bold tone of his I'd not heard in so long, 'I think I'll take over now,' and lightly snatched the scissors out of my hand.

'Hello, Mr Silverman,' he said. 'Not seen you in a while. Tell me, how is Mrs Silverman? And your mother-in-law? Still nipping at your ear?'

After Mr Silverman had gone, he dropped the cheery act and gathered us for a meeting.

'Morta . . . Lewis . . . thank you for looking after my shop. But . . . you know . . . it is *still my shop*, and I want it back now, please. Morta – your hours will be one till five Tuesday to Sunday, like before. Lewis, go back to your usual day job and your weekend hours here. My father set up this place to honour the British army, my son gave his life in the services, and not so long ago I would have happily done the same. We will keep going as before. If either of you defy me over this, I will throw you out on the street. Understand?'

When he had finished his piece Morta said, 'I speak from my brain. You speak from yours. Then we'll all get along fine.'

Though it wasn't always obvious, there was still a little fire left in both of them. But Morta knew who was boss. She called the child-minder, explained the situation and accepted the return to our previous state. Her English was getting better by the day and I was proud of my small part in her education. Also, I noticed she was developing a pleasing accent which seemed to be placing itself half way between Vilna and Manchester. She nodded at me, sneered at Dad and was gone.

After Dad's speech I went straight into the People4Jobs office, told my boss what had happened and begged to be given the chance to return to work. Also to make my abandoned presentation to the board, at a time of his choosing, with a view to applying for that promotion. I could see my nameplate on the door. *Lewis Passman: Senior Accounts Consultant, South London Division.* (Though we were based in Manchester, we pretended to have offices in four other cities.)

Marcus thought the idea over for a moment then said, 'Sure, Lewis. We might as well give you a chance to fuck it up. Why not?'

I used to admire Marcus and I would always be grateful to him – but I was beginning to think too much recruiting was turning his brain mouldy. I ran back to the Victory, fed Mum, told her the news, went home and concentrated on thinking about how excited I was over my big presentation and what it might lead to. Christy would say that in the amount of time it took me to fuck up my presentation, ten Romanian foundlings would die from exposure. Sometimes I wished the Christy in my imagination would just say good luck.

CC: I took a helicopter over the city today. I wrote this when I
landed:

HIGH AND MIGHTY OVER NYC

The helicopter takes off, banks high, swoops low,
we all hold tight to seat and side,
stomachs spinning as the pilot combats wind and water
shaking our little machine.
Left at liberty's statue, right round Empire State,
over the ferry, the pitches, the warships,
to see what is not there –
the yawning hole below
where business used to live.

All vantage points face here now.
Effigies are erected, statements made, fights started,
without permission, in the name of that space.
And meanwhile, down there are printed lies:
Here stood! says the plaque, *Here stood!*
What we all stand for.
But if we are going to pray for the wronged dead,
let us make an honest prayer.

The helicopter dives once more, coming to the tour's end –
our insides go with it, and gurgle, and splash.
Hopeless beings with beating hearts
dived desperately from the place that isn't there,
without a chance.
Ugly excess was met by ugly excess.
Which was, in time, returned with more.
The city still bubbles, sings and spits,
we still worship the rich and damn the poor,
and the helicopter lands safely.

HFN-I: #225

16

Every Day Is a New Year

Saturday.

I got up early, washed my face in cold water and drank a pint of milk to help start me into life. That always takes time. I laugh when I hear about these born-again types who have one big clang in their brain which changes everything for ever, because I feel like that every morning. It's like seeing the world for the first time, coming bleary-eyed into existence, unknowing. Chuck used to be the opposite. Like he'd never gone to sleep. Like he was always going to be awake and alive. But don't think about that.

Yawning, naked, swaying unsteadily, I leaned over to flip the kettle on and took out my black folder reading 'Believe it Can Happen!' on the side. I remembered nothing of my plans: I just gazed half-awake into my briefcase; evidence of Christy filled the space where emptiness used to be. The new, softer, ethical music she had introduced me to. The books designed to show what was possible with a little money and a lot of will. On waking up, the idea that I should be standing in front of the promotion board on Monday morning seemed like a cruel joke, but soon my mind was full of ideas. That old adrenalin that came with a big sale pumped through me. I thought about the future and bubbled inwardly with naughty excitement – some days, for a moment, when I let myself stop feeling guilty about it, I really did love my job. How many people could say that and mean it? I was an idiot for thinking about abandoning it. And I was lucky to have a boss who was prepared to give me another chance.

I had been kidding myself for seven years that I was on the verge of leaving the People4Jobs team; since Christy I was supposed to be thinking of little else, but sometimes I just didn't want to. As a sixteen-year-old on a week's work experience I had pleaded pathetically to be allowed a whole month's unpaid employment to prove myself. Marcus called me 'a bloody poofter', told me I was totally unqualified for the post, insisted I had no chance of succeeding, then employed me on the spot, saying, 'I can't lose! You already surrendered! Now off you go and make me some coffee!'

I made the best coffee I could and have been proving myself ever since.

The part of the office I first started out in, back in the days when you could fit the whole company in one room, is now part of an entire wing that's basically under my control – though nobody says that out loud. If Philip the great popcorn entrepreneur knew about that, he'd crack up. With family, life is just one ever-extending list of exposures that can be stacked against you as you get older, until no one can take you seriously any more. There is nothing of the People4Jobs rising star that they'd recognise in the over-sensitive, pliable walkover they know, but it's amazing what you can do when you go fresh into a new place. You start again. None of the old set ways. And the guys at work have never seen my bedroom, plastered head to foot in soft-focus images of the places I'd like to visit but haven't; never seen me sulk over a sly comment made at the dinner table; never watched me ruin a head of hair with a clumsy sideways chop. They only see the confident, swashbuckling Lewis, who smashes targets for fun.

My rise at People4Jobs has been swift enough, even in the last couple of years when things have been slower, so why go elsewhere? How would that save the foundlings of the world? Steady, quiet, regular promotion is the most effective way of being kept happy, whoever you are, and it's how all the most energetic industries work. Moving the hot young things sideways and upwards, between projects, until before you know it the twenty-nine-year-old regional manager has 300 people under him and is heading for the stars. The lower down, older, less successful employees roll their eyes at that kind of thing, but they don't understand that's how the best companies grow. By spotting those with the most potential and fast-tracking them to big posts. I still dream of rising effortlessly to the top, like I used to when Christy and I sat in the sun eating our sandwiches in the school playing fields and talking about the future.

But I should stop dreaming.

It was morning. I was in my flat. It was Saturday. I finished my mug of tea and closed my file. Out of the window I was sure I could see her, standing on the road, looking up, waiting to see what I'd do next.

In my mind, Christy followed me everywhere these days, and mostly disapproved of what she saw when I was working for anyone but her. She said I was of limited use until I cleared my life of unsightly debris, and according to her the job was the most unsightly thing of all. She couldn't understand what was stopping me giving it up, but how could I explain my job was the only thing apart from her keeping me sound since Chuck? I liked to daydream about the kind of world Christy wanted to make, but it was more exciting to think about than put into action, unlike office life, which was the other way round. Anyway, the bits of money I was giving to the Hope Fund was all recruitment money, so it was doing *some* good.

I put the file in my briefcase, secured the lock and was reminded of something Marcus told me the last time I was in. Beaming that wicked victorious grin, he poked his head round my door and said, 'Wish me luck for the courthouse, I'm giving evidence this afternoon!'

'You seem cheerful. . .'

'Ah yes. Well, I like to keep at least one civil court case on the go, Lewis. It reminds me there's something worth fighting for . . . and, more importantly, helps me forget what it really is. Ha ha! Think of all that power . . . *all those people looking at you*. Trying to figure you out. Trying to crawl inside your brain and sort lies from truth. Besides, I like guessing which way the jury is going to go. Look out for me on the local news – I reckon there will be a few crews there, so I'll be wearing my new People4Jobs cap!'

'Don't you worry about losing?'

'Only those in danger of going out of business or being disgraced are afraid of that, Lewis. If you have enough money to absorb the occasional loss, and are confident enough your enemies don't know most of the bad things you've done, everything becomes like an exciting game of strip poker where everyone else has to take their clothes off and you get to sit all toasty in your full kit.'

Marcus stopped, thought, smiled.

'You know what I'm saying, right? Anyway, after my performance today, no jury will rule against us.'

He strode out of my office and into the lift, whistling 'Que Sera, Sera'. Sometimes, I felt like a part of a radical, glorious team.

This scene came back to me with alarming clarity as I locked the door behind me at my flat on the 129th day since Charles Henry Passman died somewhere on the field of battle, doing something his family could not know or understand. I left home with an all-too-familiar queasy feeling in my stomach – as if I had just been force-fed a large mouthful of lice, and was about to be made to tuck into another.

I walked to the Victory, woke Mum up gently with a kiss and soon she was in her chair under a blanket, just like any other day. Then I guessed what she might want to eat this morning, told her what I thought it was, tried to interpret her non-response and went to the kitchen to make her breakfast. When I came up the stairs ten minutes later I carried a tray with two plates on it. The first contained two perfectly cooked boiled eggs, both sitting proudly in their regular egg cups, and the second contained two pieces of toast, cut into five strips, like soldiers, smothered in butter. I had been sure to bring Mum's favourite spoon, though it was dirty, and I could have used three other clean ones. I was sure to bring her mug, *World's Best Mum!*, though I had to clean that too. I'd cut off the tops of the eggs at the very last moment so she didn't have to do it herself – but so they were still steaming hot when they got to her. I imagine those are the kinds of things she notices.

'Here we go,' I said, laying the tray on her lap. 'Want to know the latest?'

Nobody else in the house was awake yet and Mum just carried on in her usual way, so my chatter had no audience but the hamsters, the fish and the newest member of her little family, a white mouse.

'I thought they wouldn't let me come back at all,' I said, 'let alone apply for the promotion again. I really think I can do it this time. Don't you?'

Mum tucked into her food, sucking the butter off the toast before chewing it.

'I mean, why not? I always hit my targets. Nobody knows London South better than me.'

Mum picked up her spoon. Was she thinking about Chuck? Could she remember him? Did she miss him?

'They'll probably tell me either way pretty quickly. So whether I get the job or not, at least I'll be put out of my misery!'

From Mum's room, Dad could be heard snoring; Daisy and Tampa Bay were silent. I was glad they had come to join us now. It was right, somehow. That's the kind of thing people say without thinking – once loved ones are dead, and can't disagree – but I really believe Chuck would have wanted it this way. Everybody together. When Philip arrived he'd say the same. I washed up Mum's dishes, took her a cup of tea and headed for the gym. A swim would prepare me for the day.

It's hard to be sure of anything much, but even in that I'm not alone any more. Last night I was sitting at the computer in the cold of my room listening to the guy in Ground Right snoring when Christy flashed up on the screen and asked what I was thinking: sometimes it's like she can reach through the computer and right into my heart. I told her. I said: when I thought of work, or home, or her, or the future, or the past, a small nagging told me there was no point. Each time she disappeared, leaving me on my own to fall back into real life, I found myself continuing in the old ways. Worse than that: I found myself *liking* the old ways. I was stupid, lazy, selfish and incapable of change; I would always be that way, unless she came to get me. Why wouldn't she come and get me?

CC: I may seem confident – how can I allow myself the luxury of being any other way? – but sometimes, like you, I feel like I don't know anything at all. I imagine myself standing in a library so big that all the books in it can't be seen from any angle, even by God. It stretches way up into the sky and off into the distance. I'm on a stepladder at the start of the A's, picking out the first book and frantically running my eyes down the words, trying to memorise it but distracted by the thought of all the chunks of knowledge I'm not going to get to on the other side of the room. I drop off the stepladder into a pit so deep and wide it could hold all the books in the library ten times over and more – tumbling downwards, I hope I won't always be falling. Hoping someone will come and pull me out, save me, make me worthwhile. I have all eternity to doubt myself, or try to find a way out. And so do you. I'll come for you when you're ready, and not before.

LP: I won't let you down.

CC: I know. Here's your next job.

17

How I Learned to Swim

Learning to swim is one of the few things I ever really made happen on my own – I just went down to the pool one day after work and began, the Monday after the company sent a few of us on a course in maximising the kill: and I was inspired. It was also the day Christy asked about my state of physical health, studied the vital statistics I sent and returned an unhappy report: how was I going to save the homeless orphans of South America if I couldn't save myself from obesity? Nobody would take me seriously. So I bought a pair of trunks and a towel, paid a year's membership and got straight in the water, imagining Christy's delighted face at some perfect moment in the future as I removed my shirt to reveal a rippling, taut stomach you could fry free-range, fair-trade eggs on. In the last few months, my thoughts of her had become dirtier. I tried to keep those thoughts locked up, but sometimes they appeared without permission, and made me feel better than I liked to admit.

All around people swam steady lengths in breaststroke or crawl, doing their daily keep-fit quota while I stood there up to my hairless thighs in the shallow end, motionless. A lifeguard crouched down by me and prodded an arm with his finger.

'Excuse me, Sir? Are you okay?'

'Sure. You?'

I used the same tone as in the office – ready to see the opportunity and grab it. But you can't fool the lifeguards, they home in on the weak.

'Well, you just let me know if you're having trouble, all right? I'll be watching you.'

'Watch who you like. I'm fine.'

It's funny, a grown man in bright blue trunks, afraid to put his head under. But the lifeguard made me want to move. I did, and it felt good. I moved again: I didn't die. I put one tentative foot in front of the other, and soon I was walking from shallow end to the deep and back, the level of the water rising and falling about me as I did my distance like everyone else. The radio played in the background, occasional cheerful pop music punctuating the news and regular traffic reports, and I thought of those people sitting in jams up and down the country, banging horns, like I used to. Thousands of people all saying 'fuck you' to the guy in front, while I walked through water in peace. With each length I began to enjoy the experience more. The chlorine smell was soothing; the bright, unflattering lights made even the good-looking appear gaunt and helped me blend in; nobody was watching apart from the lifeguard, who was pretending not to.

On my first few visits to the pool I just walked to the sound of the radio and the swish of other swimmers going about their routine, but soon I became embarrassed at walking through water while young children splashed about me, having fun. I listened in on what they were being told by their teachers – arm up and over, down and through, legs kick, arms swoosh. It sounded easy enough. On the fourth day I put my head under water, and it gave me a rush of excitement so powerful that after the session I went to buy myself a pair of goggles, proudly paying for them in the gym shop, hoping someone would ask me how the regime was going. But all I got was the lifeguard manning the desk.

'These a present for somebody, are they?'

'Yeah. They're a present from me to me, to show me how much I love me.'

Within a week I was swimming like everyone else.

I started going to the pool every day after work, always going at the same time so I could hear the rush-hour traffic report, the same one I used to pay no attention to in the early days of People4Jobs when I'd drive both ways, crawling the journey home in the car, counting money in my head, my cut of the day's deal, and how long it would last me when I finally broke away. Now I was counting calories while counting lengths, then walking home. I rewarded myself at the end of each session with a couple of minutes playing dead in the water, looking out from my new specs into the different shades of underwater blue at the kicking legs, sweeping arms, and the chests of girls on diet and exercise plans struggling to stay in all-too-tight costumes. Flesh was the only problem, really. Flesh of all kinds. I didn't like being with other men in the changing rooms – too much strutting, pruning and grooming for my liking – but maybe one day I'd be rich enough to have a pool of my own. In the meantime, it could have been worse: I might have had to get changed with the women.

I put on my trunks at the office or changed in a cubicle to avoid public nakedness, but it was hard to escape the nakedness of others. Sometimes I'd pass a group of guys in the showers and get an eyeful of someone with their you-know-what out for all to see, rubbing it with a towel or just parading it like a prize bull. Even some of the shy men let a little show while they changed under a towel, revealing shrunken distortions and scraggy, hairy clumps. The towels always drop when you least want them to. At first you look away, but after a while you don't bother. Never get used to it exactly, just look, in wonder, at how women can find men attractive. That's always surprising. How disgusting men are.

After Chuck died I got into the habit of swimming at weekends too – it helped fill out time between work and work. This morning I was determined to get some lengths in. I got undressed, folded my stuff neatly in the locker and shook my arms out by my sides. The pool was quiet and I needed to burn up energy. The family were supposed to be going for dinner once Phil arrived and there was talk of a picnic, so the more I could relax before the circus kicked off again, the better.

Recently I had been swimming forty to fifty lengths in a session, sixty sometimes. Today I was going for a record, and was just getting up to sixty-five when someone familiar came into view in the lane to my left. He noticed me, and decided for us both that we weren't going to ignore each other.

'Hi,' he said, slowing to a stop, making me do the same. 'Lewis, yeah? You know who I am, right?'

'Hello. Yes I do.'

'So . . . it's been a long time. Wow.'

Adrian swept his hair back with both hands as if posing for a photo. It was people like him who made me hate school so much that I gave it up. We had only been friends for a few months before our relationship developed a sourness that lasted until I left for the Academy – when I returned, dislike turned to bullying, and Adrian made sure I suffered for trying to escape. He was right. He told me I thought I was better than him, and that was true. I did. Why could I not bump into someone from the Academy? Someone like Alan, the HFN regional executive Christy had been telling me about, that I used to sit next to in maths, or Rob, the New HFN accounts guy, both recently signed up for Newborns by CC. I suspected both still lived locally, and looked out for them sometimes, though Christy told me not to.

'You left at sixteen, right?' said Adrian. 'Remember when I stayed at your house and your dad took us to Blackpool to do that freaky thing on the beach? That was weird.'

I swam to the edge of the pool, climbed the steps and turned towards him.

'Are you a member here, Adrian? Because if you are, I no longer am.'

'What?'

In morning break times I walked the length of the school corridors, across the fields and back again, alone, purposefully, as if I was on my way to somewhere, timing it so I'd arrive at my next class just in time. At lunch, I skipped the canteen in favour of an hour in the computer room or the library. It would have been nice if Adrian looked as if life since school had beaten him, but the Adrians of the world usually did okay.

As I turned the corner to the shower room Adrian shouted, 'I'm a fucking solicitor now! I don't even need to *speak* to you! Hey – come back here! Do you hear me? I don't have to speak to you!'

Great. A legal man. Another one for the database.

When you leave school early everyone thinks they're better than you. No matter what you do after, how much you earn, how you talk, they still think you're a loser. They swill about taking useless tests and degrees, postponing life, building up debt from too many nights in the Student Union or the gutter, while everyone else has to survive in the real world. By the time Adrian got his first month's wages I had been slogging night and day for six years – providing for my family, preparing for the future. But he still thought he was better. I walked off without giving him the satisfaction of biting back, picked up a towel and dried myself off quickly, hoping he wouldn't follow me into the changing room.

While putting my still-damp legs into the holes of my jeans, I thought about how few friends I had made so far in life. Sometimes, on my way back from work, I looked at the people that hung around the streets, in the thousands of new bars and style cafés that always seemed to be full, and wondered how the couples, the groups of friends and the Goth kids hanging out in the Northern Quarter had managed to meet and keep and swap each other. Making ties was a sort of magic I could never access. Even the people who liked me at school were gone now, to where I don't know. That's the way friendship is. When it's dying, it doesn't let you know. It just quietly, slowly, doesn't exist any more. I calmly buttoned up my shirt, tied my shoelaces, put on my jacket and thought of what it would feel like to smash a bottle through Adrian's face.

I don't remember hating him back then more than anyone else – he was just part of the mass – so I was surprised to find how annoyed I was when storming out of the gym, leaving my stuff at the door with a bewildered counter assistant.

'Keep these. I'm not coming back.'

'But Sir – you can't just go. You have to fill out a cancellation form – there are charges!'

'I am a free man. I don't have to do anything.'

I smiled and walked away.

'But Sir! . . . Sir! You've left your membership card! Would you like to stay on the mailing list? *What do you expect us to do with your trunks?*'

Adrian must have gone on to college, then university. He must have had a graduation picture, which no doubt sat on top of a television, or on a mantelpiece, or on a wall, swelling his mother's heart with pride every time she passed or polished it. My mother's walls were covered not in graduation pictures, but in maps of fish species and hamster-caring advice she cut out of magazines I bought for her. I wish I'd had a graduation photo to give – at least to see whether she'd make room for it amongst the animals.

CC: After the Academy, it was difficult to get used to anything else – it had raised my expectations – nowhere else understood me. And I couldn't go back to expecting nothing.

LP: I do.

CC: Do what?

LP: I understand you. I feel like I do, anyway. I wish you were here now, and maybe I could show you how much . . .

CC: Soon.

LP: We could be together.

CC: I do want that, but not yet. Have you done the list of jobs I gave you?

LP: Not all. I'm finding it harder than I expected to hack into some of these accounts.

CC: Hacking is easy. The hard part is getting the money to those who need it – then convincing them they deserve it. When I was at my lowest, I wouldn't take anything from anyone. I thought I was shit. I thought all I deserved was to die.

HFN-I: #238

18

Morning Shift at the Victory, Then and Now

Things are so different in the Victory now. Only a few years ago the shop used to be buzzing on Saturday mornings from as early as seven, the old assistant would start his shift along with Dad and I would be needed from about eight-thirty. In Grandpa Harry's day at least three of us were needed on shift from first thing.

'Show me a barber who can afford to close on Shabbas,' he shouted, 'and I'll show you a rich man with bagels for ears.'

Grandpa would have made a good politician, I reckon, somewhere with a big Jewish vote. Even when we opened on Saturdays, when the very idea of God had been a joke for as long as we could remember, even when religion played no part in our lives, that lilt in his voice remained – a tiny indicator of who we used to be.

'If Hitler came in here for a trim and a snip of that little moustache,' he said, wringing his hands with wicked glee, 'the old Nazifier wouldn't need to pull my trousers down to see which team I was on – he'd smell the Yid on me before I finished welcoming him in!'

When those things come back to me, they're always accompanied by the memory of lots of people laughing along. Three or four people on the seats waiting to be seen, chatting. A couple standing at the door. The whole family milling about at the back. In those days I was too small to be able to see what head Grandpa was working on, but if he was in the mood he'd sweep me up off the floor and put me on his shoulders between customers.

'Now Lewis – don't snatch at anything or I'll put you down. You might pull Mr Johnson's hairs out, grabbing like that. And he needs to hold on to both of them!'

Seemed like the only time Grandpa Harry wasn't making a joke was the day he died. I must have been ten or eleven then. Mum and Dad were still together.

'The real cruelty of living,' he said, smiling down at me, towards the last part of his life, 'is that none of the good bits come at the end. When you're old . . . it's hard to remember them. You feel a little empty, see? Fragments stay with you – so you know there's more – but the details, they're all gone. Better to lose your memory altogether, I reckon. There's something dignified in it.'

I told Rakesh that story once, and he took it very seriously. He put his hand over mine, gripped it tight and told me, while pointing up to the sky with his other hand, 'Promise you won't ever wish for bad things. You never know who might be listening . . .'

I don't know who Rakesh's God is – I don't know if he believes in one – but I promised him anyway. I'm a sucker for doing what other people tell me.

I got to the Victory around nine and found Dad, as usual, with a regular in the chair for a short-back-and-sides and twelve minutes talk about the same old stuff. Only this time there was a cold breeze coming in through the broken window. The rest of the shop had been given a basic sweep up, but there was still a little mess around – the wind softly blew the customer's comb-over in the wrong direction as Dad worked away.

'Why don't you board that thing up?' I said, picking up a chunk of glass from the floor.

'Why don't you shut your mouth?'

'I thought this was over. Did you do something?'

'Idiots don't need provoking, Lewis. Violence comes to them as easy as breathing. Easier, actually. Now sit down while I work on Gerry, and for pity's sake be quiet.'

'Don't you want some help?'

Dad looked at me, shocked.

'Some help I can do without!'

He was sounding more like Grandpa every day, slipping into the old man's personality now he wasn't around to make those kinds of comments himself. I closed the door and sat down to wait as the customer in the chair nodded in my direction through the mirror.

'All right, young man?' he asked.

'Yes, Sir. I certainly am.'

A picture on the newspaper front page showed the Vice-President of America holding a finger to the sky, pouting like Mussolini in his pomp, in front of a military audience. He had been giving a speech to the US army, warning them how much they had left to sacrifice, and the paper was quoting big chunks of it.

'Like other great duties in history,' the Vice-President said, talking about his war, 'it will require decades of patient effort, and it will be resisted by those whose only hope for power is through the spread of violence.'

I tried to imagine Chuck bravely on the field of battle. What he might have been doing. What order he might have been giving, who to and whether it had done any good. Christy's training had taught me to ignore the Middle East – the never-ending, unsolvable extravaganza designed to take attention away from the real war nobody talked about – the war against the ignored and abandoned – but reading the Vice-President's words I felt a warm recognition in the pit of my stomach that must have been something like agreement. After all, whose side were we on?

It was strange that we kept papers in the shop at all any more – the contrast between the clean, glorious black-and-white images on our walls and the dirty new ones beside the headlines seemed like a sick joke, but whenever Dad took them away customers complained. Even when the news was the same bleak stuff every day – 'MI5 in Secret Diana "Murder"

Plot!' – 'MI5 "Not Involved" in Secret Diana "Murder" Plot!'
– 'Watching TV Causes Cancer!' – 'Watching TV Cures
Cancer!' – our customers were old fashioned and suspicious of
glossy magazines: newspapers gave them something familiar to
concentrate on while they were waiting to be seen. Same with
the radio: not that anyone did much waiting these days. This
morning there was no one else in the shop but Dad and his customer and me; whenever the front window was smashed there
was never any weekend rush. Everyone apart from the hard
core tended to stay away. At least there was no blood on the
front page – small mercies, much appreciated. I flipped over to
the sport.

'It's too quiet in here,' I said. 'At least if another brick hit, it
would break the silence and we'd have a chance of catching the
little bastards.'

'Well, yes,' said the customer. 'But did you hear about that
young Patel feller who chased a thief down Oldham Street last
week? Poor kid got stabbed. Lost his life. What for? Who ben-
efits? Let them run, I say, and please God we'll all live till next
week.'

Dad didn't reply. He just kept clipping and didn't let on the
whole thing still bothered him. What was the point getting
annoyed about broken windows? If those kids knew, they
might work out there was nothing left to smash anyway.

Years of family life have gone completely from my mind, but
the details of our many nights in the shop with Dad, standing
to attention alongside Chuck and Philip at one of his pre-
school inspections, or listening to Dad in the near-darkness
while Mum slept upstairs – those memories always came back
when I watched him work. The war-story days were before
Mum had her first major breakdown, so there was a chance
she would wake up and go crazy if she knew we were up past
our bedtime. Sometimes I imagined her catching us. Our routine was pretty strict back then. Up by seven, in bed by nine;
fish on a Tuesday, meat on a Friday, leftovers on a Saturday;

Mum used to like everything to be very ordered and I suppose she still does, but she always missed a lot of what was really going on. Even before the trouble. For years we let her think we always did as we were told, even when we were about to directly defy her, a tactic which worked for so long that we almost forgot we were doing it. When we finally rebelled openly, it made the whole thing that much worse. All at once she realised it had been happening for years, that we had been growing up without her permission, and another little part of her lay down to die.

In the thrill of staying up late, in pyjamas, imagining the glories of the past, talking so quiet we could hardly hear ourselves, that possibility meant very little.

During the late-night sessions, Dad took the shaving chair with the softest seat and adjustable head support, Chuck and Philip took the swivel chairs that were side by side in front of the mirrors, and as the youngest I brought over one of the customers' chairs from the wall. We had to keep our voices down, but that just made it more exciting. Dad's army stories worked better in a whisper anyway. Churchill looking down on us, giving the V for victory that gave the shop its name, made it all seem frighteningly real. The way Dad talked about him, it was like Churchill was Grandpa's equal partner, winning the fight from the war room next door (Aarav's the Grocers), popping in for an occasional cigar and a bit of advice from my old man. Dad had plenty of experiences of his own, but preferred to tell us about Grandpa's – because he wasn't around to tell them himself, so he said – though we knew better. The only fights Dad knew about were ones he wasn't entirely sure should have been fought at all. Chuck pressed him on it once; Dad's brief answer was this:

'Just pray to God you won't ever have to see what I did,' he said, and the conversation was over.

It was his one and only mention of God, and though we weren't quite sure what we thought about that, we knew Dad's war had been serious. And all the more exciting for being too revolting to talk about. We returned to safe, jolly Churchill, who liked a drink and liked a smoke, the war we hadn't fought and the same old happy ending. The good guys were always the winners, the bad guys always got beat, and Grandpa always returned with a handful of medals to set up the shop we sat in.

I had been waiting for what felt like a long time – Dad was still on the same customer – but the cold draught made it seem longer. And Dad is slow anyway. He treats each head, even the most pitiable and sparsely furnished, like a little hairy *Venus de Milo* that must be handled with the ultimate, steady care. Slowly, slowly. Can't be rushed. 'An art form disguised as a service,' he called it.

Out of the snipping and silence Dad's customer said, 'Tell me about the family, Clive. It's been too long . . . How's young Charles doing?'

I stood up as if someone had ordered me to. Dad lowered his hand, ushering me to sit, but didn't point to Chuck's picture or pat his heart with his scissors. Instead, he took a deep breath and said, in an off-hand, relaxed way, 'He's back for a few days, to see his mother. And the rest of us, I suppose.'

'Out at the minute then, is he?'

'He's a good boy. Fighting for America. And for us.'

Dad reached for a photograph in his back pocket.

'Charles's girl,' he said. 'My granddaughter. A clever one, you can spot it in the eyes. Sees the world as it is, that thing. Just like her mother.'

The customer nodded and Dad put the photograph back in his pocket. Dad handed me the scissors, hands trembling. I stood again.

'Lewis, please finish off Mr Feingold. I need to go to the bathroom.'

Mr Feingold waited for Dad to disappear into the back room before he spoke again, this time with greater confidence.

'So what is it you do now, son?' he asked, grinning. 'Your

father says you're still one of those layabouts.'

'With all due respect, Mr Feingold, I have a very highly respected – and well-paid – job in recruitment . . .'

'In who now? . . . Then what are you doing in here?'

'I like to help.'

'How can you do that if you've got a job? What kind of a profession doesn't need you to turn up? Sounds like a layabout job to me.'

Try explaining recruitment to anyone over sixty: they don't get it. I've had a lot of blank looks over the years, mainly from the seniors, with regard to my very modern profession – Mr Feingold was nearly seventy.

'I'm only here at the weekends,' I said. 'I'll explain what I do if you like.'

'Go on then,' he said, crossing his arms. 'What else do I have to do with my life? God knows nobody's waiting for me at home!'

He huffed and puffed and wriggled around in the chair as if I was putting him out terribly, but I gave it my best shot. Anything but return to the subject of Chuck or the big hole in the window.

'Well,' I said, 'I'll try to keep it interesting for you, Mr Feingold . . . but keep still if you can. Head back, please . . . thank you. Mostly I just put prospective clients from our database in touch with companies from the main database who are looking for someone they can rely on to do whatever it is they do – you know, consumer law, corporate finance, commercial litigation . . . then I go back and forth between them persuading the company that the client will be great at the job and persuading the client that the company will be a good move for his career. This goes on for a while sometimes. Back and forth, negotiate negotiate. Eventually I glue the two together and – hey presto! – the client has a job and the company have their man. We take a ten per cent cut of that person's wages for the following year, and ten per cent of that goes to me. Put your head forward now, please.'

'What do they need you for? Why don't they just put an ad in the paper?'

'Well, it's not really like that, Mr Feingold. They come to us because we're experts.'

'In what?'

'Moving people around.'

'I don't understand.'

I gave him the line.

'Mr Feingold, my job is simple: I find jobs for people and people for jobs.'

'What, you work in the *Job Centre*?'

'No! God no! Well . . . yes . . . I *suppose*. A very grand one. For solicitors.'

'Out of work solicitors? Never known one yet!'

'No, most of these ones already *have* jobs, but I find them better ones.'

'Well, that's a funny way to spend your days. Those bastards have got enough money already if you ask me. What about the steel workers? The miners? The good men from the services who can't get jobs when they come out? You sound like a layabout to me.'

I picked up the small mirror and held it up.

'Thank you, Mr Feingold, but we don't have much of a steel industry any more, and you'll do well to find a mine in central Manchester. Now, is the back okay for you? I can trim it a little more.'

'No, no. You've ruined it quite enough, thank you.'

Dad stood at the door to the lounge, more composed.

Dad thought he'd done his bit for his country and all that was left for him was to be able to talk to customers about what his kids were doing. What direction we took, how forcefully we walked in it. So when his eldest said he wanted to get married at eighteen, he was proud – *brave*, Dad called it. Forward looking. A sign of understanding the real meaning of responsibility. When he said he was moving to Texas and enrolling in the US army, Dad was satisfied with his work. By the time he announced he wanted to be known as Chuck, Dad was past caring about anything much. It was Mum who cried over that one. Another betrayal, perhaps. Dad just told him he was free to do what he wanted in this world, and if that meant having a name like a chicken, he could deal with it. Then he resumed normal service, calling him Charles like always. We could have been nearly anything, but as long as we were sure it was what we wanted to do, Dad would have showed off about it while cutting hair – apart from recruitment, that is. Recruitment he had nothing to say about. It was not honest or honourable or easily understood: the beauty of my art was lost on him, and he was not interested in finding it.

Mr Feingold noticed Dad coming back into view through the mirror and called across to him.

'What about the middle one, Clive?' he asked. 'Is Philip married yet?'

'Nope.'

'Why not?'

A small parp of laughter came from my dad, who shooed me away from Mr Feingold's head and took over again. Clearly, I had failed to reach the required standard, and he was going back to make perfect my poor attempt.

'He'll be fine. Fine as he's ever been, I reckon.'

'And what if he isn't?' said Mr Feingold. 'Don't you think it's a bit . . . well . . . it's not really the thing to do, is it? What he does . . .'

No more laughing. The old barber came closer to his customer and put his scissors and comb into one hand so he could point properly.

'I'm telling you, he's fine.'

Scissors back in usual hand, still pointing through the mirror.

'I brought up men, not pansies. Now, Gerry, you want me to cut your ears off or shall we finish up in silence?'

He clipped and snipped for a few minutes, keeping the anger down, but eventually couldn't help adding to that. He was easier cracked these days.

'My boys are off living their lives,' he said, a little sadly. 'Still, proper good ones I raised.'

'Course you did, Clive. Course you did.'

Now the scissors pointed to the street, just as a gust of air flooded in towards us.

'Shame they've got nothing to come home to but a big hole in the window and a sign that says their dad's a Nazi. Right . . . off you go, Gerry. You know the price.'

Gerry Feingold nodded timidly, handed over a note and was gone before Dad could offer change.

The two of us sat in the chairs for a moment. There were no bookings for today, just two for tomorrow, and you could never be sure if people were going to come in off the street any more.

'You know,' I said, 'we could get the window fixed in a couple of hours. And remember, the police said we should always report any incidents from now on. Have you called them?'

'What's the point?'

'Don't be like that.'

'I can't be any other way. You want to know how I feel, Lewis? That's how I feel.'

Dad picked up my jacket and threw it at me.

'Right . . . let's go.'

'Where to?'

'You'll see.'

'What about Mum?'

'She doesn't tell you what she's doing. Why should you tell her?'

Before I had a chance to ask any more questions he had flipped the sign to 'Closed', put on his jacket, pushed me out of the door and locked the shop with his key. The weather was bright but chilly; as we left the shop and walked towards the car, it felt like this was the first day of autumn.

'Come on,' he said, 'before the cavalry comes.'

'Where to?' I asked again.

'The tools are already in the car.'

'There's no point locking the front door, Dad. You know that, right?'

'Sure I know.'

'You're leaving it like this? Anyone could get in.'

I went back inside and secured the gate leading up to Mum's room.

'Let them take it all if they want to,' said Dad, turning the door lock again. 'It makes no difference what I do anyway. But let nobody say that on the day they broke into my shop I didn't bother to lock the bloody door.'

'It'll be too cold for you to do all this soon, I suppose,' I said. 'You can't go searching for treasure in December.'

'Watch your mouth,' he snapped. 'Always respect your father. I'm not a child.'

We drove the hour-long journey up the motorway in near silence, the only sound being the radio humming along in the background. A play, I think – it was too quiet to hear anything really apart from the gentle rise and fall of received pronunciation. Though he didn't use it himself, Dad always found those kinds of voices soothing, and the louder the radio, the calmer he seemed. I wanted to talk to him about something but there was little we could share these days. Christy remained a closely guarded secret. We could only discuss Chuck when he wanted to. And we never talked about *her upstairs*.

As we coasted along the road – always five miles an hour under the speed limit – I realised I was living many lives at once. But each had been boxed, a safe distance from the others, for too long. Monday to Friday daytime I helped professionals move sideways and upwards between firms, in the evenings I cared for Mum, at nights I was a revolutionary for Christy, and, though I paid my way, more than my way, kept his shop going, my father still employed me like a teenage apprentice at the weekends. I was worth more to Christy than my boss or my parents would ever let me be: I wanted to prove myself, and soon.

LP: So what do you suggest?

CC: Changing things one newborn at a time, through the power of *community*. That word is now seen as a dirty one, but it wasn't always that way. In the last hundred years, our governments have gradually alienated us from each other through a combination of legislation and persuasion. In 1957 the British Prime Minister Harold Macmillan told the country, 'most of our people have never had it so good', but this was a lie then and is still a lie today, no matter what country you live in. The gap between rich and poor gets ever larger, especially under Labour governments. Our general election votes count for virtually nothing. Our mass protests cannot stop wars. Official slavery was abolished decades ago but it has been replaced by sex traffic, which is allowed to flourish while the drug trade is condemned so expensively.

LP: I love it when you talk like that. Like you're talking to a big crowd – like you're losing your mind.

CC: This is serious, Lewis.

LP: I know.

CC: Well sometimes I wish you would act like it. I'm writing to you from an internet café in São Paulo. There are thousands of abandoned girls here, just left to rot or prostitute themselves. We're donating beds, blankets, pillows and books to one of the orphanages. I'm meeting with one of the women here this afternoon. Imagine the future, Lewis: Hope for Newborns homes worldwide!

LP: Is it just girls you want to help?

CC: Mainly, yes. They suffer the most. But we'll get to the boys in the end.

HFN-I: #248

19

The Beach at Blackpool

It was not sunbathing weather. There were never many people walking around the beach or the pier before pub opening time, but it was quieter than usual today; the silence made it feel more like a ghost town than a tourist spot and, though the unlit illuminations proved where we were, I felt sad as we drove past the waterfront to our starting place. Maybe that's why Dad liked it at this hour: the quietness. He wouldn't go to the place at any other time. The cafés weren't open yet. The bars wouldn't be busy for hours. The tourists were all still in bed, sleeping off hangovers. There were only a couple of cars on the side street where habit always led us to the same space. We parked up, got out and lifted the metal detectors from the boot.

'I finished near *there* last time,' Dad began, pointing towards a single, lonely looking red deckchair in the distance, 'so we can start at that point and see where it takes us. We should do this area near the North Pier as well. Usually some good stuff. You start at that end by the fence, I'll start at this one. We'll cross in the middle each time, then move down a few yards, and so on . . . we have to be thorough.'

He seemed pleased to be out of the house and that was enough for now. We began covering ground up and down the beach, passing each other regularly as Dad had said, waving our sticks just above ground and waiting for a noise. This was our time together – heading in opposite directions, in silence. It was all Dad had kept up since us boys were young; everything else had faded. He only had the shop now, and chasing Chuck, and this.

In these surroundings Dad tuned out from the world completely: if the beep on the machine wasn't so loud and hoarse he might not have found a single thing in thirty years of looking. I watched for signs of change from the old routine, but he was no different; the relief of being free, undisturbed, as if outside the world looking in, was the same on any weekend, though today the temperature would have affected anyone else's mood badly. Dad loved the English weather, and acted as if nothing satisfied him more than a good old-fashioned cloud – it was certainly a day for those – a perfectly miserable, overcast, windy Northern day. A girl in jogging shorts and a Lycra top ran past, listening to music through headphones, breasts lolling up and down as she moved, just as we were about to cross for the first time. She must have been about twenty, twenty-one.

Dad waited until we passed each other and whispered, 'Have you found anything?'

'Not yet.'

'Well, make sure you're covering all the ground . . . Leave no gaps!'

I wondered if Dad even noticed women of any shape, size or relation any more, whether he had an opinion on his daughter-in-law, his granddaughter, his wife. If he'd even be thinking of these things at all as he prepared for a day's calm on the sand. His mind was most likely an empty, clear space, except maybe for the moments when Chuck fought his way in. I swayed the metal left and right and tried to make mine the same. Nearly an hour passed, and each time we came by each other I could feel him getting further from me, from everything. He just wanted to be left alone.

Dad was so caught up in the hunt that when two people came over and tried to get his attention, he didn't notice. A woman put her hand on his arm, as if to wake him. He looked up, startled.

'Hello, can you help us please?'

The couple, who were in their mid-twenties, stood between

Dad and the road, holding hands. I went over.

'We've lost something,' said the woman. 'We were sitting on the beach this morning and went into the sea for a while—'

'You went in *there* in *this* weather?'

Dad was awake now; his ability to focus on impractical decisions was ever present. The man cut in.

'I took my ring off first and put it in a pocket of my shorts. I think so, anyway – I didn't want to lose it in the water. Afterwards we collected our things, got dressed and went for something to eat. Then I remembered the ring and noticed it wasn't in my pocket. We came back and tried to find where our stuff was but there's hardly anyone on the beach, and it's so hard to remember where's where. It's all just the same, you know?'

'That's where you're wrong,' said Dad. 'Every grain is as individual as you are.'

'Yes, well . . . We wondered if you would mind helping us look for it. You know, with your . . .' he pointed, 'Your *thing*.'

'Gold was it? Silver?'

'Gold.'

'I see,' said Dad. 'Well, take me through the whole matter from the beginning.'

The couple stood on the sand and told the story in greater detail, pointing to places they might have been. Dad listened carefully, occasionally adding an 'Are you sure?' or an 'Aaah' or an 'I see'. He became very business-like and made both of them mark out all the routes they might have taken from the beach back to the road. Dad reminded everyone it was equally possible that if the young man had forgotten to put his ring back on after swimming, he might also have forgotten leaving their spot *with* the ring, only to lose it on the way to the shore.

'These details are crucial,' he said, 'if we are going to be certain to get it back.'

I hardly said a word except to introduce myself and ask for the names of the couple – Paul and Jane – him from the North, her from the South. I followed the orders Dad gave me, deter-

158

mined to find this tiny hunk of metal. Dad's eyes had a child-like twinkle about them that reminded me of Grandpa Harry in his prime.

'I feel like an idiot,' said Paul. 'I don't know what I've done with it.'

'Aye, well. Don't worry about that now,' said Dad. 'Self-pity won't get you anywhere.'

We paced slowly over the designated area, detectors swinging in tandem while Dad chatted to the couple, who talked constantly.

'It's amazing,' said Jane, 'that you were out here with your detectors. How lucky is that?'

'Not very,' said Dad, still moving. 'This was bound to happen in the end. My sons and I have been coming out here for years. You know, I used to hide little treasures under the sand, especially when this one –' (he gestured to me) – 'was small. Used to send him off with his brothers to get ice cream before we started so I could plant a few things. I even had a stash of objects in the boot for a few years.'

'Why?' asked Jane.

'So they could tell their mother they'd found something at the end of the day . . . old coins, that kind of thing. I find all kinds of junk folk leave behind – you wouldn't believe what they forget to take home.'

'Do you keep anything?'

'I drop off anything valuable with the police and concentrate on getting the cans out of the ground: they make a very similar sound on the machine to when you find gold, so I still get the excitement of a real find. Did you know that? Funny quirk of the model, maybe, but a good one for me.'

'Do you think you'll find our ring?' said Paul.

'Oh yes – if it's here, me and my boy will find it. That's for sure.'

Just then the machine beeped, loud and bassy. Dad scooped deep into the sand, taking out a crushed can.

'See? That's what I mean . . . Sounds just like gold.'

He walked ten paces towards the shore, leisurely but careful, put the can down in the rubbish pile he had been cultivating and returned ten paces to the same spot. The first square of possible ring territory was nearly covered; now we would have to move further away from the water.

Dad and I continued searching while Paul and Jane followed us around, waiting for something to happen.

'So, what do you guys do?' asked Paul.

'We're barbers,' said Dad. 'Both of us.'

I almost disagreed, but didn't.

'I worked with my dad too, for a while,' said Paul. 'Everyone thinks they can do whatever the hell they want these days, but my father was a tailor and I'm carrying that tradition on. Hand-made suits, that kind of thing – there's not much money in it, but I feel like I'm doing something he would have been pleased with, you know?'

Dad smiled gently.

'Well, how about you?' he said, turning to Jane. 'You in the family business too?'

'A different kind,' she said, patting her stomach. 'My parents were in the Met, and so was I – but you can't inherit that, can you? I'll go back to work as soon as the baby is born, but probably do something completely different. I don't feel like I'm doing much good. My parents say things have changed since they started. Too much paperwork now. Too much politics.'

Dad laughed warmly. He steadily scanned the ground in front of him, the machine humming, and said, without looking up, 'They certainly have changed.'

'Were you in the force?'

'No. The army. Same as my dad. After the Second World War he returned to Manchester, which was mainly factory outlets, factories, clothes shops, a few pubs, a market and some run-down buildings that had been abandoned for a long time; nobody could quite remember what they used to be. The one thing he thought it needed was a barber shop.'

'Good sense,' said Paul. 'He must have been a smart businessman.'

'No,' said Dad. 'What mattered to my father was Churchill, British values, his army days and everything most people of that time were proud of. He thought the shop would make people feel better about themselves, and remind them how everything they did was only possible because of the people like him who fought for our way of life.'

'Quite right,' said Jane.

'His father was one of those too – went straight into the forces after arriving in Britain from Lithuania in 1917. Thought it was his duty. Couldn't speak English yet, but already understood English pride. Tell people about that kind of spirit these days and they think you're crazy, but I've seen it with my own eyes.'

I scanned opposite Dad, searching, listening. His voice was slow, sincere, considered. I sensed him going off on one of his windy monologues.

'Dad was right about the idea for the shop. It did well. A collection for veterans filled up quickly, and had to be replaced pretty regular – as a small boy, my first job was to empty this jar and hand over the coins to the boss. Do you know I used to look forward to that? Now, when the kids attack us they always take the collection box. Even though it doesn't fill up so quickly, and there's not much to take.'

'You're still going, though?' said Paul. 'That's amazing – a small family business. All that time.'

'Well thank you, but I'm not sure how much longer it can go on. In the old days, people adapted to change without grumbling. I'm not sure if I can do that. When my grandparents arrived in the port at Hull in 1917, they thought they were landing in the USA: that's what they'd paid the boatman for. But it didn't bother my grandfather. Not much did. Do you know the first thing he said when he landed? This is how my dad told me anyway . . . translated, of course: "Well," he said, "if this is New York I'll eat my hat – but it's home now. Let's find a spot and get comfortable." He was a real man.'

As we eliminated more areas Paul and Jane became down-cast, saying several times that we had been very kind but maybe it just wasn't there.

'Don't be so negative,' said Dad. 'If it's not in the search area we've covered so far, then it means we're getting closer, not further away. Why don't you pop into the café there and wait a while? You can't do anything here.'

But just then his machine went off again, this time beeping fast and hard, louder than ever.

'If this isn't it,' said Dad, 'then I don't know what is.'

Paul, Jane and I came close while Dad dug with his hands down through the softer, lighter sand into the dark dampness below, picking out a simple, sandy white gold ring.

Paul and Jane tried several ways of saying thank you – they wanted to take us to lunch, to dinner, out for a drink – but each time Dad refused. Secretly I was hoping he'd accept the offer, but he said they'd thanked us enough, to enjoy the rest of their time in Blackpool and be careful where they put their valuables. They said they'd never forget him, if they were ever in Manchester and needed a trim they'd know where to come, and if he was ever on the coast and needed a hand-made suit he knew where he could get one for nothing. He laughed and off they went. Dad took out the car keys to show we had fin-ished for the day, and I went over to pick up my stuff.

On the way back to the car he said, 'You know, I often think to myself: Clive, it was a shame there was no decent battle for you. You would have been good in conflict – but the call never came for you. Seemed amazing that with such a messy world there was nothing for me to clear up. Except Ireland. And that's not what I signed up for.'

'No war seems like a good idea when you're fighting, does it?'

'Yes, but there are two kinds: the ones where you get applauded through the streets when you come home, and the ones where you don't. In that way, Charles and I are the same.'

'Those people were very grateful,' I said, sure not to look at him. 'We should have at least gone for a drink with them.'

'Maybe. But it was more for them rather than us, and you knew that.'

'You told them things you never told me.'

'Yes. I told a customer I wanted to divorce your mother before I told anyone else. Don't know how it happened, it wasn't even someone I knew well – it just slipped out. He asked how things were, and that's all it took . . . Shall we go home now?'

'Let's go.'

At that moment, I was sure that whatever reasons Dad had chosen for living as he had done, they must have been good ones.

The journey back seemed quicker than the one out there, and we were home by early afternoon. Dad picked his moment carefully for speaking next. Walking back up the main road to the shop entrance, detector over his shoulder, he said, 'Why did you never take that trip last year?'

I shrugged, opening the door.

'Things came up.'

'Well, take it now. Just don't think it will magically make everything all right. You've got to be going towards some-thing.'

'I know that. Perhaps it's better I didn't go before.'

'Right.'

'Before, I was just running. Now, I've got a reason.'

He unlocked the front door, wiped his feet on the mattress, reminded me to do the same, and resumed work immediately. I flipped the 'Closed' sign to 'Open' and said, 'I want to go back to the office for a few hours after I've checked on Mum.'

'On a weekend?'

'My presentation is on Monday.'

'Well, good luck with that. I don't need you.'

'We should go to the beach again soon.'

Dad continued sweeping, facing away from me.

'I wish I could go every day. Perhaps when I retire, eh?'

I went upstairs and into Mum's room. Her face was all questioning, but I would not say where we'd been. If she wanted to know, she could ask.

LP: Are you there?

CC: Yes.

LP: I thought you'd want to know – I did it!

CC: Really? How much this time?

LP: You're going to be amazed.

20

One-way Conversation

Every time I walked into a new room it was like beginning again: that morning feeling – of sleepy emptiness, waiting to be filled – was getting more regular these days, in afternoons and evenings too. The search on the beach was already hours ago. The swim was days ago. The morning's breakfast seemed months in the past.

I closed Mum's door behind me, smiled and said cheerily, 'So how are you today?'

She was at her usual spot in her chair by the window, look-ing down on the street; Mum probably recognised the top of every head that came in and out of the Victory – for someone who chose not to take part in life, she was strangely keen to know who was in the building at any given time. Just in case there was a fire or something. So when she was saving us all, running out of the burning building, a child over each shoul-der, she'd know how many were left inside.

'Aren't you going to offer me a drink?' I said. '. . . Well, I'll get one myself then. You wanting a cup? The usual? I'll just pop the kettle on, shall I?'

Asking questions was very much a part of our one-way con-versations. Sometimes it was a way of inviting her to join in – so she knew she could speak up at any time and it would be treated as normal – but it was also a plan of attack. A way of reminding her how awkward she was being. Recently I'd start-ed with insults as well, as testers. Make up stuff about the shop. Tell little white lies about things she said or did in the past. If I wound her up enough, maybe she'd eventually unravel.

I went over to the sink by her window and got out two mugs while she chewed on a sandwich. Recently Mum had taken to making her own snacks, and for a few days I thought it was the beginning of something, but it was probably just that I'd started visiting less, and she got hungry more often than I came to feed her. After all, she wasn't incapable. She cleaned herself well enough, morning and night. She knew how to use a toilet. She wasn't like a real ill person.

'I'm supposed to be away this weekend,' I said, popping her favourite tea bags in the cups. 'In Johannesburg! Christy's there for a few days' work and play – *see what was going on at ground level*, she said. But I told her I had to look after you . . .'

That wasn't true, but what did it matter? I stared out at the buzz of the main street, full of people going shopping for the afternoon, working, just spending time together. From Mum's vantage point I could see the kids flicking through the racks at the record exchange across the road, looking for a bargain. A mother and son were in the coffee shop a few doors down, drinking, picking at some food, talking. I faced away but spoke loudly so Mum could hear.

'Christy tells me the world is falling apart – would that get you out of your chair?'

Mum chewed and gazed outwards, unflinching. I imagined her saying, 'You think you're winning, don't you?' Though I could no longer remember what her voice sounded like, I could still picture her mouthing the words, and feel how it would feel to know she was right.

'Christy says I should leave here,' I continued, pacing now. 'She says it's making me ill. How can I help Newborns when I'm so busy making your tea?'

I went to Mum's chair, kneeling down at it, holding her hand.

'I want to tell you about her, Mum. She's amazing. She found me on the internet and explained how I was living, what was wrong with the way I was living, how I could change and help other people at the same time. You don't know what the internet is, do you? It wasn't popular when you were . . . with us.'

The kettle clicked. I got up, poured and took Mum's drink to her, then headed for my briefcase where I reached in for the Hope files I kept in the sealed zip pocket at the back. The precise order of everything was pleasing. There's nothing like a perfectly organised file. I knelt on the floor and began flicking through recent papers.

'The internet is pretty simple really . . .' I said. 'Remember when you used to do the accounts for the shop and you kept all the paperwork in the filing cabinet? Well, websites are like filing cabinets, just with the contents available on computers for everyone to see, if they know the password. Here are some of the account details I got hold of, for people who don't need their money. Look!'

Mum stared directly at me, but without change of expression, then looked away. That lack of response could still shock.

'It's all changing out there, while you sit in here, brooding. You're going to do that for ever, are you?'

This time I didn't wait for a reply. Instead, I took a selection of the most impressive-looking Hope files and dropped them in her lap, on top of what remained of her sandwich, so she couldn't ignore them. It was against one of the social workers' golden rules, but how could someone who had got no results object to a bit of tough love?

I went over to the big fish tank in the corner of the room, sprinkled a few flakes onto the surface and asked, 'Do you want to know something exciting?'

The fish swam to the surface and fought over the scraps. They were only interested in themselves, flapping desperately left and right. I had been getting louder, angrier than I realised.

'Well?' I demanded. '*Say something!*'

My voice was too noisy, really – noisy enough to be frightening. Dad shouted from downstairs: 'Everything all right up there?'

I went out onto the landing and called back, in my brightest tone, 'Everything's fine. No need to sound the alarms.'

I returned to the room. It was easier to talk facing away. Perhaps the fish would like more food.

'Where was I? Ah, yes . . . Christy runs this website called Hope for Newborns, which looks like a charity for unborn children to those who don't know, but is actually a charity for ones that are *already alive*.'

I turned back to Mum, giving her a start.

'People like you – foundlings, like you and Christy. Well, maybe not like you . . . these people have nobody, nothing. You've got us. Though you don't want us, we're here. Anyway, isn't that the cleverest trick? A pretend charity? A cover? Christy's been letting me help with the business side: *using my talents*, she said, *for the greatest result*. We email work back and forth – remember I told you about email? – and we have virtual meetings on the computer every week about how we're doing raising funds. Usually that happens late at night, though I have to sneak off work sometimes to phone clients during office hours. People are more likely to be more loyal when they have a personal relationship with someone in the company. I have more responsibility now, and an official title: Revolutionary UK Accounts Manager. Who'd have thought I'd turn out to be one of those? I deal with people who are donating regularly, encouraging them to invest more, and telling them how much they're making a difference. It's not the kind of difference they think they're making, but then, if we left it up to rich men, who would they help but themselves?'

Mum picked up the papers I'd put in her lap and let them fall on a sideboard, as if dropping a dirty towel in the laundry basket, and returned to the last of her sandwich. It was like she was alone and had no one to please but herself. She looked a little scared, I think. I grabbed her shoulders.

'We're forced to work this way, Mum. It's much worse than they tell you on the TV, or in books or magazines. Christy says she tried other ways, for too long really, but people were more interested in supporting the unborn than those who were already alive and she raised virtually *nothing*. Pennies! Now the money is *rolling in*. Soon we'll have the whole Newborns team in place; we'll spread and spread. We get funds through credit card fraud as well – you know, slipping a few pounds a month out of accounts abroad – but not much from each person. That wouldn't be fair. And only off people who won't notice. How can anyone object to people losing money they don't even know is there? That they're not even using? Kids are starving and there's *billions* sitting in banks doing nothing but getting fat! Doesn't that make you feel sick?'

I was talking fast, leaning forward, further forward, and Mum was too, very slightly. She tightened the grip on her blanket: I was sure she was with me.

'I know you lied,' I said. 'I thought I wasn't good enough for the Academy. You let me believe that. I understand, I know you just wanted me home – but now I know they closed it down. Of course, Christy stayed till the end. She had no choice. One day she just arrived and found the doors were locked. That was it. No more. That's private education for you. The minute the money went, the teachers did too – the caretaker, the groundsmen, everybody. Packed their bags and left, without so much as a morning prayer. The governors disappeared into thin air, like the moneyed always do; there was no one to complain to. Everyone had to find new places to go. But not everyone *had* new places to go. Do you understand what I'm saying? Some people don't have homes at all.'

Mum sipped at her tea. I let go of her shoulders. I'd held them for too long. Talked for too long – I collapsed down by her chair and spoke quieter.

'They moved Christy into a home but they didn't understand her there – she dropped out. She decided to break out. Isn't it inspiring? Christy's like a prophet. She *is* a prophet.'

Hearing me talk about being inspired made me feel more like it.

'Christy thought things had gone bad for her since that

moment when the school doors were locked,' I said, 'and wondered what had happened to other foundlings like her: the people right at the bottom of society's pile. Well, then she got the idea of helping them – Newborns, we call them – so people could see just like they taught us at the Academy – that good things were possible if people pulled together. The website has been a revelation; it's amazing what you can achieve with cash and internet links through the major search engines. We're making a *difference*. Of course, I've given the foundation a lot of my money. How can I hold on to it?'

Mum flinched slightly at the mention of money, but that was all.

'Christy has been using some of the money to see the situation for herself. Christy has been to South America, Russia, even China. She always tells me what she's doing there, who she's found, how she's going to sort them out. She calls me her Number Two. She'll come to me last. We'll travel the world together, setting up Newborns branches everywhere. I've worked hard, Mum. I've been doing well. Are you proud?'

Her response was familiar, but this time I had given more. It was like the first silence.

'Well?' I said.

Still nothing.

'Well? *Well?*'

I went up close, just like Philip had done to that boy on the bus last year. Still nothing.

'Fine,' I said. 'See you later.'

The HFN papers could stay where they were for a while. Maybe she'd have a look later, when no one was looking – even when I was giving up I wasn't really giving up. I took Mum's birthday present from my bag, put it by the door, making no mention of it, and went back downstairs where, by the sounds of things, an argument had started up. My patience with the old state was fast running out.

171

CC: Do you want to go on an errand?

LP: What is it this time?

CC: Oh – I think it's something you're going to be interested in.

21

Me and Tampa Bay Hit the Road

When I got to the bottom of the stairs most of the family were sitting arms crossed in the lounge, studiously looking at the ground, the ceiling or the walls. Daisy and Tampa Bay had gone to collect Philip and all three had just got home. This year Dad had waited in the shop: now he stood in the hallway, rubbing his hands with a towel. Nobody spoke, apart from a grumpy Tampa Bay, who was moaning quietly, and Daisy, who was stroking her daughter's cheek, saying 'Shh,' though it was making no difference.

'All right, Phil. You gonna say hello, then?'

Philip got up and gave me a hug, but the expression on his face and the weak tug he gave my shoulders showed how exhausted he was.

'No sleep?' I asked.

'Not much. How is she?'

'The birthday girl? I'd leave her be for a while if I were you. Rest. You look like you need it.'

'So do you. Been working?'

'Too much. Just wanted to say hi, then I'm going into the office for a few hours . . .'

'Right.'

I don't think he was listening. I wondered if my brother had been in this state since the cremation – while I carried on as normal, mostly pretending I felt nothing, had Philip been wandering unshaven through Toronto for the last four months, crying, moaning, letting it all pour out? I felt a sharp pang in the pit of my stomach and knew I was jealous.

The shop had mostly been cleaned up, probably by Daisy. Apart from the damage that had been done to the windows and the door, the place seemed almost back to normal, though normal was something different to what it used to be.

Dad said brightly, 'I'm going to drag in a vagrant. Anyone mind?'

Nobody spoke up so he took the broom, stood out on the porch and called out to the first person that came past, 'Free haircut, Sir? Special deal. Today only.'

The man looked suspiciously at the debris.

'Don't worry about the mess. Bit of bother with the local youth. But, some Dunkirk spirit and we'll get through, eh?'

Before the man could object Dad had put him into the chair and was standing awaiting instructions. The rest of us stood around awkwardly in the back room.

'Now, what'll you have?' he said. 'Let's get rid of this revolting pony tail for a start . . .'

Everything was happening too quickly today. I wanted to slow time down. Stop it. Or find an excuse to get away. Though everyone had just arrived, the memory of last year's party for Mum, and everyone together, Dad's tour of the shop – it all made Chuck's absence more obvious.

The prospect of having to stay with the family seemed like an impossible job, but the office on a weekend was no more appealing. The office was no fun when it was empty, and it seemed like a long time since I'd been there at all. I went up to Tampa and planted a kiss on her forehead.

'Well, I suppose I'll be off then,' I said, stalling. 'Big day on Monday. I'll see you all tonight . . .'

'Uuueeeugh,' said Tampa Bay.

'What's that?'

'Neeeuuurrrggghhh. No!'

I hesitated.

'No? You said no? Well . . . I suppose I could leave it today. Who works at the weekend anyway?'

'You do it every week!' called Dad between whistles and

reassurances to the frightened customer.

'So do I!' answered Morta, a voice calling from by the back door. 'And what thanks do I get?'

We didn't even know Morta was in. She came and went so often these days that we found it hard to keep up.

'You get thanks in pounds and pence, thanks very much,' said Dad. 'You chose to come to this country – why are you always complaining about it?'

At that, Morta appeared in the shop front, pointing.

'Oh yes – dirty foreigners! That's right. They come over here, fix our teeth, sweep our streets, teach our children, pay taxes, shovel our shit – *why don't we don't we just go back to where we came from?*'

Morta picked up a broom and began to sweep the floor.

'Daisy . . .' I asked. 'Do you want me to take Tampa Bay for a while?'

'Where to?'

'Doesn't matter. Do whatever it is you would do if she wasn't here; we'll be back in a couple of hours. I've had an idea.'

'Are you sure you know what you're doing?'

'Let him go,' said Philip, collapsing back into a chair, speaking in almost a whisper. 'Let him go.'

I lifted Tampa Bay from her spot.

'Come on, you, let's go cruise the strip. Promise not to poo yourself and I'll let you ride up front.'

'Brasouwaaa.'

'I'll see you later, Phil. How long are you staying for, anyway?'

'I . . . um . . . may be back for a while. You don't need your old room, do you?'

Daisy gave me a rucksack full of things and a list of instructions and we strapped Tampa Baby into a baby seat in the back of my car. We promised to be back soon, and I revved up the engine. Daisy had dressed her in a pink Babygro and a white summer hat dotted with cartoon flower designs – yellow, green and blue – the rim of the hat pressed onto her head like an upside-down smile. Tampa Bay's big eyes gazed up at me lovingly, without question – her little snub nose bubbled out snot.

'Which way then, Lady Passman?' I asked.

She offered up no answer, but I was used to that.

'Well then, I'll choose. As it happens, I have somewhere in mind. How do you like the country?'

Tampa clapped.

'Bbbbaaaaaaahhhh,' she said.

'Well, I'm delighted you think so. Now, shall we have music?'

I hit the 'On' button on the stereo and popped in the latest mix Christy had made me. She disapproved of hip-hop – said it was music for misogynists with Jesus complexes that were denying their slave roots – and my collection had long since been banished to the charity shop. Now she was encouraging me to find my more feeling side. On the first track, the singer was cooing so softly it was almost like listening to him talking. I turned the volume down.

'Christy is a pretty radical feminist,' I said. 'Likes to talk about how men have ruined the planet and all that. But then she says: *men sing about life, women just sing about men.* So she only gives me male songwriters to listen to: ones that *sing* like girls, about the things she thinks are important. Until women start singing about the *real issues*, they're off my diet . . . she's pretty strict. But then, I like a strong woman.'

I turned onto the motorway.

'Give me a strong woman over a wimp any day. There's nothing sexy about wilting flowers.'

Tampa Bay turned out to be excellent company. She was a toddler now, an inquisitive, bright, bubbly girl who I was enjoying watching grow up. She hadn't been with us long but it seemed like she did something new every day, and I felt like, for Chuck, I should make sure I didn't miss anything. The first time she picked up a crayon. The first time she recognised herself in a mirror and laughed. The first time she saw someone push a button and understood what that meant. Seeing how excited life made Tampa Bay made me excited too. It was wrong, but I was pleased Chuck had died when she was too young to remember him. Imagine how hard it would have been for her to see his face in her mind but not be able to find it in the world.

'Family are a funny lot, aren't they?' I said, tapping the steering wheel along to the beat. 'I suppose you'll be pleased to get a bit of a break from them – like me.'

Tampa Bay's contented silence was different from Mum's. I believed she was really absorbing in a way no one else did, apart from maybe Christy, who always answered back.

'Don't get me wrong,' I said, trying to cover that thought. 'I'm glad we're having a nice day out, but I wish I was abroad right now. Christy lives in Paris these days, can you believe that? Think of it! Paris! You should see my room. Full of pictures that Christy has sent me. The Eiffel Tower. The Arc de Triomphe. The Champs Elysées. Paris is beautiful . . .'

Tampa Bay said nothing.

'I heard from Anna again last week . . . she's got a bar job in Tanzania now . . . says they let her drink behind the bar. Tips are good, she says she likes it, way better than the last place, but there's still no mention of those Vietnamese babies. Every time she writes she asks if I've forgotten her – how can I when she won't leave me alone? – but it's different now. I don't know how to explain that, so I just tell her I'm fine and I hope she's having fun. And I remind her she said she wasn't going to write!'

Tampa Bay was looking out of the window.

'I probably shouldn't be telling you this, but we had sex once. Anna and me.'

I indicated and took a country road off the motorway. Tampa yawned.

'Givup,' she said. 'Givup, givup!'

'Am I boring you? We're here now.'

I pulled into what looked like a large country garden centre, with an elaborately designed sign at the gate:

HEPBURN HOUSE

Official residence of John William David Henry III, 15th Duke of Cheshire. Owned by the International Hepburn Foundation. Lunches, Teas, Tours. Please come in and look around.

'See? We're going to my old school. I don't know who that new owner is – the guy has four first names and no surname! Let's go inside, shall we?'

I pointed.

'Look, darling. There's the playing fields . . . that building used to be the old gym . . . there's the library . . . oh and there's the bench Christy and I used to sit on!'

Tampa Bay didn't seem hugely excited but didn't object either so I picked her up and took her out of the car to see more. It felt nice carrying that warm little bundle of arms and legs in the summer hat, and my mind raced forward to a time when Christy and I would stand together, perhaps in this place, with a gaggle of little Tampa Bays.

As we went up the winding pathway leading to the front entrance, I pointed out some more of my favourite old places to her – my spot behind a boulder in the woods, the big steps leading up the language block that was now a toilet block by a cordoned-off patch of grass.

'It's great here, isn't it?' I said. 'Not too much changed . . . When break time came round, I used to walk to one of these places, sit a while then walk back again, like at my other school. That took up the time easily. But unlike the old school, I wasn't alone. Christy would come and find me and we'd sit together, somewhere quiet.'

I pulled open the main door and we went inside.

'Breathe it in,' I whispered.

Tampa Bay sneezed.

'I'm not sure how they do things in Texas, but maybe you'll be staying here now, eh? Just in case you don't see anything like it, I'm going to show you round. And we're going to do a little scouting for Christy while we're here.'

LP: What happened to you?

CC: The government closed the school down – there were a lot of debts – from gambling, they said. The Duke. Anyway, it never re-opened. 'We're sending you back where you came from,' I was told. And then they sent me to a home where the children beat me into pieces every day and nobody did anything about it.

LP: Why did the children turn on you?

CC: Because I wanted to learn and wasn't ashamed of it. Why else?

LP: I'm sorry.

CC: Don't be. It made me who I am.

22

The Tour

I've always liked going on guided tours. I don't take much in, but that's never affected my enjoyment – I just like the sound of someone speaking like they know what they're talking about. It feels good to hear information that sounds important, stated like there can be no doubt over its truth. Just after Chuck died Rakesh and I took the city bus tour around Manchester, to see what they thought was worth knowing. Names of buildings, places of interest, stories from the city's past – I learned a lot. When the bus came past our shop the guide didn't mention it, so I stood and called out, 'The Victory Barber Shop, ladies and gents! Serving great British scalps since 1945!'

'Please sit down, Sir,' said the guide. 'There's only room for one know-it-all on this ride.'

The crowd of tourists, all huddled in raincoats or holding umbrellas to shield themselves from the spitting rain, chuckled along as if it was all a set-up and Rak nearly died with laughter, but I really wanted people to know where we were. The very next weekend we took an afternoon geology tour at the university museum. Listened for an hour on the subject of plate movements, how limestone turns to marble, heard all about rock formations. I remembered nothing but came out feeling like part of the world. It's not always like that. Rak says that mostly I act like I'm just drifting in and out. Slipping into thought, back out into reality, back into thought again.

'Geology brought you into focus for an hour or two,' he told me. 'We should go more places.'

For a while I got the feel for seeing other things apart from the inside of the shop and the People4Jobs office. A couple of times I ran away, not knowing where to go, just thinking I should go somewhere. One day I just left the office at lunchtime, got in the car, still in my suit, and drove north until I hit water, pulling up in front of a bed and breakfast on the coast and booking myself in for a week. I got up the next morning and looked out of my window at the magnificent bleak windy Scottish Highlands, the dazzling morning sunshine, the choppy Pentland Firth, the natural beauty of the view. Then I got back in the car and went home. But after a while I began to dream of a time when I would be able to see all the world, and calm down for long enough to enjoy it. Whenever Christy landed somewhere new, that occupied my mind more. At each stop, she'd email and describe everything. We talked about doing the same trip, step for step, together one day. When Mum was well. When I got the courage to tell Dad I was leaving. When I had cleared my life up. Always when something.

It was twenty minutes until the next tour of Hepburn House, so we sat down to wait in what used to be my geography classroom but was now an old-style English Tea House; the place still retained the ornate cornicing round the edges of the ceiling, but nothing else. The old blackboard area was now a coffee machine. The corner table which used to be piled high with copies of educational magazines was now a till with a selection of chocolates dangling in a nearby basket. I ordered drinks and put Tampa Bay in a high chair offered by a grumpy waitress wearing a name badge which said 'Claire' on it. Underneath the name someone had scratched the words *is a wench*.

'I know,' she said abruptly, seeing me looking. 'They won't let me take this off until I pay for a replacement badge. Which I won't do. I didn't graffiti my own badge, did I? Bunch of bastards. Anyway, what do you want?'

'Nice place you run here. I'll have a tea. Organic. And Her

Ladyship (I gestured to Tampa Bay) will have an apple juice, with straw.'

Claire grunted and walked away.

I picked up a nearby tabloid and read bits of the news to myself, foot tapping nervously on a table leg. The pages were full of the details of wars I didn't want to know about: the rich English Prime Minister was sending another regiment of poor people from outside England to the dangerous place whose name I could no longer say out loud. But when I had spoken to him, over a crackling line, just weeks before he died, Chuck told me most places were safe. When I asked how a war-torn country could be safe he laughed cruelly down the phone and reminded me the war had already been won. I can't think about those kinds of wars any more. It's hard to tell who's winning. I know which kind I can be involved in.

Next to the horoscopes was a list of people Mum shared her adopted birthday with.

'Here we are,' I said to Tampa. 'Who's celebrating today, then? Herman D. Koppel, Vladimir Horowitz, Jimmy Carter – and Julie Andrews, of course. A couple of pianists, a president and a prime dame!'

Tampa Bay looked up.

'What else is going on in the universe? Aha . . . Page Three. There's a girl with very few clothes on here – just a little St George's Cross thong actually – explaining that she thinks England have a really good chance in the World Cup next year if they get the midfield formation right – though they'll probably go out on penalties in the quarter finals as usual. They give Page Three girls a voice these days, can you believe it? That's modern feminism for you . . . *This little beauty from Islington and her pair of little 32B beauties reckon China should be pressed more thoroughly on the subject of human rights when Hu Jintao visits next month. We'd certainly like to press her thoroughly, wouldn't we?*'

I kept flicking.

'A nice human-interest story, perhaps. There's a young

woman here called Alexandra who's had hiccups for eight years, though she's quoted as saying it doesn't affect her PhD in Referential Poetics. Or, crucially, her performance in other, *less academic* areas . . . What do you think of the royals, by the way? . . . The Queen is in Australia this week; from these pictures, they seem to like her. Cheering and waving their flags like crazy, they are. Oh, and someone who used to be married to a soap actor has split up with her boyfriend . . . but she's able to talk about it now, and is saying that helps her move on. The sex wasn't very good anyway. Here it says he didn't like to . . . er . . . never mind that. She has a fitness video coming out in time for Christmas, so says the interview: *Flabby to Fantabulous in Ten Days*. That should cheer her up!'

Tampa looked up at this latest piece of information, and as she stared at me I began to hope she had taken nothing in. A stern voice called out.

'The tour will begin in two minutes. All those taking part, congregate in the hall!'

The four or five other people on the tour with Tampa Bay and me got up, shuffled out of the tearoom and over to the starting point. A French couple started taking photographs, reading the plaques, typed history lessons and bits of advice that were plastered up by the front entrance. A man in a duffel coat took notes.

Hepburn House is probably one of the most exciting properties owned by the International Hepburn Foundation. The proximate land is home to over two hundred species: hedgehogs, badgers, a small herd of fallow deer and even polecats. Also, the humble dormouse is making a reappearance after many years of hiding away, so look out for him! In terms of other attractions, they are many. The stained-glass windows of the Main Hall of Hepburn House are best viewed in the summer months shortly before sunset, but are pretty at all hours. Well worth a look is the Hepburn Aquarium which includes the direct descendants of a pilchard species

(Sardinia pilchardus) and an anchovy species (Engraulis encrasicholus) given as a present to the 10th Duke of Cheshire, John William David Henry, by his Cornish mistress in 1709 – a gift which he kept a secret from the then Duchess until confessing infidelity on his deathbed, shortly before dying of TB. On hearing the news, the Duke's wife killed most of the fish in a rage, though the few to survive were quick to reproduce.

Also, do visit our splendid Hepburn Gardens, which from above look like a cocktail glass with a cherry on top, and have been rated as one of the best in England.

'Ignore that,' I said to Tampa. 'It's not what we're here for.'

Our tour guide was a tall, thin woman in her sixties with a posh voice who wore a purple dress that almost reached the floor and a gold necklace with matching bracelet. Her glasses had string attached to either side running round the back of her head and she was forever putting them on, taking them off, putting them back on again. 'Now see here,' she said. Or, 'Listen carefully, everybody!' or, 'Well then, here's a piece!' or, 'For your information,' or, 'If you please . . .' It was hard to tell if she thought she could see better with or without glasses, and this made me even more annoyed than I already was. The building was still impressive, my mind was buzzing with memories, but the woman's colourful history had completely erased our Academy.

The grounds seemed smaller than I remembered – as we walked through the rooms, hallways, museum rooms with pictures of anonymous seventeenth- and eighteenth-century figures in official or military dress covering many of the stairways, the tour guide explained that the building had first been an old castle that belonged to the fifth Duke of Cheshire. It stayed in the family through many generations until about thirty years ago, when the then Duke, short for cash after a gambling spree, sold it to a private buyer who sold it to the National Trust for a profit. After a more successful stint at the roulette wheel the Duke bought it back and became the founder of Kindler's Academy for Gifted Boys and Girls. The tour guide didn't tell me that though: Christy did. The guide was telling a smoothed-over version that reminded me of the safe chats Dad used to have with Chuck: the old classrooms, she was telling us, were now show rooms sometimes used for harp lessons for local children. No mention of their previous life as dorms. 'They noticed there were more important buildings in England that needed more urgent protection,' said Christy, explaining why the National Trust got rid of the property so soon. According to her, the report giving the grounds up and selling it to Kindler's Academy said it was 'nothing but a rich man's house', would be 'no great loss to England's heritage', and 'could probably serve society better in some other capacity'. For a few years, that was the case. Now, as part of the Hepburn Foundation, it just looked like a rich man's house again. Though the tour guide was making every shabby portrait sound like the *Mona Lisa*.

Tampa Bay's arms gripped my shoulders as I carried her around, jiggling her up and down as I had watched mothers do. Meanwhile, no one in the group seemed to be greatly affected by what they saw, or what the tour guide was describing. A bust of an old general. A portrait of someone who used to be in charge of the estate early in the sixteenth century. The stuffy English aristocracy portrayed in the pictures looked more like members of an embarrassing secret boys' club than a great tradition to be proud of.

The guide led us in to the next room, saying, 'Now see here! To our left is the library, where, it is said, the ninth Duke spent a great deal of his time working on his unfinished epic poem, *Gateway to the Lord*. Rumour has it that this was where the Duke's firstborn was conceived – in the middle of the biology section! Apparently, ladies and gentlemen, the ninth Duke had a particular liking for . . . relations . . . in *unusual places*. His French wife was also famous for her pastry making . . .'

I felt like the one place I had been happy was being trampled all over and could keep quiet no more.

'Excuse me?'

Everyone looked round.

'Yes?' said the guide.

'Well, I was just wondering if you were going to mention Kindler's Academy at any point. You have mentioned every stage of history except the most recent one.'

'Ah yes,' said the guide, taking off those glasses again, with studied seriousness. 'Every so often, an ex-student or teacher mentions that place.'

The rest of the group seemed interested, and I wondered whether they were going to start taking pictures of *me* now. The guide tried to wrest back control. She spoke louder and more assertively.

'Ladies and gentlemen – for some years in the nineteen eighties and nineties, the then owner of the estate decided to abandon everything his ancestors stood for and set up a school for children who, for one reason or another, *didn't fit* the mainstream system. He felt he was doing them a service, probably, but in the end he helped no one, not even his own conscience. It closed down with great debts that are only now being paid back by tours such as the one you are currently taking part in.'

'But you were happy to talk about where the Duke and Duchess had sex! Why not talk about the school? Why not explain what happened to the children that came here?'

'Because those tragedies are too recent to be amusing. Come back in a hundred years. We may joke then.'

'But that's terrible!'

'You were obviously a student here.'

'And you were the Deputy Head. Do you remember me?'

'Young man, three hundred children passed through these halls in just a few years. Many of those faces I have made an attempt to forget. With some of them, I have succeeded.'

'Do you remember Christy?'

It was no longer as if the rest of the group were there. Just me and my old teacher:

'Yes,' she replied, sadly. 'Some students never go from your memory. I hope that girl is well, but I doubt it. There was something . . . *unstable* . . . about her.'

'You don't know what you're talking about! What are you doing here anyway?'

'I could ask you the same question – but I am here because I am an old friend of previous owners and I am dedicated to these grounds, whoever is the owner. That kind of loyalty is rarely understood. Perhaps you should leave now.'

But Tampa Bay and I had already begun to do that.

Instead of turning back down the spiral staircase and into the tearoom we went straight on towards the library where I used to meet Christy after school. I recognised it, even with the furniture changed. It wasn't being used as part of the museum – too small for that – so there was a red rope in front to show it wasn't to be entered. I didn't need to go inside anyway. I just wanted to see. I looked for a while, Tampa Bay in arms, and said, 'They'll be sorry for talking to us like that.' But security had been summoned, were quick to arrive, and we left without a fight.

LP: Why go back to the Academy at all?

CC: Because symbols can be powerful. And because it's good to think grandly.

LP: But the Academy already has an owner.

CC: So did Germany before the Allies went in and divided it up – we just need to make enough money to buy it off them. Everywhere has a price. Besides, the Academy is where we were happy.

LP: We would need . . . well . . . a LOT of money to buy it back. We're not really going to bid for it, are we?

CC: Not now. But wouldn't it be good? Maybe one day. What was the old place like?

LP: Just like I remembered. You would have loved it.

CC: Really?

LP: Really.

CC: That's good: I feel so far from home sometimes. Oh, by the way. I want you to wire across what you've raised this month and put it into the new account, No: 00114429, Sort: 88-38-59. I had to close the old one. I think the bank were getting suspicious.

HFN-I: #280

23

A Pair of Stubborn Old Birds

By the time we got back it was late afternoon. I arrived at the Victory holding Tampa Bay in my arms, hers wrapped round my neck as it seemed they had been all day, leaving a warm fuzzy feeling at my neck. Some days nothing happened. Whole weeks went by without anything worth mentioning. Some days everything happened at once.

'Mum!' I said, amazed. 'What are you doing out here?'

Daisy looked up from her crossword.

'Your mother is joining us for a drink in the sunshine. Isn't that nice? And perfectly ordinary?'

She twirled a large measure of red wine once round her glass then knocked the whole thing back. Mum was on the far left of the bunch, sitting on the pavement outside the front of the shop in the red deckchair, with a white sun hat a bit like Tampa Bay's partly covering her face and a pair of tracksuit bottoms rolled up to the knees. She looked defiant. She looked like she was saying to the whole street, 'See? I can do what I like!' To Mum's right was Daisy, who sat in the blue deckchair; to her right was Morta in the green one; to her right was Phil in the red; and to his right was Rakesh in the pink and white. These days, I sometimes forgot Rakesh was around at all. These days I forgot lots of things.

Everyone was eating food off paper plates, using plastic forks. I handed Tampa Bay back to Daisy.

'What's this?'

Rakesh spoke while chewing.

'It's a hello present from Ross, the owner of the new Deli

next door. Lasagne: it's incredible. He says there's more if you want any . . . or you can have some of mine.'

'Since when was there a Deli next door?'

'Since today. Hence lasagne.'

'What happened to Tsunami?'

Rak put down his fork in amazement.

'Lewis, that place closed down weeks ago. People don't like drinking in somewhere named after a disaster – they should have switched the name after last Christmas – I told them, but they wouldn't, would they? Nobody listens to me.'

'Aw, that's not true,' said Daisy, patting his knee affectionately. 'I do.'

'Really?' I said. 'Tsunami is gone? Weeks ago?'

No one answered, so I went inside to get the last chair and brought it out into the brightness, parking myself down by Rakesh. He insisted I taste his food.

'So why are we closed? The sunshine? Or was it just quiet?'

'Neither,' said Rakesh, pouring out a mineral water for himself and a straight gin for Morta, who looked like she needed one. 'Your father had a fight with mine.'

'No!'

'Yep. My dad went in for his trim – didn't even need it, really – it's only been a few weeks since his last. He was just trying to be nice, you know . . .?'

'Never mind that. What happened?'

'Israel. And Palestine.'

'Who the hell cares about that?'

'I know!'

'Well?'

'My dad said something about the West Bank, tutted loudly, said "Bastards," and your dad just lost it. I'm not taking sides – everyone saw it. Am I right, guys?'

He looked at Morta and Daisy, and they nodded.

'Your dad started pointing and shouting and said there was only one way for *us* to deal with *you lot*. That's the way he put it. *Us* and *you lot*. Well, then *my* dad lost it. There they were, both completely nuts, standing in the middle of the shop. A lapsed Hindu and a lapsed Jew, in Northern Europe, fighting about Islam in the Middle East. Crazy.'

Rakesh shook his head.

'You should have seen it – my dad left with half a haircut. He's up in his room right now trying to neaten it up in the mirror . . . Mum's out the back laughing her head off.'

'You sure there was nothing else?'

'Honest, Lewis, that's everything there is. One minute they're laughing about the football, next they're sworn enemies pacing the shop like two boxers getting ready to go at it. Morta had to step in.'

At mention of her name, Morta raised a glass in acknowledgement.

'Not much hope if those two can't get along any more, is there?' said Rakesh with a sigh. 'Stubborn old birds. Anyway, at least the sun's out . . . in October! Everything will be back to normal tomorrow. You just see if it isn't.'

'I don't know.'

'Of course you don't believe me. Nobody listens to me.'

'How can you say that?' I asked.

'Aw,' said Daisy. 'I listen to you, Rak . . . Lewis?'

'Yes?'

She lifted Tampa Bay up and smelled her.

'This baby has been swilling in stale shit for God knows how long.'

I had a polite sniff from distance – and then the stink hit me.

'It was a pleasure to look after her,' I said, haughtily. 'Don't expect to see me for the rest of the night.'

'It's your mum's birthday,' said Daisy. 'Stay. We're having fun.'

'Do you want a drink?' asked Morta.

'You know I don't do that,' I replied.

'Yes. And look at you. Stiff as a board.'

She poked my arm with her finger, once, twice, three times. 'Stiff!' she yelled. But Morta was under the influence of drugs, and I wanted more control over things, not less.

'I've had enough of this,' I said. 'Enough enough enough . . .'

Leaving the scene, heading for home, there was something satisfying in knowing I'd not even said goodbye. But I'd still knock on Rak's later. To apologise. We couldn't go for a drink any more, but maybe a coffee or something.

LP: You talk like no one I know. Like you've thought everything out in advance and the words come out smoothly, perfectly. I wish I was like you.

CC: I thought we were past that. Is there something wrong today?

LP: Nothing more than the usual. You know, I'd do anything for you.

CC: Then show me.

24

Recipe for Living

When I returned to my room, another of Christy's essays was waiting for me. The others hung proudly on my wall, in order. They usually arrived when she'd been having a bad day and she just needed to let go for a while – it was her way of doing it. Instead of banging her head against a wall, or getting drunk, or starting a fight, she got on the computer and put down her rage. She said her essays were for everybody at HFN but I suspected that at least a few were for my eyes only: and I felt I was seeing a layer that nobody else could. We were concentrating on one thing, focusing our energies for the greatest effect, but Christy saw much more, she saw the world as it truly was, and I understood that. These essays were the evidence of it and I loved them. Here was one more.

After *Understand Your Nation and Reject It*; after *Reclaim Currency for the Revolution*; after *Fight Pornography With Fire*; after *All History Is a Prelude to Nuclear Disaster*; after *Ten Days to Save the Rainforests*; after *History Is Written By The Most Efficient Criminals, Do Something Every Hour to Apologise for Your Ancestors, Today's Punk is Tomorrow's Prime Minister, We're All Fiddling While Rome Burns, Sport is the Real Opium of the Masses, Why Penises Are Always the Enemy, Fashion Strangles Us All, Supermarket Shopping = Defeat, Swearing Is the Laziest Way to Shock, The Internet Should Have Freed Us but We Are Still Prisoners, The Only Human Response to Poverty Is Action, Homophobia Still Rules OK, Travel the World and Build a Well Wherever You Go*; after *The Past Gets Bigger Every Day and One Day Will*

Swallow Us Whole; after *Every Child Born in the West Is a Spit in the Face to the East*; after *All Religion Is Racism*, after *The Black Man Is a Chauvinist Too*; after a ten-page, three-part opus on *Man vs Woman as God vs The Devil*; and finally, after *Fellatio Is Slavery*, one more communication, entitled *Know When the Time is Right and Act*, was much shorter than usual. It read like this:

> Don't send the word 'Yes'. Don't send anything at all. Get out and change something big. Don't contact me until you've done it, and have the proof.

The thought of being cut off from Christy, even for a day or two, made my mouth dry, and skin wet with sweat and fear. I tried every way of getting hold of her I could think of. My emails went unanswered. She ignored me on the Hope Forum. I even tried the Paris directory to get a phone number, though I knew having her number in there would have been suicide. Every attempt failed. I had no other choice but to do what she wanted me to. And I knew exactly what that was.

PART THREE

Unanswered Communications
December 2005 – September 2006

25

Obituary for a Reborn Man

Sender: Lewis Passman

Recipients: All People4Jobs Employees

BCC: Christy Columbus, Philip Passman, Anna Saunders

Subject: Obituary for Lewis Passman

Date: 14 December 2005

Dear Colleagues

This note is to say that I am leaving my post at People4Jobs after nine years' loyal service. Lewis Passman, Senior Consultant for London South, is now dead, soon to be reincarnated as Lewis Passman, wanderer of the world!

When I started at this company in 1996 I was one of just six employees. Now there are more than sixty. In that time I have been Employee of the Month seven times and Employee of the Year twice; but times change. As some of you know, it has been my dream to travel the world for many years, and if I don't do it now, maybe I never will. So! – Cheers to all those who've supported me over the years, and a special fucking great THANK YOU to the Chief Whip, Marcus, for giving me a job back when I was a spotty sixteen-year-old with no hope and no qualifications. Now I have realised what a filthy industry this is – how lazy and thoughtless and wrong it is to do any job that ignores our world full of lost foundlings waiting to be saved – especially one so self-serving and profit-loving as recruitment. But back then my eyes had not yet been opened. Now they have, I'll spend my travelling time building homes, not skimming my 2 per cent, or sunning myself while children the world over go hungry and lonely.

I'll be leaving England on Saturday, so if anyone wants to join me for a farewell drink (I'm on lemonade, but you can have what you like . . .), I'll be in O'Toole's from seven on Friday. All welcome. Thanks again – I just feel that if I don't take this opportunity now I don't know if I ever will. Goodbye, and remember, only you can make your dreams come true!

Peace & Solidarity,
Lewis

L. J. Passman, ex-Senior Consultant, London South Division

26

The Departure of Lewis Passman

Sender: Marcus Davidson, MD

Recipients: All People4Jobs Employees

Subject: IMPORTANT – The Departure of Lewis Passman

Date: 15 December 2005

Dear Colleagues

This note is to explain the sudden departure from People4Jobs of Lewis Passman. Many of you will know Lewis as, until today, Senior Consultant for the London South Division. He joined the company in its infancy and was a crucial player in the early stages when were establishing ourselves as a vibrant new voice in the UK recruitment market. That can never be taken away from him. But yesterday he offered his resignation and emailed the entire company with an inflammatory message before packing his things. Our internal email system picked this up, blocked his communication and alerted the technical team, who alerted my secretary, who alerted me. And that's why you're all receiving this instead of Mr Passman's intended farewell. I would not usually take this odd, public step, but email was his choice of format so it is mine. In future, others who wish to fire off one last dramatic shot before departing for the high seas may think twice before clicking 'Send All'.

A reminder: The Christmas party, complete with two free glasses of sparkling wine, is next Thursday from seven on the second floor of the main building. Unfortunately I am out of the country on the big day, but I hope you all have a good time. Behave yourselves while the cat's away! And, I expect everyone to be in bright and early on Friday, as usual!

Yours,

Marcus

Marcus Davidson, MD

27

A Postcard with a Picture of Three Bare Tanned Backsides Baking Under a Foreign Sun on One Side, and Some Very Small, Very Neat Handwriting on the Other

21 January 2006

Hello Lewis

Hope you like the postcard . . . I figured it might have been a while since you saw any flesh! I got it when I was in Greece, pub-crawling my way through the Islands, but it sat in my rucksack for a while (it's been a crazy few weeks), and now I'm writing to you from Reykjavik – where it's BLOODY FREEZING by the way! I've been having a *totally* brilliant time here, learning how to make cocktails off this girl called Kipper who's taking me on a horse trek tomorrow – yey! Anyway, hope you don't get this coz you're off somewhere cool, sipping Margarita and getting over yourself. If you're still sitting at home sulking, ignoring me and waiting for the revolution then WAKE UP, LAZY! Why don't you come and join us? We're in Iceland for another week, then a whole bunch of us are doing Scandinavia.

You'd really like Kipper, by the way. I could hook the two of you up, no worries . . . she's *totally* paranoid, dead smart, sulky as hell and sexy with it. Just like you!

Love and kisses,

Anna

28

Re: Lottery Award Notification

Sender: Unknown

Recipients: Mr/Mrs/Miss/Ms F. A. Lopez

Subject: Re: Lottery Award Notification

Claim File Number: HFN/00114222677

Date: 4 February 2006

Dear Mr/Mrs/Miss/Ms Lopez

We are pleased to inform you of the release of the HOPE FOR NEWBORNS SWEEPSTAKE LOTTERY held on 22 January 2006. Your name was attached to the ticket number 46110-932-450 which won the third category. You have therefore been approved for a lump sum pay of $814,216.00 (eight hundred and fourteen thousand, two hundred and sixteen dollars only) credited to file REF NO: HFN/028045160027. This is from a total cash prize of $25,291.210.00 (twenty-five million, two hundred and ninety-one thousand, two hundred and ten dollars only) shared among winners in this category. CONGRATULATIONS!!!

All US participants were selected through a computer ballot system drawn from 250,000 names as part of our annual promotions program. Please contact your agent, the US Claims Manager, by emailing hopefornewborns@hfn.com for processing and remittance of your prize to an account of your choice, whose details you need to send along with your official acceptance. Note: all monies must be claimed by 28 February 2006. After this date, all funds will be returned to HFN Inc. as unclaimed.

Once more, let me congratulate you on your fantastic luck, and send our warmest wishes on behalf of all our staff here in the Connecticut office. It's a joy for us to give.

Yours truly,

L. J. Passman

Chair of the Hope for Newborns Foundation USA Branch, Connecticut

29

How I Came to Know What Happens When We Die, *or* The Apple

It's been six weeks since I left People4Jobs and I thought I'd be abroad by now, but yet more delays keep me here, preparing. Always more delays – funds not sufficient yet – plan not ready – suspicions over tracking of calls and paperwork – we've been more careful for weeks now, since Christy decided they – the police, the law, whoever – were ready to come and get us, and we couldn't go on much longer.

Despite all Newborns work going on in the background, a little more Manchester had been good for me, especially since I stopped working for anyone but Christy. Returning to the shop during the days, looking after Mum (who was brighter recently, I was sure), Newborns at nights, even taking up Spanish again. I learned practical, everyday phrases off a CD: (*¿Tienes una cuchara?* – *Do you have a spoon?* – *Si, tengo una cuchara* – *Yes, I do have a spoon*). I was raising funds, but it was slow work. Sometimes I thought I'd never get on that plane. Sitting alone in my flat at nights, it was hard to imagine I would ever be happy. In my darker moments I thought that maybe Christy wasn't real. Some nights I imagined walking right through her, off a cliff and into the sea. But as she always said, when your mind closes its hands around your throat, only you can loosen its grip. Act, don't dream. Dreaming is for cowards.

So with just a small lamp for light and a bowl of pasta for company I sat up in bed, placed a pad of paper carefully on top of the large hardback atlas I'd been marking Christy's route on, picked out a Hope for Newborns pen from the stash

and began. I titled the page: HOW I CAME TO KNOW
WHAT HAPPENS AFTER WE DIE, by LEWIS JOHN PASS-
MAN, put on a little of Christy's Croatian Samba to block
out noise coming from the other flats and just started, noticing that, given complete freedom, I quickly lapsed into a
tight, formal tone on the page – like I used to when writing
progress reports at work. I loved filling in forms. I enjoyed
the strict immovability of the interview process we used to
conduct when taking on new employees. Recent weeks had
been freeing, but I missed the order of my old life. It was as if
I was creating something to be delivered, assessed and
returned, accepted or rejected. There was still something
dirty and satisfying about cold facts, simply told. No matter
the topic or circumstances, I always preferred polite order to
an unrestrained outpouring.

*I thought I was an intelligent child because people were
always saying so. Though my first words were standard
enough, I soon decided my mouth was made for grander
expressions, and made plans to learn them quick – mainly
through pestering adults. Asking about the world got me
attention and helped others confirm their suspicions about
my intelligence, so I asked everything I could think of, whenever I could think of it, of whoever was around. Mum was
pleased when she noticed me doing unusual things and often
said in later years, usually over dinner, how early she realised
what a marvel she had given birth to. I was sent to nursery a
full six months sooner than most, though barely able to
stand up straight yet, and was half the size of many of the
other children. I don't remember it now, but Grandpa Harry
used to tell how I noticed I was being treated differently to
others, and that it gave me a thrill. 'Three years old!' he used
to say, feigning shock. 'And dizzy with power!'*

*My earliest memory is my first day at nursery school. In
the morning session, while sitting in the corner facing the
wall and inspecting the lines on my palms, a teacher came*

over, crouched down and asked, gently enough, why I wouldn't play with the other children.

'Why are circles?' I replied, looking sadly upwards. 'Is it so the sun can have a house to live in?'

That day I was collected early from nursery and the following morning I found myself in a new room with slightly bigger children and a different teacher, who received me with barely contained excitement. The previous session had taught me to offer theories along with questions. Even if the answers were wrong, it would make me seem more extraordinary.

'What are girls for?' I asked the teacher, Mum still by my side, grinning widely with pride. 'Is it to make the boys happy?'

Other adults within earshot stopped what they were doing to look round at the teacher, who was tripping over her words.

'Oh! What a child you have there, Mrs Passman,' she said to Mum, 'We'll take good care of him, don't you worry about that.'

The teacher clamped an arm round my shoulder as if to protect me from other poaching nurseries, and Mum walked away proud, though she had to come back for me early again, for a different reason. When we arrived home that night, she smuggled me through the back door and stood me in the kitchen on a towel while, damp and cold, the smell of urine rose from my trousers. While she did it I stared up at Churchill, looking down on us all from one of his many places in our home, waving a hat and fat brown cigar. 'Who's my clever little boy?' Mum whispered, rushing me out of moist clothes and into dry ones. 'Who is it? Who is it, eh?' 'Me!' I shouted, forgetting my wetness, not caring who heard. 'I'm your clever little boy!'

As I got older, searching for that kind of attention became addictive. 'How tall will I be?' I asked. 'Who decides what colours are allowed in a rainbow?' 'How many eggs can you put in one basket?' As well as a source of affection, this seemed a good method of ascertaining facts that would later be useful, finding out how the universe worked, and, eventually, how I could come to be in charge of it. But not everyone was dazzled by me. I annoyed my two brothers with questions all the time, and when I was very young they had little patience – but by the time I was seven or eight they had become friendlier about my grand ambitions. The workings of my mind became an endlessly funny joke they could share with others. 'Did you hear that?' they'd say, calling down the stairs to our parents: 'He wants to know why the stars don't fall out of the sky!' So they were not in the way, but they weren't much help either.

There were other methods of getting information – Dad's shop had a small portable radio in it in those days, and we had a television in my parents' bedroom – but these machines were frustrating because they often contradicted each other, and never quite said enough. One evening, after watching a TV bulletin on Mum's knee, I turned to her and said, 'Why is the news so quick? Is that all that's going on?'

She became totally rigid, put me roughly back on the floor, threw her teacup and saucer at the wall and cried out wildly, 'Shut up shut up shut up! For the love of God – why me?'

That kind of melodrama didn't last long. She spent much of the rest of the night apologising, kissing my forehead and force-feeding me.

'Everybody likes sweets,' she said, under her breath, as she lined up an intimidating collection of chocolates, mints and jellies on the tray in front of me. 'Sweet sweet sweeties for my sweet sweet boy.'

I was sick that night but had forgotten the incident by the following afternoon – though I remember thinking that, even though I was still not ten years old, she was treating me as if I was a younger than that, almost as if she didn't want me to get bigger. The day after the sweets episode, Dad took me to the local library for the first time, where I took out one book about the Bible and one about the Big Bang. I was disappointed to discover that there were so many things left to find out in the world and upset to discover that not all facts were undisputed, but pleased that so many books were sitting there on a shelf, just waiting for me to pick them up.

I continued to ask questions for as long as people were prepared to give me answers – many adults were impressed or surprised at the little boy with the clear diction and wide vocabulary, and most indulged me. This intoxication, especially at home, was a feeling close to being above the law. But on some topics, like British history, inconvenient questions were not rewarded with love and sweets, but with mild violence and harsh words, often shouted, about how some things were just the way they were, and kindly be quiet please, Lewis, I'm trying to do the ironing. I deduced this only happened when I asked questions my parents didn't know the answer to, and I felt very sorry for them, then. To be so old, and still have things you didn't know. I couldn't imagine it. When Mum smacked me, I understood she was really smacking herself.

Even when punishing us, our parents were always saying how privileged we were, and enjoyed describing the history of our country to us, right from when we were almost too young even to know what a country was. Britain was once one of the leading nations in the world, they said. It was the head of a glorious Empire which contained many countries as far apart as Canada and Australia, who still had to bow to the Queen and take part in the Commonwealth Games – even now, we were one of the richest countries in the world and she was the richest woman. The whole planet communicated in our national language. English landowners had been at the forefront of the Industrial Revolution which transformed the way people worked and lived. We were the inventors of Penicillin, the light bulb, the tin can, the computer. And we had not been selfish with civilisation either:

we had given it to countries we borrowed like India, Scotland, Wales and Ireland, who couldn't have dreamed of such things without help; and God only knows what state Africa would be in today without us.

Once Mum showed me pictures of the Houses of Parliament, and it looked like such a grand, exciting palace that I was sure that we lived in the best country in the world. Where else could have Houses of Parliament? I told them I wanted to live there one day and they smiled like their work was done. Dad prided himself on giving us the beginnings of a good British education as well as the official ones we were getting – 'an on the knee education' he called it – and he was sure we would have a head start on other children. At eleven, I could recite the dates of all the rulers of the UK from Elizabeth I right through to Elizabeth II. It was a party piece I was expected to perform in the shop when called upon, and I was not shy about it. While my brothers heckled loudly I stood on one of the barber's chairs and listed my monarchs for the pleasure of customers. Loud and bold, from my little throat to the world, it felt like my natural domain.

In those days both my parents paid extra attention to me, but sometimes tired of my enthusiasm. One night at the dinner table I said, 'What would happen if there was no such thing as broccoli?'

'Well, Lewis,' said Mum, banging a few limp, pale-green stalks onto my plate, 'I suppose you'd have to have peas with your shepherd's pie!'

While Mum attended to the dessert, my brothers secretly sneaked a couple of bunches of broccoli into my pockets, then burst out laughing. I let the soggy food sit there, untouched in the lining of my jacket, so as not to upset Mum further. Charles and Philip had not learned to turn on each other yet, but were old enough to know they could gang up against me, and to know I would put up with nearly anything to avoid raised voices. I was twelve, I think. It wasn't long before the break-up.

My early home life, I thought, was good training for a prime minister. At that time, Grandpa Harry said a grocer's daughter had just been voted back into Britain's top job, and explained this was evidence that yet again we were leading the world – America had to settle for a rigid ex-pretend cowboy to lead them, whereas our twentieth-century Boadicea was the nutritious salt of the earth. Soon after I was questioning that kind of talk, and Grandpa Harry's opinions changed too – he no longer thought we were a nation of heroes, but a nation of vampires. I had just been accepted at Kindler's Academy, and thought I knew it all. It was around then that I stole an apple from the fruit bowl.

When Mum found out I had taken it, half an hour after I'd left my dinner, cold and untouched, it wasn't just a teacup she threw against the wall. This time, half the kitchen went.

'Who cares?' I asked, shrugging my shoulders. 'We've got lots of apples left.'

That was all it took. First the chopping board where she was already preparing the following night's meal went flying, along with the bits of baby sweetcorn and carrot she had been cutting up. Little yellow and orange chunks flew everywhere. Then she started reaching for anything near by.

'Nobody loves me in this house!' she screamed. 'Not even my favourite little boy respects me!'

I sat still in my seat, hoping Charles and Philip had not heard that, as a vase, several plates and a couple of glasses went hurling past. Once there were no more obvious things to hand, she became more methodical, going into the fridge and taking the items out one by one and sending them to the wall.

'I've had enough! You hear me? I made you a meal! Hard bloody work!'

Two pints of milk, some orange juice and even a home-made minestrone soup got emptied out onto the floor. Dad came through to find out what was going on, raced over, picked Mum up and put her down on a seat opposite, restraining her. Mum stared, hissing, eyes red and bulging, as if they were about to pop from their sockets.

'Do you know what happens when you die, Lewis?' she said. 'If you've been a bad boy who steals apples you go to HELL, and the devil makes you sit on a seat of FIRE and he makes you watch a screen where he has filmed everything you've ever done wrong. And for every apple you steal, he sends a THOUSAND BOLTS OF FIRE through you. A THOUSAND.'

'Come on, Marion, have we had enough now?' said Dad. 'Don't scare the boy. I'll clean up this mess. Go and have a lie down.'

'A THOUSAND BOLTS!' she cried.

Dad finally got his hand over her mouth, holding it there hard while Mum tried to bite at his wedding ring. Through the pain he turned to me and said, low as he could, 'Lewis, your mother puts a lot of effort into housework – that's proper work too, you know, though most people pretend it isn't – and she likes to be appreciated.'

'She looks mad,' I said. 'What's happening?'

'She just likes to be appreciated,' he said again.

They grappled with each other for a few moments until Dad overpowered his wife, then forced her back into a seat. She looked exhausted now, emptied out. When he was confident she was no longer dangerous, he turned round.

'Remember what I've said, Lewis,' he told me, 'But don't worry – you're not going to hell. That's just a word people use to get others to do what they want.'

Then Mum picked up a frying pan and clapped him once, clean and hard, round the head. He collapsed to the floor. She left the room.

I sat at the kitchen table, apple still in hand, looking down at Dad, who was only half-conscious. I was so afraid that I didn't move: after a few seconds I let out a scream that was so long and high pitched that Charles and Phil came running *and went straight to Dad, helping him up, getting him water, asking him if they should call an ambulance. I still hadn't moved, and was still screaming – loud, shrill and pointless.*

'You idiot!' shouted Phil. 'What have you done? What are you doing? Help us!'

But I was far away, thinking about Mum and the devil. I knew which side of the story I believed, and promised myself I'd be more careful about what questions I asked in future, if indeed I asked any at all. I'd brought on Mum's first breakdown – or at least the first I had witnessed – all on my own, which meant I could do damage without meaning it. And who knew if the devil was going to be reasonable enough to discount unintentional damage? I didn't know a lot about the devil, we hadn't talked about him before, but he didn't sound reasonable at all. I tried to picture him, and me next to him, struggling to escape. He was high, I was low – he was big, his hell was even bigger, and I was very, very small.

When Dad recovered he locked Mum in the spare room for two days, taking her meals, putting her to bed, but keeping her away from us boys until he decided the time was right. For safety, he said. Hers and ours. Though I didn't feel safe any more, and it gave her an idea.

Christy said if I wrote things down and discarded them, my memories might go away. And I'd be left freer, more able to help others. Sometimes it's not even about Christy any more – she's mostly in my head anyway and keeps contact limited more than I'd like, perhaps because of the Newborns workload, perhaps because I haven't proved myself yet – so this kind of living has to be for me. And it's really kicking in. I feel less dirty because of it. I wouldn't have it any other way.

30

A Polite Request to All

19 May 2006

Dear Employee/Ex-employee

RE: Financial Report, 2005/6

The Board of People4Jobs are currently conducting a series
of inspections regarding financial dealings within the company – as in previous years, this process involves a small
number of random checks on employees, also some ex-
employees who were working for the organisation during
the period of assessment (in this case, Tax Period
05/2004–04/2005). If you have received this letter you are
or were employed in a department due for a check; please
read the attached questionnaire, answer the appropriate sec-
tions and return the form to the address below. Even if you
are not personally aware of any irregularities, you may be in
possession of information that could help us make sure there
is not, so please answer thoroughly.

These searches are the most effective way of keeping the
company in good shape. If deemed necessary, one of our
investigative team will be in contact to discuss the matter in
more detail.

Yours truly,

F.D.R. Samson

F. D. R. Samson, Finance Department.

*NB: This is currently an internal investigation, but may in
the future become external, if significant irregularities are
confirmed.*

The Emperor's New Clothes, the Florentine Maid with the Ordinary Smile and the Reason the Time Has Come

Some things I did without thinking.

Closing the broken door behind me, I tossed my clothes about the place and headed for the computer. I used to be so tidy: now there seemed no point in that. I kicked off the shoes on my feet and pushed them in any direction, hurled my trousers on the nearest chair, shirt and socks right behind – and soon I was sitting at the keyboard, fingers hovering above the buttons. Passwords, codes, entry screens. I jumped the barriers on auto-pilot. As I went into my Hope account, a surge of energy drew up inside me, so big and powerful that I wanted to burst. I knew it was coming. I knew it. The style would be the same as always. She'd explain the latest place she'd been, report the horrors, then we'd talk all night:

Dear Lewis –

I'm never going back to France. Today I had a few hours spare between meetings so I wasted my time chasing down the most over-hyped piece of art in the world in the Louvre – a portrait of an ugly girl who is more sulky matron than alluring model of beauty – a figurehead for a multi-million-pound business in novelty pens. When I finally got through the crowd I was so annoyed by it, security-guarded in that disgusting palace of excess, that I wanted to reach through the glass and strangle her.

Frame a ball of string, put it behind bullet-proof glass and wait for the cameras to start snap snap snapping. No matter how much real treasure you put on display around it, no one will notice. Like the Florentine Maid, sitting proud, dull and ridiculous in the Louvre, surrounded by greater works that lie ignored while tourists gawp at what they are told to, we are dizzied by the light and give not a thought for the darkness. I went back, Lewis, the next day. I couldn't believe that so many people could be so wrong about something, any-thing: *but it is precisely because of the mass that nobody notices. With a single day's* Mona Lisa *mug money, you could feed a thousand foundling girls in China for a year. And yet it was me, and not the organisers of this dirty conspiracy, who spent a night in jail for trying to alert the people. Six words: 'Hope for Newborns! Reset the Scales!' were enough to get me arrested. Now I'm tired and have no more energy for museums, grand buildings, sunsets. Dead gaps between the beauty have ruined everything.*

I try not to use the quotations of the dominant sex any more – they have had plenty of oxygen in the past several thousand years, while greater women were kept silent or finished off for speaking out – but occasionally males say things that are difficult to ignore. Henry David Thoreau wrote that Man (and he was talking exclusively about man) *is only rich in proportion to the number of things he can afford to let alone. Bear that in mind when you're tearing yourself away from your junk. Bring your preparation pack and travel kit, but nothing else. There'll be no room for sentimentality in our new life.*

We'll be together soon. It has taken longer than we expected, but it's best that you were ready first. When we first spoke, you were desperate – you would have accepted me no matter what. But now I think you understand. Send the word 'Yes' and travel to the address below at the allotted time on 01/10/2006.

CC

My hand went straight to my back pocket where, as instructed, I kept my passport, ready for any order. So when I looked up again I was surprised to find that the address on the message was not in Rio, Buenos Aires, Mexico City or any of the other places Christy had been fundraising in recent months. The address was a flat on the other side of Manchester. I lay down on the bed, unfeeling. Set no alarm. Drank no water. Thought nothing. It was here, and I was not ready for it.

PART FOUR

Union
October 2006

32

A New Start

It was the happiest day I could remember, with everyone chipping in, doing what they could for the good of the Victory. I was jumpy with excitement, but the atmosphere was upbeat anyway so nobody had any reason to suspect the cause. And I wasn't about to tell them what it was. Dad put some old sixties soul music on the jukebox, after a while I put on a Mongolian drumming album Christy sent me last week, Daisy replaced that with some Country thing, and we spent hours laughing and joking together, hardly noticing the time passing, or that we were working at all. Even when we stopped for a cup of tea or something to eat it seemed like there was always someone working on a part of the room, which was turning quickly from the old red, white and blue to just plain white. Phil was keen to get the back wall finished before the end of the day so he hardly took a break at all, but it didn't bother us, one person taking over. It wasn't like he thought he was better than us; he was just enjoying himself. I hadn't seen him or Daisy laugh so much in months. She and Phil got on so well these days – better than Chuck and Phil ever did, really – sometimes they went on walks when Morta looked after Tampa Bay. I didn't know what they talked about, Canada maybe, but whatever it was, it seemed to help. When they were happy, everyone was – we hardly talked about Chuck, and I forgot to disapprove of the way we lived. By two o'clock we were all feeling a little giddy with the sight of the change. Somebody mentioned celebrating, and though it was a little early for that, there was plenty of enthusiasm for the idea. For a second I

thought about having a real drink, just to join in – until I
remembered why that was a bad idea. In the end I went for
lemonade, the others had a beer, Daisy toasted the new place
and we soon returned to the decorating. Every day closed was
a day without income. There wasn't much time.

The redecorating was a messy job, but nobody worried too
much about that. The whole room was going the same colour
anyway, for the first coat or two, and Dad had put down a covering on the floor, even though that was all going to get ripped
up. Dad said he wanted to do the refit with dignity, but when
Tampa Bay dipped her palms into a pot, hands spread out like
a celebrity putting her prints in Hollywood Boulevard, and
placed them on his overalls, delighted with herself, even he
couldn't help but give in to a big belly laugh. Tampa Bay was
turning into a curious child, full of joy – always waddling off
somewhere, picking things up, chucking them about, putting
them in her mouth. Today, she could hardly keep her little
mitts out of the clutter.

It was difficult for us all to lose the barber shop, but in the
end it was not a tough choice, even for Dad. That last, frightening storm of bricks. It didn't even seem like we were being
defeated – just freed. Nobody could have put up with those
attacks, so we hardly had a choice to make. And, as Phil said,
'There's nothing Grandpa Harry would have hated more than
defeat. Better to change than sink like the bastard *Titanic*.'

Towards the end it was costing us a fortune to keep replac-
ing the glass out front – the insurance company had long since
got sick of shelling out – and we were all desperate to set up a
place no one could object to. Also, somewhere that wouldn't
remind us of Chuck, though nobody said that. The important
thing now was to keep the spirit of the old place in a very general way, so we all agreed that Grandpa Harry should get a
mention on the front window where the old sign used to sit in
the painted-on Union Jack. As of this morning the window,
now without flag, read:

THE VICTORY, MANCHESTER

SERVING THE GREAT BRITISH PUBLIC FOR OVER SIXTY YEARS. FIRST OPENED BY HARRY PASSMAN IN 1945.

PROPRIETOR, C. J. PASSMAN. COME IN FOR A SMILE AND GOOD SERVICE, SEVEN DAYS A WEEK.

That was true enough, and it pleased Dad a lot. But there was another reason why he was so cheerful today. He'd just received a letter which had given him hope that Chuck's case might be looked at again.

'There may yet be justice in this bloody country,' he said, plunging his brush happily into the pot.

It would have been a shame to spoil Dad's mood. The rest of us decided not to say how many other investigations were going on into the deaths of soldiers on foreign soil, none of which appeared likely to be concluded any time soon – or remind him that people were paying less attention to that part of the Middle East these days anyway because of the newer, sexier wars going on elsewhere. Not that you'd know there was a war going on anywhere. The collection for the servicemen was long gone. The daily papers had been banished long before we closed for the refit. Before we shut down, one of the last, loyal customers asked what Dad thought of the recent fight between Israel and its enemies in Lebanon, and spoke like it was his last word on the subject:

'Nothing to do with us, that. Let the Jews do what they like – I'm not one of them any more; let armies kill who they like – I'm not a fighter any more; let the bombers do what they like – I don't bomb anyone any more; let God strike down whoever he fancies. I don't lose sleep over what bullies do.'

It was as if he'd never thought the opposite – or would have been if he hadn't still been monosyllabic with Aarav, who took the aftermath of their own personal battle better than Dad did, acting happily enough, assuming the problem wasn't with him and carrying on as if nothing had changed. He, Mira and Rakesh were at ours even more regularly these days. Rak's two younger sisters, Shivani and Sita, came round too when they were back for the weekend from university in Leeds, where they were doing degrees in business studies. When neither shop was open, their whole family would be round sometimes, and I'd try not to look at either of the two sisters for long in case I blushed, and they realised how embarrassed they made me: double shame – they were both pretty, and were both training to go into corporate management. Anyway, we liked having the whole family round. But their link was with us now, not Dad.

He had been becoming more inward, talking less, spending more time in the back room watching the box and pretending nothing was happening, anywhere. He had bought a TV package that gave him fifteen 24-hour sports channels, and now ate his dinner off a tray with his eyes rarely off the screen. He had developed a fierce interest in games he'd previously ignored or disapproved of – athletics, cricket, even that most extravagant of pastimes, golf. (Christy said that if the grass used for golf courses was used to grow vegetables, no Newborn would go hungry.) Dad went crazy for the World Cup. The Test matches. The Open. The Formula One grands prix. Because there was something to watch at most hours of the day, most days of the year, he rarely had to interact with the rest of us; and when there was a disgrace in any of these sports, a bung maybe, a drugs cheat, a lie exposed, it was opportunity for him to say how it was proof the world was going to ruin. 'I'll be glad to die,' he'd say, filling the grumpy space Grandpa Harry had left. 'I won't have to see any more of it.' He revelled in that kind of comment. Until today. It wasn't clear what had changed, but now, as I looked up from my paints, I wondered how long it had been since I'd seen him holding Tampa Bay. He was crouching down, cuddling her, pointing out some of the songs in the jukebox, and trying to get her to say the word.

'Jewbox,' said Tampa Bay. 'Play the Jewbox!'

'Ha! Not many of those around here, my love!' Dad cried – but more in joy than anguish. Husband, warrior, barber, Jew: these days it seemed like he left parts of himself easily. He picked up Tampa Bay off the floor and brought her face close to his. 'We're not in the ghetto now, are we, darlin'?' he said, kissing her on the nose. 'Thank God!'

'Ha!' spat Morta, crossing herself with her paintbrush. 'Listen to him talking about God!'

Morta and I didn't discuss her Lord any more. Over the last few months there had been some bitter arguments. I told her I wasn't much interested in deities who did nothing for the welfare of abandoned children. She told me, with great pride, that she wasn't much interested in anything else. I ignored the comment and returned to my work. Soon I would be in a place where my views would be welcomed.

It was time for some old family favourites – Dad told Tampa to hit a button on the machine, any one, and she chose one of the early World War One tunes Grandpa Harry used to sing on the job before the weight of years and too much research turned him bitter. The machine whirred lazily into action, picking out the vinyl with a dusty arm and setting it, crackling and hissing, into action. Dad danced to the song with Tampa Bay, singing along to 'Pack Up Your Troubles in Your Old Kit Bag'. He knew all the words:

Private Perks is a funny little codger
With a smile, a funny smile.
Five feet none, he's an artful little dodger,
With a smile, a funny smile.
Flush or broke he'll have his little joke,
He can't be suppress'd.
All the other fellows have to grin,
When he gets this off his chest, Hi!

The rest of us clapped and cheered, singing the words where we knew them. Everyone put their brushes down:

Pack up your troubles in your old kit bag,
And smile, smile, smile,
While you've a Lucifer to light your fag,
Smile, boys, that's the style.
What's the use of worrying?
It never was worth while, so
Pack up your troubles in your old kit-bag,
And smile, smile, smile . . .

Tampa Bay squealed with happiness. 'Again! Again!' she said.

This time she chose 'Who's Going to Take You Home Tonight?', and as the song kicked in, for the first time, I felt closer to my family and to Christy all at the same time: I'd be with her in just a few hours. At the thought of that meeting I shivered so hard that my whole body shook and Morta was spurred into action, thinking I was cold. She ran out the back and returned a few seconds later with one of her shawls, a big purple fluffy one, which I tried to shake off, laughing. But she wasn't having it, and neither was anyone else.

'Wear it!' she ordered. 'You'll look worse in your grave.'

So for the next half an hour, that's how I painted – in her purple shawl – happy to look ridiculous. When Rakesh popped in to see how things were coming along he nearly broke a rib laughing. But I could already picture myself in some Brazilian shanty town in six months' time, telling the story; writing home, telling them what I was doing; making them proud. I wanted to cry with happiness.

By the end of the afternoon the shop was almost unrecognisable as the one we'd operated for years, faithful to Grandpa Harry's design. And once we'd put the ladders, paints and brushes away, the whole room looked more spacious too; I was beginning to imagine what it would be like when it was finished. But then, I wouldn't see it for a long time, would I? Maybe never. I was always forgetting the new life that was coming.

We finished work for the day and Morta put the kettle on. She leaned up against the kitchen cabinet, stretched out a bony finger towards me and asked playfully, 'Hey, you! Any plans for next week?'

CC: We don't enjoy breaking the law. We're driven to it.

LP: I love that you break the law.

CC: You do it too.

LP: Yes, I keep forgetting that.

HFN-I: #400

33

The Victory Coffee Shop

There had been plenty of ideas as to how to present the all-new Victory Coffee Shop, especially when the subject of the grand re-opening came up. When I broke the news about the barbering and asked her to stay on with us, Morta described the change well.

'Ah, I see,' she said, nodding seriously. 'Keep the winning, lose the war.'

It was good to see her English coming on, but she had a bad habit of talking directly.

'So, are you with us or not?' I asked.

Morta pinched my cheek with her thumb and forefinger, her red face now more excited than exhausted.

'You bet!' she said. 'I'm sick of cutting off heads!'

Then she jumped into the air and clapped like a little girl.

The nostalgia aspect of the Victory was still important to everyone, and we all had plenty of suggestions for what it could look like – especially over who would get framed photographs in place of where the old maps and regiment photos used to be, a subject which had hogged conversation for most of this afternoon. We would be sad to see a lot of the old stuff go, particularly Winston (Dad suggested keeping him out the back somewhere, maybe in the bunker), but we all agreed on the sporting theme. And everybody said Bobby Moore would make a fine replacement for above the door, in the middle of the new sign – holding the World Cup, of course.

'Some decisions are for the Gods to make,' said Dad. 'Only the devil, or a Scot, would deny Bobby his rightful place.'

We planned to be less partisan elsewhere, coming up with many weird and wonderful sporting moments that might lure people inside for a latte and a muffin at a competitive price. Alongside the more obvious football choices, Diego Maradona's Hand of God made the cut, as did the Russian linesman who helped us to the World Cup, and Cristiano Ronaldo's infamous wink from just a few months ago, which seemed the natural choice to represent this decade. Daisy and Phil made sure North America was represented, with images from ice hockey and basketball being insisted upon, though none of us knew who they were talking about. (Those pictures could go in the back room.) I didn't know Philip could be passionate about anything played on a field, but the way he talked about American football it was like it was the only game on earth. Dad asked him how come he knew so much about it, and Phil said his flatmate in Toronto was a Superbowl nut. He'd just picked it up. No big deal. Nobody believed that, but nobody questioned it either.

Daisy popped out for a takeaway, I cooked a simple omelette for Mum and everyone else went through to the back room to watch TV. Then Phil and I decamped to our old spot out front, sitting on the pavement, watching the Goths going into the rock club across the road. Sunday night. Pretty much the same as every other night, these days. The kids seemed to party all the time now and I liked how reliable that was – sometimes it still seemed like the Northern Quarter was the centre of the world.

'Do you miss home at all?' I asked. 'All this?'

'Sometimes. But it's changed a lot. Manchester isn't the place I remember any more.'

'You sound like an old man.'

'No, actually I think it's better here now. Since the IRA came to town and took out half the city centre, they've improved it. Look at what happened to the Royal Exchange.'

'Here's to the IRA then,' I said, smiling. 'Good deeds, done accidentally.'

Phil raised his bottle of beer.

'Yeah – here's to the IRA – are they still going, by the way? There's a few other places in England I could think of that might benefit from a good blowing up.'

As Phil and I sat talking I began to feel sad we wouldn't be doing this again, not for a while anyway, and I wanted to be friendlier than usual.

'You're getting on now, old man,' I said, soft as I could. 'Why don't you just tell them your secret?'

But Phil's mood darkened when I said that.

'You're one to talk about growing up. Anyway, it would kill them.'

'You'd be surprised. Stephen's a businessman. He and Dad would get on. Why don't you at least tell *him*?'

He shook his head firmly.

'There's no need now.'

He reached into his back pocket and drew out a wallet, which he opened to reveal a photograph of a handsome man in a suit, crouching, with his arms wrapped around two small boys, each smiling naturally for the camera.

'He's a looker,' I said.

Phil ignored that.

'I took the photograph,' he said. 'I didn't need to be in it. You see?'

He shook his head again.

'They weren't being cruel – it just didn't occur to them that I should be part of the picture. I should have got out then.'

'But you loved them all . . .?'

Philip sighed. 'I had to, didn't I? It would have made life difficult if I'd admitted I didn't like the kids.'

He laughed coldly.

'And I didn't, Lewis – they were real brats, you know? They got worse as they got older. I don't like children.'

'You don't mean that . . .'

'It doesn't matter what I mean, does it? They were old enough to know they didn't want me or anyone like me around. What kid wants a step-parent? No kid, that's who. And I wasn't even that. They called me Lodger, even after we got married, because they knew it upset me.'

I was stunned:

'You got *married*?'

'Oh yes, you can do that over there – though I wish they'd kept the damn thing banned now. The problem with gay marriage is you open the trapdoor to gay divorce.'

'Do you have a photo of the big day? I'd like to see it . . .'

'I don't want to talk about it, Lewis. It's not easy for me.'

I looked down at the pavement, avoiding Phil's eyes. If he'd left this until tomorrow, I might never have known. I waited for a pain to hit my gut, but it didn't. No feeling of rejection that he didn't tell me about it, or invite me to the ceremony. No horror or pity that it was over. These days, I felt invincible sometimes. Like the greater sufferings of people far away made the ones closer to home more bearable.

'The kids knew, right?' I asked.

'They knew.'

'That must have hurt.'

'Ignoring it? No. *That* I understand.'

Phil spoke with surprise in his voice.

'They're much more relaxed in Canada – not half as many Christian crazies as America – but even over there, I didn't tell many people. It was just easier not to. Mum and Dad were thousands of miles away and still I couldn't open my mouth and say the words. You know. What I am.'

'So is that it?' I asked. 'You're not going back?'

'No popcorn, no man, no home. We'll build a new empire here, eh? On the old street? I've got a good feeling about it . . .'

'Ah yes,' I said. 'I've been meaning to talk to you about that. You see . . . I'm not going to be around . . .'

When I started talking, I was sure he'd understand. But as I tried to explain about Christy, about Hope for Newborns, everything I wanted to do, the good work I'd started, the funds I'd raised and how I'd raised them, Phil's face became paler and his eyes more afraid. His breath swirled around in the cold evening air. People walked on past like nothing unusual was going on. They had seen plenty of our games recently. Philip started shaking his head, getting faster, like it was going to speed up and spin right off his shoulders. I just kept talking, telling him everything, as fast as I could in case he stopped me, but I'm not sure if he was listening at all. I wanted him to be proud. He wasn't. My invincible feeling was gone.

When there was no response at the end of my speech, I got up and went inside. Phil followed a few seconds later; but as soon as we returned to the shop, all that was forgotten anyway.

LP: I dreamt about it again last night.

CC: Me too. But tell me yours first.

LP: Well, we were abroad. Somewhere hot. We met in a restaurant. In disguise.

CC: What was I wearing?

LP: Sunglasses, and a long black coat . . . but nothing else.

CC: What happened?

LP: You stretched out your leg and put it up against me while we ordered.

CC: Couldn't the waiter see?

LP: Yes. But he just smiled, then walked away.

CC: And?

LP: We ate in total silence, then you went to the toilet and I followed a few minutes later. We fucked on the floor. You screamed so loud that the manager came running in and caught us. He thought someone was dying.

CC: Your fantasies always involve me screaming. And they always end in us getting caught.

LP: Of course. I have never been close enough to make you scream; and, some days, I think of little else but exactly how we will be caught.

HFN-I: #411

34

Mum Crushes the Rebellion

No one was in the shop and the music had been turned off. Phil and I ran upstairs without a word to each other to find Mum's room full of people, her crouched in one corner in an ankle-length white nightie, legs tucked into her chest, arms wrapped around her legs, rocking slightly while the family stood arguing in the carnage. We had enjoyed forgetting about her for most of the day. It was as if she'd disappeared or died – but now she had reminded us that wasn't quite true. Every one of the tanks had been smashed, dead fish lay all over the wet floor, and some of the empty cages which had previously held hamsters and rats had been stacked by the door, probably by Morta. A couple of the other animal containers were strewn around the floor, straw everywhere, mixed in with seaweed and stones. Dad knelt by Mum and faced her.

'What did it, then?' I asked.

'Not what you think,' said Dad gently, without turning round. 'Another one of the fish died.'

Philip was angry.

'*That's* why there's rats loose now? What the hell?'

Dad ignored him.

'It jumped out of the tank, I reckon. Two in two days, it is.'

He let out a sad little smile.

'Three in three years, if you like. So she killed the rest.'

'How do you know?' I asked.

'I do know some things, Lewis, without being told. Besides, she stamped on the poor bastard afterwards. That's it there.'

He pointed.

'The one in the corner. With the eyes squished into the carpet. That'll never come out, you know . . .'

He carried on stroking Mum's head: she never openly resisted anything, but the grimace that usually appeared on the rare occasions when Dad touched her was not there now, and as he moved his hand and a damp cloth over her forehead and down onto her cheek I thought I saw the beginnings of a smile.

'Why was I not told things had got this bad?' said Dad, dabbing her forehead, soft and steady.

'Actually,' I said, 'there's been an improvement recently. She made her own tea last week.'

Philip began storming about the room, shouting.

'A bloody goldfish! When is someone going to get a hold of this family?'

Dad stood up and turned round to face us all.

'I am. Now. So calm down, all of you. Philip – help me get your mother back into bed. Lewis, tidy this room, and Morta, bring in some chairs please. Put them in a circle. Include Marion. Then you can go. You're not employed to listen to us shout at one another.'

Morta snorted and clapped her hands together.

'Ha! In that case, I have been working for many months when I could have been at home bathing my blisters!'

Sometimes Morta acted like our arguments were too poor for the title. I always thought that if you're from where she's from, anything less than a full-blown war is just friendly chat. But then, I didn't really know that much about where she was from. We never asked and she never said. Not all cultures make a fuss about suffering.

Dad gave orders and for now, for a little while anyway, we followed. He requested tea and Phil brought it through on a tray without comment. Morta arranged the chairs in a circle with a gap where Mum's bed was, so it at least appeared like she was to be included, Dad nodded approval at his employee and she left with another snort, but no words. The old ways were back. Then Dad sat down next to Mum, one hand resting

241

on his own knee and the other softly holding her arm. 'Shh,' he said, 'Shh.' It was almost as if they had never been apart. As we all waited for something to happen I felt an unfamiliar rush of heat inside my chest that reminded me of the sticky feeling that took me over each time I got a message from Christy. I was due to meet her in an hour. Soon, I'd have to tell them all.

Everyone took their seats and waited for Dad to speak, which he did with calm determination.

'The thing someone is about to say,' he said, hands clamped onto his knees, leaning forward, talking with quiet fierceness, 'that this is final evidence of your mother's insanity and we should quietly shuffle her off somewhere medical – is not the solution to anything. It would only be the beginning of a new set of problems.'

I interrupted.

'Dad, nobody has said anything yet.'

'But it would be a good idea . . .' said Philip. 'Mum needs support.'

'Well,' I started, '*I've* been providing that!'

Dad stopped the rising noise by raising a hand.

'I don't believe I had finished speaking,' he said, detached but insistent. 'Had I?'

He pressed his hands onto the front of his forehead, drawing them slow and tight over his hair to the back of his skull.

'You lot talk too much,' he continued. 'You've had things too easy. Well, not any more.'

There was a sureness to his voice that had been absent for some time, except when talking about Chuck. He was certain, and that was enough to beat anything. But after a few moments Dad realised Phil's opinion was one some others shared, and his certainty was gone again. His face turned an angry kind of red; he saw the looks on our faces and could not hide his disgust. He pointed at Mum, who was sitting up in bed, worn out from her fit. His finger waved wildly, close to her nose. He raised his voice for the first time.

'This woman brought you into the world – seven hours in

labour for you, Lewis! And nearly twelve for the twins! You think you can just toss her in the bin?'

'Dad, we're not saying . . .'

'I know what you're saying. You're saying you want rid. Well *tough*!'

He folded his arms and surveyed the circle, looking for support. He turned to Daisy and tried to speak in a softer tone, though even his soft seemed aggressive.

'Join in, love. What do you think?'

But I didn't let Daisy speak. I stood up straight, head spinning with the fear of being trapped for the rest of the night, fighting, when I should have been gone. Mum's room stank, it was clammy, the design seemed ugly in a way I had never noticed before, all sickly beige sunflowers and harsh red lines. I never wanted to look at it again. All I could think of was having to tell Christy I wasn't coming.

'Dad, we can't just all hang around here for ever,' I said. 'We have *lives*. Things have changed since your day . . .'

'This *is* my day, Lewis, I'm not dead. Sit down and stop being the big drama queen. And I'll thank you not to refer to *for ever* as well. You know nothing of that word. You're a baby.'

I sat back down, numbly listening to Dad resume his speech, unbelieving, unable to strike back. Nobody moved. Not even Mum, who was like a big, pale, sad old statue. I didn't know what Dad was saying any more. Why listen? Finally, someone cut him short.

'What are you suggesting?' asked Phil.

'Roles for everybody,' he said. 'From now on we'll all take an equal share of the burden.'

Mum twitched at that word. Dad didn't notice.

'It won't be *for ever* –' he grunted – 'though if it was, you'd have to put up with it.'

'Dad,' I said, 'When was the last time you did anything? Where have you been?'

But he was not shaken by that. He knew it was coming and

took it well. He composed himself, as if swallowing the insult, digesting it fully, with patience, before answering.

'I have been working hard, to pay for the heating that stops her from freezing, to pay for the water she uses to make her tea and the tea bags she uses, to pay for a licence for the television she watches morning noon and night,' he said, 'But, from now on, we'll be a proper family. Your mother needs me in another way. I see that now.'

He gripped her hand. She gazed into the middle distance.

'We need each other. And you lot too.'

He let that comment settle for a moment. Or maybe he'd said it without meaning to, and was as surprised as we were.

'Now, Marion and I will be staying in tonight. Why don't you kids do something together? You too, Daisy. Go out. I'll take care of the little one. Don't worry, I know how to look after a child. I raised three boys, you know – they turned out well enough.'

Philip had been sitting in his chair, arms folded tightly, ready to explode. Daisy put her hand on his, much like Dad had put his hand on Mum's.

'Phil?' she said, tenderly. 'You there?'

After Philip opened his mouth there was a gap of a few seconds before any noise came out. We all waited for his response, which he delivered without looking at any of us. I envied that old Passman family steadiness, which seemed to have slipped by me.

'That is one point of view,' he said. 'But just now there is one person caring for Mum – he has been doing it a long time – and that person has not kept her safe. Tonight, she could have killed herself, or someone else. She has severely damaged this room, which now stinks of dead animal, and probably will do for weeks. It's a wonder we're all still alive. There are vermin eating away at our home as we speak. These big speeches calling on our dedication are all very moving, but they mean nothing. They are driven by guilt. I say we can't take any risk; God only knows what a local doctor will make of her. We put Mum in a private home first thing tomorrow morning. The shop will be back up and running soon. We'll find the money. This madness can go on no longer. You say she refuses to move, but two big men could have her out of here and sitting in a comfy chair looking out onto the seafront before you could say "nutcase". Which is what she is. Let's not pretend anything else. She'd eat her own face if she could.'

Philip wasn't finished, but that didn't matter. Now it was Dad's turn to explode. He stood, thrust his chair out of the way, went right up to his son and shouted. Philip gripped his seat and took it, spit and all. It was the kind of outburst that reminded me of what Mum used to be like, before the silence.

'Nutcases!' he screamed. 'Vermin! Madness! Private hospitals! What a nasty piece of work Canada has made of you, Philip. Charles would never have used those words. What kind of fairy world have you been living in, where working families magic money into existence in order to dishonour their parents? Eh? No wonder your business went to the wall! Well, you won't kill this one!'

The meeting was over.

One by one everyone left the room and soon I was left alone with Mum, taking the chair next to her bed. As I approached she looked up at me.

'Say something,' I said. 'If you can, do it. Help us.'

I imagined her opening her mouth. I wanted to beat her into speech. If I lashed out, maybe she would cry. Maybe she would speak of her own free will. But though there would have been no better time, she did not, or could not, speak up. Sometimes it seemed she was so broken that even if she tried to talk it wouldn't have been possible.

'Tell me what you want,' I said. 'It doesn't matter what it is.'

I waited, expectant, but it didn't come. I had nothing left.

'Happy birthday, Mum. I'm going now. Do you understand? Going.'

The smell of scattered fish and water seeping into the carpet rose up in an unholy stink. Two dead hamsters lay stiff on their backs in a cage by the bed; the remains of the omelette I had made sat on her bedside table, going hard. Downstairs, everyone was arguing again. The meeting had lasted no more than ten minutes, the silence no more than two; I buried my head in the sheets and screamed. I knew we had let her down and said so, repeatedly. Mum tapped my shaking hand with hers as if to show me she understood, and our conversation was over.

CC: I miss you so much.

LP: I miss you too. How can anyone know you better than I do?

CC: No one does.

35

The Barber's Chairs

An hour later I was still at home and we were back to long silences. Dad was upstairs with Mum, doing the first shift – he said she should be guarded at all times – but it was obvious he needed to be with her anyway, danger or none. It was odd to think of him wanting to be with his wife after years of pretending she wasn't there. Strange even to see them in the same room. She had finally blinked, and now he didn't want to win the game any more.

Once Dad was safely out of the way, Philip went to his suitcase, retrieved a bottle of red wine and three mugs and brought them to the shop front where the rest of us had gathered. The label said the wine was over twenty years old, and I noticed that a little dust flew out into the light of the shop as the cork popped out.

'Supposed to be a present . . .' said Philip, opening the bottle as Daisy returned from putting Tampa down for the night.

'Don't you want to go out to do this?' she asked, taking the bottle from him. 'Wouldn't it be easier?'

'I don't want to go anywhere,' said Philip. 'I pay my way like anyone else. Or at least, I will be doing. Soon.'

'Well then, you'd better serve up. For Lewis too, okay? Make up and drink up, you two. I know there's something going on. Hell, everyone else is against you – can't you just get along?'

I covered my mug.

'None for me, thanks.'

'Let's talk about something else,' said Philip, pouring for himself and Daisy. 'I've had enough of this.'

'No,' I said. 'I'm not finished. Nobody lets me speak.'

Every time the temperature seemed about to drop, it shot back up again. There was little opportunity in our family for people to say what they meant, and I couldn't let this one go. This evening's episode was proof that I had been doing a bad job, to everyone but me.

'I've done my time. What's wrong with you?' I said, turning on my brother. 'Why don't *you* look after Mum for a while? Or are you afraid of getting trapped here?'

Though we were talking in lower voices, we hadn't calmed down. It didn't take much to set Phil off.

'That's you, Lewis,' he snapped. 'Not me. You never talk about what you do or where you go, you hide away in a rancid little flat no one has even seen, secretly plan your big escape, talk like a deluded romantic revolutionary. But you bounce around here acting like the one good boy! Just because you do a bit of dusting doesn't mean you're a saint.'

'Nobody appreciates what I do.'

'No, it's just so bloody obvious that you don't want to do it, that no one *wants* to appreciate you. You think no one notices your attitude. You stay, but you resent it. Chuck was right; you'll be here the rest of your life. You'll take over the shop, run it miserably into the ground and wonder why nobody thanks you for it. Well, it's not happening. Because I'm here now, and I'll be in charge.'

'Fine – I'm glad! I'm going tonight! For good!'

Daisy raised her eyebrows, took a gulp of her wine.

'Then why are you still here?' asked Philip, and knocked his drink back.

I never thought anyone would be anything but grateful for what I've done. I thought I was good, but even my closest ally disagreed. He spoke with such venom. Philip's hands were clasped tight around his mug as if stapled there for safety.

'We can go back to talking about sport now,' said Daisy.

'No,' I said. 'I don't deserve to be attacked. I never attack anyone else.'

249

'Is this over now?' said Philip.

'Sure. No more. Not from me. You can all go to hell.'

'Stop!' said Daisy. 'For God's sake, shut up! Both of you!'

I was behind time. I hadn't even packed my things. Hadn't explained things properly. But there was nothing I could do – my legs wouldn't move.

Daisy made Philip and me shake hands, say sorry, like naughty children, and then we sank back into the barber's chairs. There was no noise from upstairs apart from the sound of Dad snoring. He seemed too young for it, but these days he fell asleep anywhere, anytime. Daisy poured wine into Philip's mug until just after he told her to stop, handed it over, then she did the same for me, removing my hand which was still covering the mug with an expression on her face that seemed to say, *Get it down you, or else.* I wasn't sure, but it seemed like the sort of time when I should do something dramatic, something unexpected of me. And anyway, even when Daisy was stern it felt like she was being friendly, so I wanted to do as I was told. Phil looked across, seeming to dare me, so I took a first small sip and had to stop myself from gagging. The wine felt thick, metallic, hard, sickly, all at the same time. An unfamiliar sting.

'God,' said Daisy, settling into Dad's main barber chair, trying to stifle a grin. 'That man upstairs! He should be in bed too, with a hot water bottle and a whisky, instead of sitting with your mum. That's probably what he wants. You do know that, don't you? Hey, if she breaks out again, he'll be the first to get a fish in the face!'

We laughed, and with the tension broken the three of us brought all the chairs together into the centre of the room, facing each other, just as we had done upstairs. Daisy had an amazing talent for making big problems seem very small.

'Come on,' she said. 'Everything's fine.'

As we sat in the near-darkness of the shop, leaning back in the chairs, looking up, marvelling at the work we had done today, Daisy explained about her own family; it made ours sound perfectly normal, perfectly sane, and I began to understand why she didn't want to return to it. No matter how often she said she was staying with us for her dead husband, it didn't seem like that to me. As Daisy spoke in a matter-of-fact tone about her home, how she joined the army to get away from it, how she had no choice but she wouldn't change it if she could, there was a trace of sadness in her voice along with the strength and determination. Where were Daisy's moments of weakness? Didn't everyone have them? I would miss her more than anyone.

Half an hour or so passed and my reservations about the wine faded. After the first drink there didn't seem much point in saying no any more, and the more I had, the less it stung. Two mugs went down. Though I wanted to leave, I didn't feel ready. It was too soon. I didn't want to spoil these last moments by bringing them to an end.

'There you go,' said Philip, each time he filled me up from a second bottle he took from Dad's secret stash in the loft. 'That's a boy.'

It felt good to make him pleased. I wanted to do more of it. Then Daisy lowered her voice.

'So . . . Do you want to know where the bricks were coming from?'

Philip and I leaned forward.

'Well,' said Phil, 'we caught them once – but I didn't recognise them – did you?'

'No,' said Daisy. 'But I did find one of our little attackers this afternoon – leaving a present – and I interrogated him.'

'Who was it?' we both asked, almost together.

'The youngest of the three Jarvis boys. His dad used to come in the shop all the time.'

'Jarvis? I hardly know them,' I said. 'I'm not sure if I know who they are at all. What did you do?'

'I said I was going to take this one to the police, but the poor kid crumbled. Made me promise I wouldn't tell his mum. Seemed a shame to shake it out of him, really – but I don't think you'll have any more trouble.'

'Why?'

'Not because of the refit. It's just that – your dad isn't seeing Mrs Jarvis any more, that's all – so they've got no reason to carry on. She ended all that last week. Which might explain his . . . current state.'

I was so annoyed I couldn't speak. We had known about Dad's little past affairs, we just thought they were over years ago – so yes, I was annoyed with him. But I was more annoyed that the attacks had nothing to do with politics.

Philip and I sat, quiet. Finally, I said, 'But – the slogans? The graffiti?'

Daisy smiled, looking satisfied, and for the first time I could see she had enjoyed the whodunnit.

'They knew it was going on,' she said, 'but didn't want anyone else to. Everything else was just an excuse. We should have known they weren't attacking us because of the shop. Who cares about wars and armies round here? If people really cared they'd do something about it. Get up and change something.'

'What about the anti-Iraq war protests? Thousands got up and did something . . .'

But Daisy was pleased with that.

'A perfect example. People chanted and walked for a single day, and when nobody listened they went quietly back to their homes.'

'That wasn't the point.'

'No – *you're* missing the point, Lewis. Those Jarvis boys just hoped they could frighten your dad into backing off without their own father finding out. They knew he'd work it out, and wouldn't prosecute.'

'So what was he dropping off?'

'Oh . . .' said Daisy, smiling. 'It was more a present from their dog. A parting gift. I put it in the trash. Double wrapped. Still, I wouldn't go too close . . . it smells pretty bad.'

Sometimes I thought I knew nothing about anything. But just then Philip started laughing a dirty laugh, Daisy did too, and for the second time in a day I was doing the same without quite knowing why. Daisy finished her mug of wine in one, dumped it in Philip's lap and said, 'Well that explains this evening's madness then. See you tomorrow – goodnight! Be good to each other, boys. Chuck can't knock your heads together any more. Don't make me do it.'

She kissed us both on the forehead, then went upstairs, where she slept, as always now, in a single bed next to Tampa Bay. Philip and I were left alone. A few minutes later I heard a noise from her room, but Philip said he couldn't hear anything and reminded me of my overactive imagination. There was definitely something though. Crying? That didn't fit into my preferred view of Daisy, so I tried not to think about whether she was lying in that room, wide awake, clinging to her daughter and missing her man.

On the main road, drinkers wobbled home after nights out, girls in groups sang, couples huddled in close to protect themselves from the cold. Some looked in the window as they passed. I wished I had gone to Christy after the family meeting and left everyone to fall apart – or better, gone in the morning and never known about this. Left with good memories and a warm feeling in my gut. I was still at home, still burning up on the starting line. But now it was time.

'I am going, you know,' I said to Philip, so gentle I was hardly speaking at all. 'I really am.'

'Do you need a lift?'

'Thanks, but no.'

I gave him a hug.

'I haven't got much stuff. And I can walk to the station from here.'

'Are you going to be away for long?'

'I don't know . . . But I'll call when I get to New York!'

The sentence sounded too sad to be convincing. I didn't even know if I would be going to that city. I just always imagined I would since Christy sent me the poem from there, the one about the helicopter. I reached for my jacket and put it on.

Phil said, 'What are you going to do?'

253

I brightened.

'Go to places. Reset scales. Move on. There's a proper plan – we know what we're doing, don't worry.'

'Be careful. I want you to promise.'

'I promise,' I said, glad that at least one person was making me do that. 'Don't worry. I'd better go. I'm late.'

Then he put something in my pocket, which I saw later was a small roll of cash, bound by an elastic band. Not much. Enough for a few nights in a hostel, maybe. But we always needed money. I kept my hand in my pocket as I left home for the final time, holding on tight to what he had given me.

LP: No more.

CC: Soon.

LP: No more.

CC: Please, Lewis.

LP: I can't wait any longer.

CC: I'm not ready . . .

LP: You'll never be ready, will you?

CC: I will. I am. Nearly.

36

Not Quite the Short Route

I went back to my flat to pack: just a few things – not too much, like Christy said – but as I ticked off the checklist in my mind (Hope files, a few changes of underwear, socks, a couple of T-shirts), I got the urge to take down everything from my walls and bring it with me: the essays and late-night messages that I'd printed, stuck up above and around my bed; the pictures and Christy's emails. But what would I need those for? Soon I would be able to *look* at her. I headed for the station, walking but not running, via Rakesh's place – I wanted to be with her, but was so afraid of how it would go that I was still using every excuse I could to put the meeting off. Wait for something for two years and, whatever it is, you can't help but get used to the waiting. If the trains are regular enough, you can always just say you'll wait for the next one.

Rakesh offered me tea but I declined, refusing even to go in. I explained everything, fidgeting while he stood on his doorstep, and I tried to talk as quickly as I could, afraid that someone from my family would come by and my escape would be over before it had begun. I told him the story honestly, hiding nothing, while he listened with an expression of horror on his face, looking at me as if he was sure I was about to make a huge mistake. He pleaded with me not to go. He too gave me money. He tried to make me promise not to break the law. But I couldn't do that: what's the law got to do with what's right? The comment just showed how out of touch he was. With me, with the whole world. Ignoring Rakesh's pleas, his request to stay one night at his house and decide in the morning, maybe talk to his parents, get some advice, rethink, calm down, I put my hands on his shoulders and told him I didn't know when I was going to see him again. I can't remember most of the words I used. I can't remember the ones he said back, apart from that he was going away too, next month. Some management retraining course down South. Another reason not to stay, then, I said. Everybody leaves home in the end. Soon there'll be no one left, I'll be the only one here – waiting, still waiting. I can't wait any more, I told him. I'm sorry I haven't been a good friend. Then I left. Before I knew it I was back out on the road, running, running to the train station, out in the middle of the road, dodging people and cars and taxis, just to feel danger.

The autumn wind was strong, it whirled around me, and as I paced ever quicker to my platform I felt totally unbound. I wanted to be out of here. I wanted to be in a place where everyone blended perfectly. In Manchester people hung around in groups of their own, looking sideways at each other, circling each other, rarely crossing. I always tried to smile. Especially if they looked lost. I wanted to go up to strangers and kiss them. But that wouldn't be anywhere near enough.

My big adventure had started with a short journey; I was already at the station, which was buzzing with weekend activity. As the automatic doors opened for me I realised that I had been running, and that must mean I was no longer afraid, no longer putting it off.

LP: If you don't tell me where you are, I'll come and find you. I don't care. I'm coming.

CC: Calm down. You're frightening me.

LP: Well, I'm frightened too. I don't think I can wait any longer – I'm losing my mind. I'm so lonely, so scared they're after us now – I've taken so much money, so much – sometimes I think about . . . just giving up. Don't you? Ever? I know we've been doing the right thing, but how can I be sure people will understand that? That the law will understand that when we're caught? What if they separate us and make us betray each other?

CC: Be patient, Lewis. Soon. Soon.

LP: No – I've had enough of that. Now, Christy. Now.

CC: Okay, okay. Just give me some time to make arrangements – and promise me you won't hurt yourself.

HFN-I: #421

37

The Journey

My train had started out in London and was going right through to the airport via everywhere in between; it was delayed twice – there were works elsewhere on the line. This one route was scooping up everything that had been left behind by the other abandoned ones, resulting in the kind of passenger chaos that would cause a general strike in less decent nations. I squeezed through the closing doors. My breathing was quick and sharp, my chest tight, and the few mugs of wine I'd had at the shop were beginning to make themselves known. An unfamiliar swaying sensation made me want to hold on to something steady. My hand rested on the shaking side of the machine. I willed the shaking to stop.

The euphoria hadn't lasted long. I didn't want to know how late I was. Late night, weekend, and it was hot, cramped and clammy in the carriage. My knees were pressed together, both rubbing the underside of the table, legs and arms clamped between those of bigger men all around. The train was full of drunkards and it felt like I was touching most of them with one limb or another: a tourist flicked through a celebrity magazine opposite me, listening to dance music too loud on headphones, the thudding of the beats bleeding out into the carriage, taking me right back to being on the night bus in the days when I had two brothers, when I was so quick to condemn.

By the exits on either side were two groups – one stag party, one hen – competing for the attentions of the other passengers. Each group was of about ten or fifteen but seemed like double that, all in matching pink and blue T-shirts for their respective celebrations – BIG SUZE TIES THE KNOT!, MATTIE'S CRAYZEE BOYZ – fully grown men and women acting like teenagers, chanting across the carriage, drinking beer from cans, eating foul-smelling burgers-with-cheese in plasticky buns, kebabs and hot dogs, pulling up T-shirts and down trousers to show off to their lot on the other side like they were deep in some primitive multiple mating ritual, not in control of their own libidos. Office workers let loose from their lives and inhibitions for a few lousy hours; it reminded me of People4Jobs, which reminded me of the money I'd stolen and where it had gone to, which reminded me of the investigation into the money I'd sliced off from the profits, which reminded me of the letters I chose not to open and how the sooner I got out of the country, the better. As I gripped my bag and looked out of the window, trying to block out the madness around, the sleazy flirting, the desperation, I felt more like a prudish old spinster than a fit young man at the beginning of an exciting journey. But why did sex always have to draw attention to itself? My phone beeped, showing up a message from an unrecognised number.

'Where are you?' it said. 'You're late!'

I tried to send something back, but the messages were rejected. That was her, for sure. Shadowy right till the end.

If I'd been able to hold it in, I would have. But we'd only been going a few minutes when I had no choice but to rush to the toilet to be sick, squeezing hurriedly by the hen party on my way, trying to keep my head down and my mouth shut. The shout went up, 'Hey, ladies, here's something fresh!' and a red-faced woman with fingers like blunt little knives pressed her nails into my backside. I jumped, forced a smile, moved on, and she soon worked out that I wasn't for plucking. Sweating, sickly, nervous, confused, I felt like I'd stumbled into another world and already missed the one I'd left.

It was out before the toilet door was properly shut, and a cry of happiness broke in the corridor in response as the cream bowl turned red with splashes of Philip's wine and the Indian takeaway Daisy had bought us – once I was done I felt weaker, not stronger, for draining. Before braving the train again I crouched at the bowl for a few precious seconds of peace, thinking about how I could have said goodbye to the folks better, remembering how actually I hadn't said goodbye at all, not to everybody. Not Tampa Bay. Not Daisy. Not Dad. The carriage swayed left and right, rattling, rattling. Coming back out into the corridor, closing the toilet door behind me, I saw the crowd had swelled. We'd picked up more passengers at the next stop down the line and now the gaps between carriages were crammed too. There was no space anywhere. Suitcases littered every gangway. I was just thinking I'd never get back to my seat when the train jolted, then lurched, then stopped.

In the action that followed the announcement – something on the line, the conductor said, nothing to worry about – passengers broke into life and began communicating, some to shout, some to speculate, some only to ask when they'd get home or discuss how long the delay might be: real concern didn't last long, except with the sensitive few. English speakers were busy translating for tourists, and messages were passed down carriages. It was leaves on the line, said a regular; the usual for this time of year. It was an animal, said someone else. It was a person. Rumour was, a young girl. A woman in a suit got annoyed and said they didn't usually announce these things, why didn't they have a system and stick to it. I sat still, waiting for it all to pass, trying to control myself. Sometimes I can't. Sometimes I can. Christy could have been angry by now, but it'd take a while to clear up all the bits of body on the track. We'd have to wait. No choice.

According to a man standing in the aisle, who told someone who told me, there had already been two suicides on the network this month. They set each other off, he said. One kid jumps onto the track and five others hear about it on the news and remember they don't like life. Tonight, all over Britain, newscasters would set in motion another chain of tragedies by explaining what had happened in between items on possible interest-rate rises and the debate about whether people should be allowed to wear the veil – as if either of those things mattered when the world was full of abandoned children who *needed me*. I looked out of the window, seeing only darkness and my own reflection. But that didn't stop me imagining men and women searching for bits of teenager, praying the rumour was not true. I was starting to feel sick again.

Then: 'Ladies and gentlemen,' said the conductor, 'the bags of rubbish some friendly kids left on the line did not survive the impact of the crash, but rest assured they will be given the proper burial service, in good time. I believe they were Church of England.'

He chuckled into the microphone.

'Barring any other tragedies, we'll be moving very soon. Thank you for bearing with us.'

A spontaneous round of applause started up in the carriage and the weekend partyers took the conductor's speech as permission to celebrate twice as hard as before. Christy and I wouldn't cross too many stag or hen groups on our travels – where we were going, people would be more concerned with staying alive than getting drunk. And the surroundings would be prettier too. I wondered whether the last girl who jumped to her death had a moment of doubt in mid-flight. Whether, leaping off the grass into the bright beam, she changed her mind and hoped to reach the other side safely. Whether she thought about her mum, dad, boyfriend, girlfriend. Whether she had any of these. Whether she was committing suicide at all, or just running.

We arrived at the end of the line after nearly fifty minutes, finishing a journey that was supposed to have taken twenty at the most; as the engine wound down to nothing I checked my pockets for essentials, wiped my hands dry of sweat and waited for the carriage to clear before I moved. A dirty, wet film all over my body had worsened during the journey – during the stop I broke out in little sweat pools on my back and chest – and now my shirt was damp. Already that decision to bring nothing with me seemed stupid, not smart. It felt like a long time since I'd left home. At first I wanted to go travelling to meet people. I remember saying that to Anna once, and she laughed. Now all I wanted was a shower, a service that departed and arrived on time, an empty platform and sweet silence otherwise.

Though I'd never been at this station before, it looked similar to the one I'd left, right down to the adverts currently doing the rounds all over the city, which I could see from my seat in the carriage. A billboard of a smiling woman eating an apple. A large photograph of a woman reading a magazine and gasping with pleasure. A poster of a smiling woman applying moisturiser to her bare shoulders. A cardboard cut-out of a smiling woman holding up a car wheel, blowing in the breeze as she gripped the official Industry Tyre of the Year 2006. The adverts in every shop window, on every corner, in the middle of the street – you'd think women were easy to please. They get excited at any old thing. Even tyres. When you're alone those coy, teasing smiles follow you everywhere – but none of that applied to me any more. That would take some getting used to. A pretty girl from my carriage jumped into the arms of a handsome man and walked away with him, smiling. The drunkards reeled off last, chanting and cheering and fighting, probably heading for their connection to somewhere in Europe. Amsterdam. Prague. Somewhere sleazy. Eventually the queue of people getting off before me dwindled and I stepped onto the platform.

Watching the other passengers meet family and friends, I realised how much I wanted to be picked up. After all this time, I deserved a moment like that. Christy might have come to get me – she could have been hiding somewhere – but there was no sign of her, or of anyone who looked as I imagined her, so I hurried towards the station exit. Now everyone was gone and I was alone apart from an old man nursing the end of a coffee in the station café, being politely hurried along by a waitress who was telling him she wanted to go home, and a few people straining to look up at the arrivals board, not far away from me.

One of those people looked like Anna only with shorter hair, coloured bright red, and a large tattoo of several Chinese letters on her left forearm. It could have been the dizziness making me imagine things, but hadn't Anna said she was coming back one day? I had begun to ignore her postcards a few months ago when they had descended into drinking stories and sexual exploits. I think she had been trying to shock me – but now she was right there. It was her. I was *sure* it was her. The sight of Anna standing there looking upwards at the board made me stop, and I stood there for a few moments, still, waiting to be noticed. Thinking about approaching her. Whether it could really be her. What I could say. The thought of being caught, still here, two years after she'd left, filled me with a hot shame and I ran away just in case. I'd been seeing a lot that wasn't there recently. At the station exit I took out my copy of the map Christy had sent and examined it. I don't trust maps: I wish she'd given me directions instead.

Once I was on the street I slowed down a little, surer that Anna hadn't seen me, and I caught my reflection in the shiny metal of a street cash machine: though it was a bad angle, I could see quite clearly that I was thinner now than when Christy first came for me. My hair was longer – almost down to my shoulders – and I was proud of having lost ten per cent of my body weight in the last couple of years, despite putting on a bit of muscle from the swimming. I tried to imagine taking Christy's hands and moving them round my sides and downwards so she could feel what she helped me achieve – but no image came. The not knowing was a familiar feeling now. It was normal daily life. I stepped out into the main road, which didn't seem that main at all, and thought, as I began to follow the map, that they didn't make postcards of these kinds of places. Maybe Christy had wanted somewhere quiet, where we couldn't be traced. Every movement had to be a careful one. The idea of a secret HQ was thrilling. I turned off the main road into a side street.

From the centre of the new road I heard the sound of voices having a discussion. Some were angry. A woman was shouting out of an open window. An old man appeared out of another, emptying a bucket out onto the paving. On each side of this small street were shops on the ground floors of buildings that were several storeys high. Each had flats above. The meat in the butcher's shop hung in uneven lumps from large metal hooks: though the shop was closed, a fat man in an apron hacked at animal portions on wooden slabs in the evening half-light, the sound of his radio covering the chopping sound of cleaver on bone. Outside the chemist's was a dirty cardboard cut-out of a child with toothache clutching her mouth that made me think of the woman gripping the tyre. The void in my stomach twisted and pulsed. The road took a sharp turn and became narrower. There weren't even any shops any more. Just high stone buildings on either side of a narrow trail. I took out the map, getting a strong feeling that I was close to where I needed to be. Then I turned a corner and the view opened up in front of me, like a drawbridge coming down to reveal another world. I didn't move. I waited. Then looked up. Then knew.

Christy's flat was on the top floor of a large bright yellow stone block flanked by others of different colours on all sides; grey to the left and right, but with red, green and white all as part of the same chain. The narrow trail was already a distant memory, as now there seemed to be nothing but space everywhere. Directly below Christy's was a large European-style square, complete with a row of cafés and bars with chairs out on the front paving that reminded me of some of the newer parts of the city centre – empty streets, run-down buildings, half-demolished blocks, in sight of slick, clean, brightly coloured drinking boxes – just far enough away from the old city for businessmen to spend time in them after a hard day's work without the sour sight of poverty spoiling their night out. An anomaly in this city, the scene was something like the images of Budapest Christy had sent me, but a more muddled version. Like someone had come in the middle of the night and shifted a few things round, done a quick paint job for a joke and run away.

For a while I just stood looking at her building, but didn't know why I was doing it. Not straight away, anyway. I hit the buzzer and the lock was released immediately, though nobody spoke to welcome me. By now I was visibly shaking, and all hope that I would be able to remain calm and in control was given up right then. I pushed the door and climbed, going right up to the top, and as I passed the first floor, combing my hair nervously with my fingers, tightening my belt, slackening it, tightening it back up again, trying to ease the hurt in my stomach, it occurred to me that maybe Christy's flat in Paris had never existed. Looking back on it now, I suppose I was quick to spot that, but I was slow to work out much of the rest.

CC: It's going to be beautiful.

LP: What if I don't know what to do?

CC: You will.

LP: But what if you don't want me?

CC: I already know I do.

38

A Room for Living In

I thought I had the wrong person. It was a few seconds before she spoke.

'Hi,' she said. 'You came, then.'

'Of course.'

'Have you been drinking?'

'A little.'

'I thought you didn't drink.'

'Except for on special occasions. Sorry I'm late.'

'Yes . . . don't worry about that – you had no way of letting me know. The food is cold – but never mind. Follow me.'

But she didn't move yet, and I couldn't. All those times I'd begged her to send me pictures, all those times I was angry that she insisted we wait till we saw each other in the flesh; I was wrong. Christy was worth waiting for. I was sure I could feel my heart swelling with how beautiful she was. My insides were so hot – what other reason could there be?

Yes, there were a few things different – her hair was longer now, she was a little thinner than she used to be, she wore no rings on her fingers or coloured nail varnish, and for some reason I imagined she would – though now I think about it I realise how stupid that is. Still, she was what I hoped for. Christy's black hair fell over the top of a simple white T-shirt, which she wore with a pair of plain blue jeans, no socks and no shoes. It was not hot outside but the heating was on full in the flat. I cleared my throat and spoke without thinking.

'So . . . you got dressed up for me, then?'

'Why not? Don't I deserve to treat myself?'

I thought we might have hugged, or kissed, or devoured each other right there on the doorstep, but there would be time for all that yet. Still we didn't move. I didn't mention what I'd left behind, the late train, or the emptiness I expected to disappear the moment we met that was skipping about inside me, trying to find a way out.

'Are you okay?' I asked. 'You're not nervous?'

'No. Why would I be? Give me your bag.'

I handed it over, trying to see more from side-on as she turned away, taking in as much as I could. Tall but not taller than me. Small breasts, cupped by a flower-design white bra showing slightly through the T-shirt. A nervous stride. Soft white hands. That skin – so smooth, pale, much paler on her face. And the accent, not the international mish-mash I had expected.

'You've changed,' she said. 'You're not the same boy any more.'

'Really . . .?'

'Yeah.'

'How?'

'I don't know.'

Her hallway was just two white walls, a narrow corridor and a dirty, cheap white carpet, full of muddy marks. We hadn't touched yet, but were closer.

Christy said, 'So, what about me then? Am I how you imagined?'

'You're a fraud. On paper, you're a dictator. In the flesh, you're all sweetness. So yes – you're exactly what I expected.'

She smiled.

'You like me, right? I'm okay?'

'Of course you're okay,' I smiled. 'You'll do.'

She was still assessing me as the front door closed, but she laughed lightly, and that sent a wave of relief through me: it would get easier now.

I followed Christy through another do or with a sign on it reading STAY AWAY in a reckless, childish scrawl that must have been her handwriting – but it was hard to imagine her essays written in that hand. Someone had written IN YOUR DREAMS underneath in red. She had written NO, IN YOURS. Once it was closed Christy locked the door behind us in three places – top, middle, bottom – each one a big, chunky piece of metal that would have secured a prison – then let out an audible sigh of relief, her manner changing from nervousness to confidence as the clicks bolted us inside.

'That's better,' she said. 'Thomas is having a party tonight, so it's best we stay put.'

'Who's Thomas?'

'You might meet him later, I'm afraid.'

'Is he one of us?'

'No.'

'Who is he?'

'No one. An idiot.'

It was not a big place – the whole flat was uncomfortably small – but Christy's room was expertly planned and looked more like a show room than one that was actually being lived in. It was full of unusual features, most notably a single French window opening out onto a small balcony, overlooking the rest of the multicoloured spread of buildings and bars across the way. In front of Christy's door, by a low single bed, was a filing cabinet with a computer, printer and phone on a mahogany desk, which also had a large set of silver scales sitting on it that looked like a real-life version of the ones that headed all of Christy's communications. I was in the hub now, wasn't I? I could feel it. The scales were in pride of place, and it seemed the rest of the room was arranged to best complement them. Next to the desk were two tightly stacked bookshelves, neatly categorised, covering the adjacent wall from top to bottom. The Newborn office maybe; though there wasn't all that much evidence for it. She must have tidied up for me. Another wall was blank but for a large notice board, empty but for a tornout page from a paperback, pinned to the wall, which Christy did not stop me from inspecting. Typically, she had taken the trouble to cross out the references that didn't apply to her. Very efficient. Very like me. She had written in red pen underneath: DON'T BE LIKE THIS ANY MORE. It read:

Women have this tendency to think things will be better if they wait longer

  ie when

  – ~~I get away from my mother~~
  – *when I live with the man-I-love*
  – *when I get away from the man-I-love*
  – ~~when my mother loves me more~~
  – *anyone loves me more*
  – *when I finish the diet/buy new clothes/get a haircut/buy new make-up/learn to be nicer/sexier/more tolerant/turn into someone else*

Directly above the computer screen was a set of carefully carved square holes in the walls, with photo frames resting inside – one contained an old Academy photograph with Christy bottom right, me bottom left; another was of two people who couldn't have been Christy's parents but looked like they might fit the role. A fourth wall had a half-size oven and hob crammed up against it, a microwave sitting on an impeccably stylish but very small worktop, and a table for two in the corner. A black-and-white chequered cloth lay draped over the table, two glasses, two sets of cutlery and two mats covered much of the space, and I wondered whether there would be room for plates at all.

'This place is amazing,' I said. 'When are we leaving?'

'Oh, don't worry about that now. Look around some more . . . I made everything myself.'

'It looks like home.'

'Yes,' she said defiantly.

It was impressive, this world she'd made for herself, so different from mine, which I'd left without a thought or a note to my landlord, or even taking my rubbish out. Christy ushered me into a tiny en-suite bathroom, which had an impressive bright white shower and bath with polished chrome taps that sparkled clean in the corner. Standing on the tiled white floor, the night sky was visible through a large window looking out on to the square. The evening was clear enough to be able to see the moon and many bright stars, sending the sky spinning above me as I watched each one sparkle in turn. We were next to each other now, touching hands, briefly, while looking up. I could smell her. No perfume, of course. It made sense that she didn't wear perfume. She smiled, just a little, and I smiled back.

'What's going on?' I asked. 'Have you got the tickets?'

Christy smiled again, but more sadly this time.

'Too many questions. It's good just to be together – isn't it?'

'Of course.'

'Well then. Sit down in the other room and wait to be waited on.'

She was enjoying herself now. A little, anyway. Christy opened what appeared to be a large cupboard, inside which were another two apparently blank white spaces, one with a fine line round the outside in a rectangular shape at head height. She looked round at me once more, then pressed the side of one wall in firmly – out popped a fridge door, behind which there was a stash of white wine. Christy took a bow.

'You could live in this room!' I said. 'You'd never have to leave!'

'Well, yes. I do like to spend time here.'

'This must have cost a fortune!'

'Not really. It's amazing what you can do with your own materials and a bit of time. Though I don't earn much, so I don't know if I would have been able to do it without our fund.'

The buzzer went, and the pleasant atmosphere was punctured instantly, as if Christy had forgotten we were not alone, and was annoyed to remember. Somebody opened a door in the room next to us, passed through the hall with heavy tread and buzzed whoever it was inside with the words, 'Hey! Come on up!'

'Don't think about that,' said Christy, opening a bottle of wine and pouring me a glass. 'Think about this instead. I hope you're hungry . . .'

I found it hard to imagine a moment in the future when I might ever be hungry again. The front door opened and five or six voices could be heard laughing as they piled in, one by one. It always seemed like everyone else was having a good time. But there was important work to do. When would we get down to business?

LP: Do I need to prepare?

CC: You've been preparing for long enough – there's nothing else you can do now. Just come to me. And be careful. You never know who might be following you.

39

This Rope's Getting Tighter

Christy produced two meals from the fridge and put one of the bowls down in front of me, taking the other for herself. I picked unsurely at what looked like a tomatoey vegetable roast which had gone soggy and flavourless. I wanted to tell her how good she looked, or talk about our plans; talk about how we were going to escape. I wanted to show her my figures for the last month, marking out my biggest idea yet, the Lottery Notification Scheme, and discuss ways to keep it going while we were on the move. But though I was desperate to talk about these things, she showed me, without words, that we couldn't discuss certain topics – and we stayed away from anything dangerous. We discussed my journey. My day. My week. Nothing about her. Nothing about where we were going or why. She didn't even say where our first stop was going to be. Perhaps they were listening in on us. I was unsure, and edgy – which made me reach for the drink more regularly as the meal went on. As I filed mechanically through the lies I had prepared, avoiding all mention of anything she might not like, I began to sweat harder. She hadn't packed anything. If she lived here, or used it as a base, there was little evidence of Newborns on the walls. Surely there would be a map, at the very least? My home had become an office full of Newborns paperwork, bits of her.

'Where are all your records?' I asked.

Christy put down her knife and fork, held my hand, took a deep breath and said, 'You don't think I keep everything here, do you?'

I pulled away, looking down at my meal as I spoke.

'But you work from home. So do I. And I can't get anything done without my notes.'

'Not everyone works the same way, Lewis.'

'Perhaps.'

'Yes. We have to be careful.'

'So . . . what happens now?'

'Can't we enjoy ourselves before making plans?'

'I thought you'd already made them.'

Christy gripped her knife and fork tightly, twirled her glass like mum had at Benny's. Then she looked at me with an expression that was not excitement about our trip, or nervousness about who might be coming after us, or concern over whether I was enjoying the meal. It was fear. She knew what I was going to say, and could not stop it.

'You lied to me. Didn't you?'

'I'm sorry?'

'You lied.'

Her game was over, and she was not having fun any more. She did not answer straight away, and it took all my strength to stop myself from jumping over the table and attacking her.

'I said, *you lied*.'

Finally, she spoke, so quiet.

'I meant everything I said. Reset the scales; all that. But you knew it was a lie, right . . .? We couldn't really do it. I thought you'd worked it out. If not before, then on the way here.'

'What?'

My voice didn't sound like mine. The weak whine now coming out of my mouth was a long way from the confident boom I used to use on the phone to clients. Not that I could go back to that.

'The homes all over the world,' she said. 'The other members. Everything. I'm sorry, Lewis. It just kept . . . growing. Can you understand?'

I couldn't. I had confronted her knowing we were not going anywhere tonight. Knowing there had been some fantasy. That had hit me when she looked across the table and I could see she was afraid of being found out. Realised there were no other escape routes. But I didn't think – I hadn't had *time* to think – how *many* lies there had been.

'What?' I said again. 'What?'

Christy became impatient. She didn't want to have to say it, and I didn't want her to, but though I searched for something to make it better, that something wasn't there. My world was spinning away. My eyes began to sting. My legs went numb.

'What is it?' I said, faintly. 'What's happening?'

'It's over. We have to stop . . . Everything you've done. We could get in trouble . . .'

'Well, yes – then we have to get away! We have to go tonight! Grab the passports and let's go before they catch us! My old bosses are on to us, I think . . . I was going to tell you . . . I've stolen so much . . . *so much* . . . We have to stick together though, right?'

But that didn't satisfy her either. Now came a new, sterner voice, more like the one in her essays.

'I can't go anywhere, Lewis. I haven't got any money. I spent what we made in this room, and on clearing my debts. I have to stay here now. And I can't leave the country – I have a criminal record.'

'What about your fundraising?'

'I haven't been doing any. I've been working.'

I was standing now, above the half-finished food, though I felt like I might fall over. She seemed to shrink below me, and I knew it was all going to come out.

'Then what have you been doing in all those places?'

'I haven't left Manchester.'

'But what about your poems – the one from New York?'

'I found it on the internet. It was written by a New Yorker.'

'What about the *Mona Lisa*? You were in prison in France . . .'

'Who hasn't seen a picture of the *Mona Lisa*?'

'But what about the photographs you sent me? You were in Argentina! Chile! You sent me your tour diary from Cuba!'

The more annoyed I got, the more defiant Christy became.

'It's very easy to doctor photographs, Lewis. You know that from the Newborns site . . . and didn't you ever wonder why I wasn't in them?'

'You've been all over – saving people. You saved me.'

'I wanted to, yes. But I've been too bad for too long – and it can't go on. You forced me into meeting you. You made me do this. Do you understand? This has to *stop* now.'

'You *did* save me . . . You *did* . . .'

'But I couldn't really achieve anything real . . . out there. It's too big.'

She gestured towards the balcony.

'But you're a great leader! . . . You've got ideas!'

Her anger was turning to something else, something less controlled. More vulnerable.

'But how could someone like me . . . do anything?'

I was shouting now.

'Where is that person who has been talking to me?' I screamed.

'Don't be angry.'

Christy left the table and flopped on the bed, facing away from me, as if she knew what was coming next.

'The money!' I called out, realising one last, horrible thing. 'The money! *How could you?*'

I felt cold and lonely and tricked, but then Christy started crying and that became all that mattered. Without a thought I went over to the bed to hug her, hold her, marvelling at how warm her neck was, how soft. I had the urge to kiss it, which I did. She pulled away, trying to clear the tears from her face, but they were coming too fast to catch them all.

'You lied too . . .' she said, trying to drag herself up. 'You pretended too. And I still wanted to help you.'

Only then did I think I totally understood. I was not nervous any more. It was like all the night's alcohol drained from my system in a second and I was sober again. Alert.

'So how long have you been following me for?' I asked.

'Not as long as you might think. Not for the first year.'

'Were you in the shop?'

'Not when you were there. I wanted to see what you were hiding.'

'I *had* to hide that. You wouldn't have understood about the shop, my brother, the army. I didn't do any harm. But you led me on.'

'I wanted someone to talk to. And didn't I make you feel better? You just said I made you feel better.'

At that, I broke down and called out, 'We have to leave . . . we have to leave . . .' Christy cried with me, hard, and said sorry sorry sorry so many times that for a while there it seemed like the only word in the world.

After the tears, there was a lot of silence.

When we finally had the energy to talk again it was with greater freedom, and I was surprised to feel relieved, not angry. I looked at her wet face and shaking hands and saw she was no less beautiful. She was no less heroic. We ate the rest of the cold, damp meal. It seemed like the obvious thing to do – and then we lay on her bed. After a while I felt dizzy, then fell asleep, without dreaming.

CC: What do you think it will be like?

LP: What, the first time?

CC: Yeah.

LP: How do you want to do it?

CC: We should decide before. .

LP: Okay . . .

CC: I want to be really soft. And slow.

LP: Okay. We can do that.

CC: Almost like in slow motion . . . And I want you to tell me you love me. No matter what you're thinking, I want you to say it out loud.

LP: That won't be difficult.

40

It Was Still Night

I had a fuzzy, dirty film on my tongue, an unusually strong headache, and a hot, restricted feeling in my chest, like there was a belt tightening around it.

Light was coming in through the gaps in Christy's blinds – lamplight, probably – but I was glad. It helped me come slowly out of sleep into early morning. I was facing the window and felt through the covers that I was still clothed, with one arm hanging out over the side of the bed. I moved a foot to see if the sleeping warmth next to me was also dressed. She was. A noise came from her mouth – somewhere between a sigh and a groan – and then she turned over towards me, bringing her face close to my back, breathing on it. I turned over to face her.

She smelled stale, of white wine and sleep, but I didn't mind that. Only small loves needed cleanliness to make them real, and I had waited a long time to be close to her. To anyone. I moved my foot down her leg, slowly, as steadily as I could, and as I reached the end of her body I felt her toes curl in recognition as if to welcome mine. I lay there, the side of my face pressed tight into the pillow, imagining looking at our bodies from above – hers resting in the same shape as mine, but in symmetry, with both of us facing away from each other. She moved again and I wondered whether that movement was intentional. If it was, what it meant. Then she turned round and began shuffling closer, curling up so much, like the boy on the bus, that it was almost like she was hiding in my back, afraid something was coming to get her and only I could protect her. Christy put an arm out towards me and let it fall on my stomach. Then the hand at the end of that arm clenched, half-opened, clenched again. She sighed, yawned, sniffed. Then her weight shifted. Until then, I wasn't sure if she was awake.

To start with, we followed the plan and each kiss was gentle, caring. Soft, defensive, more like a tester than a demand. We were together then. But as each item of clothing was removed, I began to think Christy was trying – and failing – to hide her disappointment that I wasn't going about things differently. She kissed like she needed the compliment to be returned in a very specific way; I was too clumsy. Too tense. Too nervous. Once, she sighed and shifted me very definitely from one side of her to the other, almost lifting me off the mattress and placing me, like a doll, to her left, though I was certain I didn't want to move. In her hot, awkward embrace, I was surprised to find myself thinking of Anna – longing for that careless confidence that made sex less like a serious competition and more like a meaningless game – and I wondered if she was happy, wherever she was. She had been kind; I was sorry I hadn't stopped to say hello. Remembering her orders – 'Hold me like a man!' – I wanted to be stronger, more impressive.

I don't think about it all the time. I rarely feel it. But the rush of terrible energy that zipped up and down my arms and back and legs and head and erection and fingertips and eyelashes and toes as I held Christy was a familiar one that took me back to the city-centre backstreet where I bubbled and began to fear what was underneath me. I even thought I could smell the same smell as that cold night when I was lost, something like boiling tarmac. I feared being caught and exposed for not being a gentle good resetter of scales but a coarse, filthy human being like her and every other who steals and cheats and abandons those who need him most. As I drifted further from her and further into myself, Christy's voice – the sound of her half-pleasured, half-frustrated sighs – took on a different tone, more like that one I would never entirely forget but could put safely away in a box for weeks on end: the sound of that other foundling in my life being disappointed in my choices. I gripped her arms, hard. I clutched instead of softly touching.

'Don't kill me!' said Christy. 'That hurts! Ow! Let go!'

'Sorry . . . I didn't know . . . I was doing that.'

'Relax. Kiss me. Gently. What's wrong with you?'

'There's nothing wrong with me, is there? Okay. Okay. Sorry. Let's start again.'

And we did.

It didn't last long, but it finished with a moment of absolute dreamlike togetherness which felt the closest thing to paradise I had ever experienced, and Christy said time only mattered to fools. She kissed me and we settled down for sleep. We were hardly awake anyway, and there would be plenty more chances to get it right. I returned to sleep in sureness of tomorrow.

Hope will not let you down.

CC

END OF EXCERPTS
CASE No. 00337/418/3x
Greater Manchester Police, October 2006

41

Hope for Newborns

In the morning I woke to find Christy doing sit-ups against the bed. She was dressed in long black jogging pants and a grey T-shirt, sweating out the night before. When she saw me open my eyes she moved towards the doorway to the en suite, where she began to pull herself up onto a bar just below the frame. That was something I could get used to, I thought. Watching my lover. But I smelt no coffee, saw no lover's breakfast, and she didn't seem pleased to see me. She came over for no kiss and said no good morning. Just this:

'I slept in. I didn't want to. I must have been tired.'

This time I would not be left wondering. I sat up and said, 'You want me to go, don't you?'

Christy stopped her exercise and smiled sadly.

'I'm sorry.'

'But I've only just got here.'

Christy's tone was so formal that I was sure she used it to stop herself breaking in front of me.

'It would be more convenient to carry on,' she said. 'We could keep trying, but what would be the point? I really thought it would be okay, even after last night. But it isn't. It doesn't feel right. It was better in our imaginations.'

'I can't go home. Is that what you want me to do?'

She seemed confused by that.

Christy came over to the bed, sat down and said, quiet and kind, 'I'm going to get in the bath in a minute. I'll close the door for a while. That will give you a chance to get your things together without feeling I'm staring at you. Then you can go.'

And with that she did exactly as she promised, finishing off ten or more pull-ups at the bar before undressing without ceremony and closing herself in the bathroom, as if she was just popping out to the shops for some bread and milk and would be back for another kiss in a moment. She didn't bother to cover herself from me. Did that mean anything? She walked without self-awareness and with grace. Her nakedness brought to mind the men I used to see in the swimming baths, walking undaunted, despite ordinary bodies. I was jealous. I watched her disappear.

After a few minutes, Christy called out from the bathroom. 'Are you still here?'

'I'm waiting for you to change your mind.'

Her voice was kindly, but I could tell that underneath it she was impatient to be rid of me.

'Lewis – please go,' she said, her voice starting to turn into a sound more like tears. 'I can't see you.'

I thought of many answers I could give to that, but each that formed on my tongue sounded bitter, or angry, or cowardly, or cold, and I didn't feel any of those things. I couldn't say what I felt at all. All that waiting, all those words – and now, nothing.

'Okay,' I said. 'All right. All right.'

And with that I picked up my clothes from Christy's carpet and got dressed. The distance between some of the items was a reminder of how recently I had been careless. As I pulled on yesterday's socks, I wondered distantly why there were no more tears from me now. Maybe I had none left. Maybe this wasn't happening and soon I would arrive outside her door for the first time, press the buzzer, walk upstairs and be excited to see what I might see, and fall in love with a woman who would not tell me things I didn't want to hear or send me away for a reason I could not understand.

I knocked on the bathroom door and said, 'It's okay. Goodbye.'

I met Thomas in the corridor. He was still drunk from the night before.

'You all right, man?' he said. 'You look terrible.'

'Thanks. You look pretty good too.'

'What did she do to you?'

'Nothing.'

'Okay. Fair enough. She's okay, really. You want a drink, buddy? There's plenty left over. Beer? Wine? You smoke dope?'

'Thanks, but I'm not sure about all that.'

'Okay, be how you want to be, but there's plenty. That's all I'm saying.'

Thomas leaned on the wall in the corridor, blocking my exit.

'Where you off to?' he said, all casual.

'Not sure.'

'Be careful, okay? You look wasted, man.'

'Yeah, well. I'll be fine. Thanks though.'

He stood aside to let me pass, and I realised as I closed the door behind me that Christy probably needed me gone fast for a reason.

Once I was in the open air I hid close to the entrance to Christy's flat and waited for her to come out of the front door. When she did I went after her, making sure to keep a safe distance. After a few minutes she arrived at an old pub, which was next to a car park on one side and a newsagent on the other. She went inside and I waited, looking through the window. I saw her say hello to a couple of people behind the bar. She disappeared into a back room for a few minutes and then returned wearing a yellow-and-green uniform and cap which was dirty from a past shift, a black T-shirt and a white apron wrapped around her waist. Her hat read: 'Ask me about our Beer and Burger Deal!' I waited, peering in for a couple of minutes, straining to see. Watching her expressions. Then I walked inside. Then I changed my mind again, and turned to leave before she saw me.

I took my bag which contained so little, slung it lazily over my shoulder and looked around one more time to see if anyone was following me.

HOPE FOR NEWBORNS

BECAUSE THE LOST JUST WANT TO BE FOUND

Acknowledgements

Thanks to:
My agent Jenny Brown, my editor Hannah Griffiths and all at
Faber Towers (especially Sam Brown, Kate Burton and Sarah
Savitt), Trevor Horwood for the copy-edit, Ross Wood for
photos, Gemela Forman for www.rodgeglass.com, and the
Scottish and English Arts Councils for financial support. Also,
to those who gave advice, especially Haim Shalom, Alan
Bissett, Claire McCallum and the many great minds of Room
104; and to Liz Lochhead who was poetry advisor on 'High
and Mighty in NYC'.

Credits:
The idea for Chapter 8 came from an event witnessed by Colin
Clark.
     Hepburn House from Chapter 21 is the name of the Scottish
Literature Department of Glasgow University, where some of
this book was written.
     Christy's essay in Chapter 24, *The Past Gets Bigger Every
Day* . . . is named after a lyric by Ross McConnell, who also
helped with several drafts.
     The page on Christy's noticeboard in Chapter 38 is from the
novel *The Trick is to Keep Breathing* by Janice Galloway.
     The title of Chapter 39 is from a song called 'This Rope's
Getting Tighter' by Emma Pollock.

Thank you all for donating support, ideas, words, cash. A
novel is a joint effort.

Also:

thanks to
the friends and family
who suffer
while this
and other books
are being written.
I promise,
one day,
to calm down.

RG